# Across The Tracks

# Across The Tracks

Donald Jones

**To order additional copies of this book, contact:**
Xlibris
1-888-795-4274
www.Xlibris.com
Orders@Xlibris.com
774818

# CONTENTS

Hello, readers! This book is designed for people who are open-minded and who realize this world is made up of people who are just different from others. In other words, different strokes for different folks! First, I would like to give you a poem written by a personal friend of mine by the name of Carl Kirkendoll that hits home for me!

AMERICA, THE TWO SIDED STORY!

When it comes to describing America, there are two sides of it . . . Some people hate it while others love it . . . Seen from different eyes you will get different views . . . So please hear them both out before you begin to choose . . . Some people might tell you this is the land of opportunity, where you can get a good education and live in a safe community . . . They will say this is the place . . . where you can advance despite your sex, religion or race . . . Hard work can get you anywhere and the government even treats you fair . . . For their country they feel nothing but pride . . . But that's just one side . . . Now let's go to the other side of the tracks . . . Where people might just tell you the opposite of that . . . Where there's no sunshine, only rain . . . No joy, only pain . . . The neighborhoods around here have crime rates that are way too high . . . and the kids that live there don't care if they live or die . . . The streets are controlled by drugs and gangs . . . And the cops don't even show up until they hear a gun go bang . . . Kids are forced to be grown before they leave elementary . . . That's why most end up dead or in the penitentiary . . . No need to vote, march or put up a fuss, because the system is not broken, it was just never made for us . . . This is a tale of one country with two different insights . . . And no matter whom you ask, they'll both be right!

My name is Ray, but everybody calls me Ray Ray. I guess if the first Ray didn't get my attention, the second one would, I guess, so here is my story!

It was a very hot day in mid-July, and there wasn't a breeze blowing in either direction. In fact, it was so hot that the only thing moving around were insects and they even seemed to be lazing around. I was almost five years old at the time, but it's just amazing that I can remember all the things even from way back then.

One thing I would like for my readers to know is, I'm a very big dog lover, even now, because of my puppy, Fluffy! One of the best and worst memories that stuck in my mind today was my little puppy, Fluffy. He meant the world to me as a child. In fact, I still get a little choked up just remembering some of the times we spent together. You see, he was much more than just a dog; he was also my best friend. Everywhere I went, you could best believe Fluffy was right there, tagging along on my heels.

He was all-black, with four white paws and a white-tipped tail. (I know, cute, huh?) He was given to me by one of my mother's church friends to keep me company when my older brothers and sisters didn't want me tagging along behind them, and I'm telling you right now that was pretty often. Now I also had my childhood friends who lived right next door to us, and they had older brothers and sisters just like I did. But most of the time, it would just be Fluffy and me hanging out.

Roy Gene was the older of the two little boys who lived next door who were pretty close to my age, and he was also the ringleader of mischief. Earl was his little brother and was the same age as I was. Roy Gene knew how to get us to do just about anything he wanted. I guess it was because he was a little older than the two of us.

We lived close to some railroad tracks that we were all forbidden to be anywhere near, and this was not a request. This was an unbreakable rule that was not negotiable by any means! You see, there were too many bad things that happened on those railroad tracks, and that's just a plain, simple fact! So don't be surprised when you see the frown on my parents' faces when I tried to give them a good reason for being down on those railroad tracks.

One day, we were all sitting around, bored, as all little kids get from time to time; and it was raining hard outside. Roy Gene came up with this brilliant idea to go race our Popsicle sticks that we had saved from the ice cream truck. Like I said before, we were all bored, including Fluffy, so it didn't take much convincing at all. Our mothers were nowhere around, and my dad was in the back room, listening to the baseball game. So Roy Gene convinced us that we could go down there and have some fun before anyone would even notice we were gone. My older brothers and sisters were all at school, so we didn't have them to worry about at the time. As soon as the rain let up a little, we grabbed our Popsicle sticks and went outside to race them alongside the curb that ran down into the creek alongside those railroad tracks that we were supposed to be nowhere near.

Now we had the type of parents who didn't ask for respect; they demanded it! Getting caught near those railroad tracks was definitely a punishable offense that would make most kids want to move in with Grandma just to avoid it. But we didn't think about that at the time, and Roy Gene didn't mention it either. So away we went!

Back in those days, we didn't have the technology that we have today, so we did things mostly outside, with our imaginations to create our own games. We would take the Popsicle sticks and place them alongside the curb and let the water from the rain carry them down the stream to see who had the fastest Popsicle stick. But this game was a bad idea because we had to cross those same railroad tracks that we were all forbidden to be anywhere near to follow the sticks to the creek, but we went anyway! It seemed like as soon as we got there, Earl stepped on a rusty nail, and it went straight though his shoe and into his foot. The fun we were supposed to be having went downhill fast!

His foot started bleeding profusely, and we all went into panic mode. Even Fluffy started barking like never before, as if he were saying he knew it was a bad idea from the very start. Earl fell to the ground and started yelling in pure agony, as if his foot had just been chopped off! I could see the panic in Roy Gene's eyes, and for the first time ever, he seemed to be speechless! I was watching him with great anticipation for instructions on what to do next, and I've got to tell you, judging from his facial expression, it wasn't looking good! He tried to respond by putting on a brave face and calling his little brother a little girl, hoping it would toughen him up enough to maybe make him stop crying.

And just when I thought it couldn't get any worse, a school bus stopped right on those same railroad tracks, and my two older sisters came running off that bus with their mouths moving a hundred miles an hour. (You see how bad things happen on the railroad tracks.)

I looked over to Roy Gene for what to do next, and he was gone. The boy's shoes were still there, but his body was gone! I mean, the boy literally ran out of his shoes and left a chewed-up path in the grass to indicate which way he went! So much for our leader Roy Gene because as soon as he saw my sisters getting off that bus, he made his exit faster than Superman going to rescue Lois Lane! Earl started crying even louder now because he knew the outcome of this wasn't going to be good at all once we got home, especially since my sisters had arrived on the scene.

Fluffy was turning in circles and barking now, and my sisters were talking so fast that they had to stop for a minute just to get some air to reload again! We finally got Earl up after a while, and we started that long journey home. Actually, the walk wasn't that long, but the consequences we were facing made us walk very slowly. Ms. Johnson is my mother, and she does not play when it comes to kids not doing what she told them to do. I'm not only talking about just her kids; I'm talking about kids in general. Once she called the house and told me that if the trash was not emptied when she got home, she was going to knock the black off me when she got home.

Readers, you already know that I'm not going to play with that, so I jumped to my feet like a marine sergeant and took that trash out; looking down the street at the same time just to make sure my mom was not in the vicinity already. On the way back in, I started to think about that threat and went and took a shower with a Brillo pad just to see if my black would really come off. Well, needless to say, I was a good kid from then on because if she could slap me that hard to knock the black off me, I don't want to mess with that.

My sisters Dee and Bobbie were like assistant prosecutors to my mother, like the ones you see on TV. So Earl and I were interrogated over and over until we reached the block that we lived on before they eased up a little. Then my sister Dee asked me, "Ray Ray, you want me to see if I can come up with some of your old baby diapers? They may take some of the sting off your butt when you get your butt whipped!"

Then you know my other sister Bobbie had to put her two cents in. "By the way, it hasn't been that long since you were wearing them."

Now I didn't see the humor in that at all, but they obviously did because they fell on the ground, laughing and holding their stomachs with tears coming from their eyes. Now how can that be funny when I'm scared to death? They were laughing so loud that my father must have heard them because he stepped out on the porch, asking what was so funny. Then he looked over at Earl's bloody shoe and asked what happened.

Well, before Earl and I could even say anything, the assistant prosecutors took over the whole story. After my dad finished listening to my sisters, he looked at Earl and me and said, "Y'all might want to double down on those diapers that your sisters were talking about." And he turned around and walked back in the house with a big smile on his face to go finish listening to the baseball game. Now I know the man liked baseball, but I know he saw his son was going to need some help on this one. And I needed him to get that before my mom came home.

Earl fell back on the ground and started crying all over again, and the butterflies filled my stomach so fast that I thought for a second that they were going to literally fly out of my mouth! You see, my dad's punishments were mostly verbal, so that made him cool to me! But my mom's was just the opposite when it came to things like this. So I was hoping that some of dad's cool would work on Mom if he attempted to get in front of what I had done!

My sisters made so many jokes out of this bad situation that I almost started laughing too. But as soon as I saw that long black car pull into our driveway, I got a little dizzy! Roy Gene was in that car too, and I immediately started thinking that something was wrong with that picture. The car sat there in the driveway for a minute before the door opened! But when it did finally open, it was like Cyclone Debbie had just arrived! Roy Gene's mother had him in an ear lock when she brought him out of that car, and he was crying with the snot coming out of his nose. Now you know some serious hurt is going down when you see snot on a kid's face. (I'm just saying!)

I looked at my sister Dee and asked her if she really knew where some of the diapers were because this just got serious! She looked at me with this big smirk on her face and said while laughing, "If you tuck and roll, I think you will be okay, Ray Ray. But make sure you tuck before you roll, or it won't work! Make sure you get it right. That's important."

I wanted to just run up on her and kick her or something, but she had already bloodied my nose before, so there was that! I just looked at her like she was crazy or something because I was not about to walk into that windmill of punches again. Nope, nope, nope!

"Yeah, Ray Ray, I think that ship has sailed already, and if the tuck and roll don't work, don't worry about it because you will flat line soon." Now she was laughing so hard she was holding her stomach. "Ray Ray, you should see your face right now because you're as white as a ghost, and I didn't think that was even possible." She was laughing too hard at that "white as a ghost" joke part. Even though I should have been offended, she was laughing so hard I started laughing too because I am dark-skinned and there is no way in hell my black butt is going to turn white.

"Ray Ray and Earl get in the house right now" was what my mother said. "You girls got homework to do, I'm sure, so my suggestion to you is to go get started on it right now, unless you want to be a part of this!" Well, you don't have to be a brain surgeon to figure out how my sisters kept good grades in school (Ms. Johnson's after-school threat and homework program).

My mother was very polite, more polite than usual, when we were in trouble! For all the kids who were in trouble, you would have thought we were all about to go on a picnic or something with the way she said, "After you, children!" On our way to being marched back to the bedroom, I glanced over at my dad for maybe a little sympathy, and he gave me the shoulder shrug kind of look, as if I weren't going to drag him into this. I started thinking about how that tuck-and-roll thing might go because it didn't look like this was going in my favor. Maybe I should have taken my sisters' advice and doubled down on the diapers or something.

Now you remember how I mentioned earlier about how my sisters acted like assistant prosecutor? Well, now it was time to face off with the head prosecutor, and a law had been broken. Somebody had to be held accountable or have a very good reason why we were down by those railroad tracks or it was about to go down right here, right now! As soon as we entered that room, that nice, polite mother went away fast. We were asked to sit down and tell the story of how we ended up down by the creek and those railroad tracks when each one of us knew better.

Roy Gene went first, and I didn't know why he tried to lie because our parents had a pretty good idea who the ringleader was behind this anyway! The boy was sitting there with no shoes on, so there was that. It was already looking bad for him way before he even started trying to explain because the no-shoe thing was a dead giveaway. In the middle of telling them what happened Fluffy pushed the door open with his nose, as if he had been listening outside the door for a minute and he had heard enough! He started spinning around and barking, as if to say that that story was not even close to being right and that he tried to tell us before we even went down there across those railroad tracks that it was a bad idea! It was at that point that I realized that puppies are smarter than kids and probably most people in general.

We all got spankings, and still to this day, railroad tracks make me nervous.

# Moving On

By the time fall was arriving, I was getting pretty close to turning five years old, and the talk of moving was in the air. But I didn't pay much attention to it because I was just a kid, doing what kids do. My father worked in an oil field, and sometimes he would be gone for days. Sometimes, that work would consist of him working underground; breathing air that I'm sure was not healthy. The doctor would give him medication to fix one problem but would create another! The side effects of the medication would outweigh the problem it was supposed to be curing!

One day, Earl and I were outside playing with Fluffy, when my older sister Carol came outside to tell me that we would be moving to Kansas City soon so I could start school. Now Carol was older than I was, and people say we look more alike than anybody else in the family. But there is one sure way to tell us apart! She is pretty much the one walking around with the devil's horns growing out of the side of her head. Other than that, we pretty much look like twins. If my parents wanted to know who had done what, she was the one they would ask, and she enjoyed telling it. She made trouble for all the kids in the neighborhood because she told everything she knew, and if she didn't know, she had a theory about how she thought it went. So I just figured this was one of these things that she didn't know, so I just put it in the back of my mind and kept on playing.

After dinner, I overheard my dad telling my mother it was almost time for me to be starting kindergarten and how much better the schools were in Kansas City. I hadn't had those butterflies in a while, but when I heard that, they came flying in first class on the most reliable airline. I didn't want to move to Kansas City or anyplace else. I started thinking right away if Fluffy was going to be able to come with me because after all, he was my best friend in the whole world, and I had never been away without him before. This was just too much at one time for an almost five-year-old to process right now, so I picked him up and went into my room to just think for a minute.

I had always heard that I had cousins already living there, but I had never met them before. So they were strangers to me as far as I was concerned. Grown-ups have a way of not letting kids know certain things until they are ready for them to know. Most of the time, if it's not early news, then there's a strong possibility it's bad news!

I can still remember the look on Roy Gene's and Earl's faces when they found out the news. My entire family felt bad for me now because I was walking around holding Fluffy in my arms, and I didn't want to put him down, even for a minute. My older brothers and sisters tried to explain to me that I would make lots of new friends when I started school. But I didn't want new friends because the old ones were working out just fine with me.

Fluffy brought joy to all he came in contact with, so I automatically thought he was going to be making that trip with me. That turned out not to be the case at all; I quickly found out that my puppy was not coming along on this trip, and my little heart just dropped to the floor. I didn't sleep the night before, as you might imagine. Instead, I held Fluffy in my arms and cried for most of the night, and he tried to cheer me up by licking my tears off my face as they ran down one by one. I started to wonder whom they would be leaving him with because I wanted him to be happy too if I had to leave him with someone.

Everyone got up at the crack of dawn, packing boxes, but I just stayed in my room with my puppy until I heard my name being called. Then it came. "Ray Ray, let's go, honey. It's time to go." The first thing I saw when I came out of my room was Roy Gene and Earl standing there with big tears in their eyes.

Then my dad said, "Ray Ray, your friends are going to take care of Fluffy for you."

Now I definitely didn't want to leave my puppy, but I did have some small piece of comfort knowing it would be them taking care of him, though only a small piece. The decision had been made whether I liked it or not, and it was time to move on. I handed Fluffy over to them, and everyone in the room had tears in their eyes. But they tried to smile right through it so it would be easier on me, I'm sure. As the family put the last items in the car, Fluffy started barking, like he was asking me to take him too. At least that was what I wanted to believe. My parents grabbed me and made me sit down and face the front of the car because my little eyes were almost swollen shut from crying so much already. Even though I couldn't see him, I could still hear his little puppy barks, and I started to cry all over again until I fell asleep on the highway.

By the time I woke up again, we were pulling over for gas and something to eat. Of course, I wasn't hungry, but my dad insisted that I at least try to eat something anyway because it would be a while before we stopped again. I remember trying to eat some graham crackers and milk because they were my favorite sometimes, but I didn't have much luck with that because all I could think about was my puppy, Fluffy! After they all finished eating, we jumped back on the highway and I slept mostly all the way there.

I woke up shortly before turning on the block where our new house was located. I remember looking out the window and thinking how much better looking these neighborhoods were than the one I had just left, so maybe this new place wasn't going to be so bad after all. There were so many green trees in every direction that I looked. Kids were outside, playing all sorts of games. Dogs were running around, like everyone had one except me. And of course, Fluffy came to mind again, but I didn't start crying again because there were all this other stuff going on at the time, I guess.

As I told you earlier, I already had cousins living there whom I never met, and they were already at the new house, waiting for us to arrive. Danny Ray was the cousin who was more close to my age, even though he was two years older. He was outside with a football in his hand, along with a few other kids from the neighborhood. The family got out of the car to go inside to check out the new house, but I stayed outside with Danny Ray and the boys to see what they were about. Danny Ray was a very high-energy kid who seemed to know everything about everything, and you would just be beating a dead horse if you even tried to tell him different. He loved to talk, and he talked so much that I think if he would have closed his mouth for five seconds, he would probably fall asleep. At the time, that was cool because I really wasn't in the talking mood yet anyway.

The first thing he told the other kids was that I was his little cousin from Texas and that I was coming to live in this house. Right away, I started to feel at ease with him, and that was something that I needed at that particular time. I will never forget that one little kid who asked me what my name was. Before I could even respond, Danny gave him my name, rank, and social security number. Well, maybe not the social because I didn't have one yet, but he would have if he knew it.

"Dang, man, how many Rays y'all got in the family?" the little boy said.

Danny Ray smiled and said, "I don't really know, but there are more than just Ray Ray and me. Now I do know that much!"

The next thing I knew, we were in this big yard, playing football, laughing, and talking about all kinds of stuff that little kids talk about. My family all came out on the lawn to watch me for a while with big smiles on their faces. They were just glad to see my mind off my puppy for a minute, knowing how that had to be pretty dramatic for someone my age. Shortly after, my parents called me inside, so I gave Danny Ray and the rest of the boys a high five and went inside. The new house was all set up, and everything was in place. And, I must say, it looked very nice. For the first time since I left Texas, I caught myself smiling with delight.

School was starting tomorrow morning, and I was starting to be a landing strip for those butterflies again. They were flying in again straight to my stomach area, and it was starting to give me a little gas. I got up and went to sit on the toilet seat and just sat there, rocking back and forth because the standard old way wasn't doing anything. You know how sometimes when you have eaten too much of the wrong stuff and it takes you anywhere from ten to fifteen good rocks on that toilet seat to finally get a very small piece of comfort? Well, it was one of those days and right before school too. I was so constipated that I probably weighed a little more that day than two days later.

The morning of the first day of school, I didn't sleep much, but I was sure that was normal for any kid on the first day, especially if he put in at least thirty rocks on the toilet seat the night before. My mother was already up, cooking breakfast and laying out school clothes when suddenly, a knock came at the front door. I looked out the window to see who it was, and it was Danny Ray, coming to walk my sister Bobbie and me to school. I opened the door and let him in. He seemed to still be in a cheerful mood from yesterday, and I needed that because it was the first day of school and I didn't know what to expect. We had to wait on my slow sister Bobbie because she was still in the mirror, trying to get everything in place, I guess.

"That's why I always beat my sister to the bathroom in the morning because they will take forever," Danny said.

Bobbie came out of the bathroom and looked Danny Ray right in his eyes and told him, "Don't get beat up on the first day of school by your girl cousin because I don't think that will carry over too well on the football field with your little friends."

Danny stopped smiling and looked over at me! I shrugged my shoulders and told Danny Ray to "come here." I pointed to the knot on the back of my head and said, "Look what she did to me, cousin, and it's still sore."

Danny walked over and took a look at my Afro. "Dang, Ray Ray, she knocked a patch out of your fro, man. What the hell happened?"

"Man, my friends and I were outside playing baseball one day, and here she comes wanting to play. She would never let me play with any of her stuff, so I wasn't going to let her play baseball with my friends and me. But she was a bully, and she was bigger than any of us. So what we gonna do? She took the bat from one of the kids and made the other kid pitch the ball to her, even though he didn't want to. I was the catcher at the time, so I was standing right behind her when she got ready to swing that bat! When the little kid pitched the ball to her, I wasn't going to let her hit my baseball way down the street somewhere. Nope, nope, nope. So I jumped in front of her to steal the pitch!"

"Wait, Ray Ray, you jumped in front of that bat?"

"It's my sister, man, and I knew she was not going to swing that bat. But she did! Man, she swung that bat and knocked a patch right out of my Afro, man. And now I walk around with this sunroof, or maybe I should call it a half moon roof because of the position it's in."

Danny was laughing so hard that it made me start laughing too.

"Hair doesn't even grow right there anymore. If I were you, I would play it safe and not let her hear you saying nothing bad about girls unless you can fight! I don't know about KC, Danny Ray, but in Texas, girls can fight. And they don't mind doing it."

He still had this confused look on his face when we went out the door on our way to school.

# The First Day of School

It was only four blocks away, but it seemed like it took forever to get there. There were so many kids walking in the same direction that my sister soon peeled off from us and started walking with some girls she met along the way. As soon as she left, Danny started talking smack. "Man, I thought I was going to have to kick her butt in there."

I tapped him on the shoulder and pointed to my sister, and she was looking straight at him, holding her fist up at him, and shouting, "I heard you, cousin, so I guess we will see about that when school is out!"

Danny turned and asked me, "How can she hear me way over here?"

"Man, I'm telling you, the girl is not normal. She has superpowers. I think she rides a broom at night. Who really knows? I mean, I'm asleep. I don't know what she's doing when I'm asleep. All I know, she is always up first when I wake up, like she never even been to sleep! If my mom didn't call her daughter, I would second-guess her being my sister. That's all I'm saying, man. I think maybe she is really from Gotham City or something. You know, where Superman is from? I mean, think about it! She did just hear you, didn't she? Well, don't rule it out is all I'm saying."

"Ray Ray, that's not funny, man."

"Nah, man, it's not. Actually, it's kind of scary when you really think about it, so let's not think about it right now."

"Lil Ray Ray, you're a funny guy."

"Was I smiling when I said it?" I asked.

As soon as we got to school, the bell was about to ring, so we all scrambled to find our assigned class. Anthony and Robert, who had played football with us, were in the same class I was. At five years old, I didn't even like girls yet, and it was probably because I thought they all were like my sometimes-mean sisters. But as soon as we got in class, this one particular girl kept looking at me like she knew me from somewhere or something. I was much too shy to even make eye contact with her, but it didn't matter because right away, the teasing from Anthony and Robert started anyway because they had seen the whole thing.

Everyone had to stand and give their name, and I almost fainted when it was my turn because she was still looking at me, smiling. Her name was Marsha, and she had pretty blue eyes. And that was different for me because I had never seen that before where I was from. I used to stare at those blue eyes when she wasn't looking right at me, wondering if they really worked like mine did.

As soon as class was over, I was the first one out that door. I was halfway down the block when Danny caught up with me. "Ray Ray, why are you running so fast? Is someone after you?"

"Nah, man, if that was the case, I would have just told my sister Bobbie because she is a lot scarier than you are!"

"Ray Ray, that is definitely a fact, lil brother, and there is no argument on my part!" Then we both slapped high five on that and laughed.

Next came Anthony and Robert, exaggerating the whole thing; by the time they finished telling their version of the story, Marsha and I would have been walking down the aisle by Wednesday, getting married, and it was already Monday. I didn't even like girls like that, so it was a little embarrassing at first. But they made so many faces with their jokes that it made me start laughing too.

By the third week in that class, I wasn't shy anymore, and Marsha and I became good friends. She was just as smart as she was pretty, and she always offered to help me with my homework. That never seemed to work because I would always end up looking at those blue eyes rather than paying attention to what she was saying! The girlfriend jokes never stopped though, and they traveled all the way to my house and the football games in the neighborhood. I got used to it after a while and just enjoyed the popularity that came with it. All the guys wanted to be able to say they had a girlfriend after the school year ended because girls were cool now, and playing with little hardheaded boys all the time kind of make you want to have some girls as friends as well.

Marsha moved away to California, and I started to pay attention to girls just a little more. My mother worked in the suburban area for the more blessed, as I like to call them. It was not until I got a little older that I realized my older sisters and brothers had always chipped in to make all our lives a little more comfortable when things got a little rough financially. My dad worked as a coal miner back in Texas for many years, and still to this day, I'm sure it drove him to a much-earlier grave, leaving my mother with a lot of beautiful memories.

By the time I got to ninth grade, I was not only good at football but even better at basketball, and I was playing both sports at school. So you know a brother had skills. In fact, I picked up a nickname (Mad Skills) playing sports, and it followed me for a while. My dad loved sports too and used to attend all my games until his health took a wrong turn! His illness had been apparent for years now, but now it was being more visible than usual. My dad loved all sports, and so did all of his kids. I still talk sports with my brothers and sisters, even now. His favorite sport was baseball, and if I had known how much they get paid, I think I would have put a little more interest in that sport. Now when we would go to church on Sundays, my mother would always ask for special prayers for my dad, and that would always concern me very much!

By the time I made it to high school, I made first varsity on the school team, and Danny Ray couldn't beat me at basketball anymore, although he would never admit it. I was much too quick for him, and I could stop on a dime and pull up for a jump shot from anywhere on the court!

One time, I was on my way home from school and decided to stop by the basketball court to watch the big boys play on the court. I had never played with the big boys before, even though I always wanted to. They played hard and rough, but that didn't scare me at all. I had another cousin playing who went by the name of Hershel, and this guy had mad skills on the court. He was much older than I was and never let me play with the big boys because he thought I was just too damn young. Anyway, that was what he always said when I wanted to play on the big court.

On this particular day, they were running hard, just like the Lakers or something, when one of the guys on the opposing team twisted his ankle coming down from snagging a rebound. The guys needed another player to take his place in a heated game, and their captain picked me as that guy's replacement to be on his team. Hershel thought I was way too young to be on the court with the big boys and did not want me to play, but the guy had seen me play before and had the utmost confidence in me to handle the point guard spot. Hershel chose to defend me at the time because he wanted to scare me into getting off the court, but I was having no fear from his smack-talking!

The game was tied 10–10, going to 12 for the game, and I still had my school clothes on that I was not supposed to be playing basketball in! Danny was one of my teammates and wanted me to pass the ball to him because he thought I was intimidated by my big cousin Hershel, but I wasn't! I had mad handles on that basketball, and when he tried to steal it from me, I crossed him over and stopped on that dime that I was ever so famous for and drained the shot like I was Allen Iverson or somebody. Now of course, Hershel didn't like his little cousin hitting a shot over him like that, so he dared me to try it again! Teenagers on the sideline were definitely paying attention to me now because nobody had ever crossed Hershel over like that! One point to go and I was not scared to take the last shot, so I demanded the ball again with Hershel tightening down on his defense! I knew he would be trying to pick my pocket because everyone was watching! When he went for the steal, I took the ball behind my back and pulled up for that famous jumper and banked the ball off the glass, calling the bank shot before Hershel could even turn around and see the ball coming through the net. Game over!

Danny started teasing Hershel, and of course, he didn't like that. Hershel was so embarrassed that he ran up to me and picked me up and threw me in a mud puddle with my school clothes still on! When I got home with mud all over my school clothes, I was sure that I was in trouble, but after my parents heard what happened, they went out and bought me a basketball goal for me to play with my friends in the neighborhood!

Now let me just tell you how my cousin Danny Ray was when we were younger. Danny put a whole bar of Ex-lax in a Hershey's bar candy wrapper and brought it outside to share with the kids. This was definitely out of character for him because he never shared candy with anybody. If anything, he would help you eat yours up and have his in his pocket the whole time, saving it for later. We were all outside, playing baseball, when Danny got in that sharing mood. At first, after we ate it, we were just passing gas and stinking up the air a little while we were still playing baseball. Then everyone broke for the bathroom just about the same time, except him. He just stood there with that bad-kid smirk on his face, taking the whole show in. Oh yeah, it turned out to be quite a messy show because everyone couldn't get to the bathroom at the same time, as you might imagine. (I mean, the boy fed us Ex-lax, so you know he had to be a conniving little boy to do something like that!) That was just one of many prank stories to tell about Danny Ray, but there were so many that I wonder whom he is pulling a prank on right now!

My parents were especially proud of me because playing sports and going to church kept me grounded and respectful and out of the trouble that most teenage boys were getting into at that time. Plus, my mom had a secret weapon—a fresh can of whoop ass if she needed to open it!

# My First Real Girlfriend

I have a girlfriend now, and her name is Stacey. Girls were cool now! I was a guy that could always make people laugh, even when they were having a bad day. My family said that I had missed my true calling because I should have been a comedian or something. My dad used to always tell me that if a guy could make a girl laugh, he was more than halfway home with her. Stacey loved that about me, and she used to throw her head to the side and make this little laugh, like Betty Rubble with a girlish giggle, when I said something funny. And I loved that about her because it was unique and unlike anyone else. There were a few girls who flirted with me, but I only had eyes for Stacey. But that didn't stop them from flirting when she wasn't around. She also was a cheerleader with a frame to die for, metaphorically speaking, and as you might imagine, she loved sports too. We really enjoyed spending time together because we had so much in common, and that is one of the keys in a long-lasting relationship. Anyway, that was what I believed.

Anthony and Robert had taken a different route from me because they had much more freedom than I did. My mom used to say that an idle mind is the devil's workshop, and they had a lot of idle time. It wasn't until I was a little older that I got the true meaning of that phrase. They both only had a mother in their lives, with no father in sight! I never quite understood why when I was younger because I had both parents in my life, and since I was the youngest in my family, it seemed at times that my older brothers and sisters were parents too, especially my oldest sister, Evelyn, because she was always the one taking up the slack when my mother was at work or something.

She had one problem though! She couldn't make oatmeal come out right to save her own life! I mean, how could she have lumps in the oatmeal? I mean, cream of wheat or something, I get; But the oatmeal? I used to spit it out when she wasn't looking right at me. You don't know how many times I burned my mouth because sometimes she took too long leaving the kitchen. I would have to hold it in until an opportunity came around just to spit it out.

My family always paid very close attention to everything I did, so there was only a small window to climb in for mischief if that was what you wanted to do.

# Losing My Dad

One day, I came home early from basketball practice with my girlfriend, Stacey, and as soon as we walked in the house, I could hear my dad's radio up pretty loud, listening to the baseball game as he always did. So I didn't think too much of it at the time. Stacey and I went straight to the kitchen to get something to eat. Then Stacey asked me if I thought my dad might be hungry too. I walked back into his bedroom to ask, and there he was, slumped over in his favorite chair. His glasses had fallen to the floor right beside his tobacco pipe that he enjoyed so much! I was stuck for a second, like being stuck in the mud on a rainy day. I called out to him because I wanted him to just be asleep, but in the back of my mind, I knew better. Or was it in the front of my mind because at a time like that, who could really tell where it is? I walked over to him to turn his radio off, and that was when I noticed his color had changed! I quickly turned the radio off, and right away, I got a weirder feeling than I already had! I touched his arm, and it was cold.

You ever knew something but you wished you didn't? Well, that was where I was at this particular minute. I didn't want to know what I knew, but it was much too late for that already because my father was gone just like that! Now I don't know about everyone else's family, but in our family, Daddy was the rock and the foundation of the Johnson family! Even now, just writing this book brings back memories that take me on a horrific journey that I don't want to revisit. I'm sure you have all been there, and maybe some of you more than once, so I know you share my pain on this one.

I was so startled that my brain just shut down, and I couldn't even breathe or talk for a very long time, it seemed. The next thing I remember, Stacey was coming into the room with her mouth wide open, mumbling something before she collapsed on the floor! The phone started ringing, and I approached it very cautiously before picking it up because I didn't know what to expect right about now! It was Gladys, one of my older sisters, and she already knew something was wrong. Gladys had been diagnosed with muscular dystrophy, but it didn't stop her from being who she was. She said, "Put Dad on the phone!"

I responded by saying, "I can't do that right now, big sis, because he is not waking up right now, and I don't think he ever will again!"

"He is gone, isn't he?"

"Yes, I think so, but I hope like hell I'm wrong!"

All I could hear was her saying, "God, please no!"

The whole family knew how really sick he was, but it was just one of those things you don't ever want to talk about because you hope one day, it would all turn around and he would be all better again! By now, Stacey was up off the floor, crying like she wasn't breathing! I looked up at her, but no words would come out! When all my senses finally came back around, my family was all standing in the front room, along with the paramedics from the ambulance that had arrived. I didn't know how they all got the news so fast, but I'm thinking it was my sister Gladys or her daughters.

My mother was also standing there in disbelief just like the rest of us. Now we have all heard the expression "The calm before the storm." Well, that was kind of like my mother because she would take bad news very calmly before she switched into Hurricane Sara or something! She walked around the rest of the day without shedding a tear, but when that storm finally did arrive, it showed up like a category 5 hurricane! She cried for days!

The funeral was huge, and people came from as far back as Texas to show their respect for him. He had touched a lot of lives just by taking out the time to talk to people because that was worth more than money to some. He used to always remind me to be courteous and considerate to people up until a point! When you have to go past that point though, make sure you always get the first punch! Being a man is about standing on your own two feet and taking care of your responsibilities, even if you have to go outside the box sometimes. Sometimes, it's not so much what people say as it is what they do, and you have to know how to decipher between the two.

"Ray Ray, always remember, trust is number 1 in this thing called life, and if you can't trust a person, then you definitely should not be around them. Trust is earned, not given, and that goes for everybody! Son, all people will eventually reveal their true colors. You just have to pay attention to what is said out of their mouth. You get what I'm telling you right now, son?"

"Yes, sir, I do! Watch what I do and watch who I do it with."

"Yeah, I'll take that one because you're on the right track even if you're not on the right road."

My dad used to say stuff like that to make me think and keep me sharp! I know we have all heard that expression that "time heals all wounds." I don't know if I agree with that. I'm still hurting from losing my dad because that was my guy! It took a while for the family to get past that day, if there even is such a thing. I mean, we only get one dad, so what do you think?

# The Fork in the Road

Shortly after that day, I broke my leg in basketball practice and had to sit out for a whole semester just to let it heal. It was my junior year in high school, and Stacey was a senior. She had already started receiving scholarships from prominent colleges, so she had started having dreams of her own. When I returned to the team, my leg wasn't as strong as before and I wasn't as quick as I used to be. I lost my starting position to a rookie as far as I was concerned, but I have to admit though, the boy could ball!

After a while, I started to lose interest in sports altogether, and Stacey graduated early with high honors and picked Georgetown University to attend. We started to drift apart because now we were on different paths, even though I didn't realize it at the time, but I was about to find out how different soon enough. My mom and dad had been together forever, and I always thought Stacey and I would be too. But preparing herself for college was starting to take up most of her time now, and we weren't hanging out as much anymore. Stacey had been my one and only since ninth grade and I just took it for granted and thought that she would always be there with me. I mean, I was just a young and dumb teenager, and she was my first; so you know, I was open like 7-Eleven! Sometimes, I would just be daydreaming about her girlish little Betty Rubble giggle, and I would catch myself smiling too. And yes, I did watch the Flintstones too.

I remember one day when she asked me how I knew that I loved her. I grabbed her by her hand and looked her straight in her eyes and responded with this: "Stacey, you're the first thing I think about when

I open my eyes in the morning and the last thing I think about before I close my eyes at night when I go to bed. What else could it be?"

She pulled me to her and said with that giggle that only she could make, "I always thought it was your puppy Fluffy, that you loved, Ray Ray."

"Fluffy who?" I said before I kissed her like it just might be my last. (Of course, I had told her about my puppy.)

"Ray Ray, you know the summer is almost over and I will be going off to school soon, so what are you going to be doing when I'm gone?"

"What do you mean, Stacey?"

"I mean, have you ever thought about what you're going to do if you can't play sports?"

When Stacey really wanted to know something, she put her pinky finger in her mouth and bit her nail. Right then, I knew this conversation was going somewhere, and I didn't know if I was ready to go yet because up until now, I hadn't even thought about it. But I could look in her eyes and tell she really wanted an answer to her question right here, right now! So I responded with this, "I guess I would get a job or something if I had to."

"Ray Ray, is that really going to be enough for you?"

Then I thought to myself, *Maybe I should be asking her if it would be good enough for her because that's what it's starting to sound like.* Even as a young teenager, I knew every question that was asked was for a reason. "Stacey, I still have another year left, so what's this really about?"

"Well, you know I'll be going off to college soon and will be doing my part in becoming a successful person in life, and I want you to be concentrating on yours as well for our future together."

I grabbed her around that perfect frame and kissed her again, as if saying, "I got this, so don't worry about nothing!" Well, summer came to an end, and Stacey went away to college, promising that she would call every day. And she did for a while, but then the calls started to fade a little and then even more. We started to have conversations with long periods of silence in them, and even though I was still a teenager, I knew something wasn't right about that! Once again, that feeling kicked in of knowing something that you really don't want to know, but that feeling never goes away until you do know! But when you do, that is the kind of feeling that tears your heart out! I think that statement that goes something like this has a lot of truth to it in my opinion: "You don't know what you have until it's gone." I mean, the girl was athletic and liked sports too. You can do a lot of things with a girl like that! Stuff like watching any kind of game, she would be into it just as much as you would. And the girl had a frame that looked like it was handcrafted by Toys "R" Us. I mean, when she took off those sweatpants and slip into one of those sundresses, she was all woman! I'm just saying the girl had a body!

Now do you remember my sister Carol who I told you about earlier? Well, she was the one who found out that Victoria had a secret! Victoria has been at the top of the lingerie game for a very long time, so she definitely knows something that nobody else knows because it produced billions for her. She probably noticed how men looked at women with nice frames and with the tight apparel clinging to their perfectly crafted body. I don't really know; I'm just speculating here!

Nobody's secret is safe when it comes to my older sister Carol. She is like a forensic specialist. If there is some gossip out there, she will find it. She collects bits of information in her head that she downloads on her everyday gossip with her friends. Stacey's name came up in some of this gossip, and you know my sister could not wait to tell me what she heard! Now if Carol can find out Victoria had a secret, then you know that no one else has a chance keeping a secret.

Stacey was seeing someone else and had not told me anything about it. Well, you know how most long-distance relationships go anyway. Out of sight, out of mind! I was kind of messed up for a while because Cupid had shot me in the ass! Oh, sure, we stayed in touch for a while, but soon the calls and letters just stopped completely. I was walking around in a daze, trying to figure out why. Now I don't think her leaving got to me as much as not knowing the reason why. I just think if you know the reason, the blow is not as bad, but it's still bad if you're not ready to let go!

After Stacey left, nothing was quite the same. But I was still going to church with the family because God performs miracles, and I needed one right now for sure.

# The Pool Hall

I also had started paying close attention to that pool hall that we rode by on the way home every Sunday after church, and now I was paying a little bit more attention than I had done in the past! Stacey had left a stain on my brain, and I needed surgery to get it healed. And I couldn't even come up with the co-pay! I would always see shiny new cars and well-dressed people hanging out there on the regular, and that got my attention. I had a void that needed filling because Stacey was gone. The days were dark and gloomy now, and I desperately needed some sunshine in my life!

One day, I was riding with my cousin Danny on our way to church for choir rehearsal, and as we were passing that pool hall, I glanced over, looking at the pool hall door. I saw Anthony standing there by the front door. I tapped Danny Ray on the arm and told him to pull over there, and he quickly asked me why!

"I just saw Anthony from school, man, so turn around." Little did I know how much that pool hall would become a major turning point in my life.

As soon as I got out of the car, Anthony spotted me and called me over. "Mad Skills, what's going on, man? Long time no see, brother. You still playing ball? And where is your fine-ass lady, Stacey?"

"Whoa, man. One question at a time, please! Stacey and I came to that fork in the road where she went off to college, I guess, man. And my leg never did get back like it was after that surgery, so I kind of lost interest in sports, you know? Hey, Anthony, what goes on in there, man?"

"Oh, Ray Ray, you know, a little of this and a lot of that. You want to go in and check it out?"

I stood there for a moment before I answered because I had never been in a pool hall before, and I didn't know what to expect! "Sure, man. Why not?" was all that would come out of my mouth. So we opened the glass door and began to walk inside.

Right away, Danny froze right in his tracks! "Hey, Ray Ray, what are you doing, man? We don't know anyone in there, and maybe you forgot already that we are on our way to choir rehearsal!"

Anthony said, "Just relax, Danny Ray. It's all good because I come in here all the time."

"So what you're saying, me and Ray Ray are supposed to get killed because you come in here all the time?"

"Chill out a little, Danny," I said. "Let's just take a peek at it, man."

So we walked in, and I could remember the song that was playing on the jukebox like it was yesterday. "What's Going On" by Marvin Gaye was playing, and it really seemed to fit the surroundings at the time because I really wanted to know what was going on in there. For some reason, I wasn't as scared as I was curious about all this. They were shooting pool on the pool tables and playing cards at another, and the domino game was in full effect too. Then Anthony started giving me the rundown on who was who and who did what. Some of these people had names that I knew weren't on their birth certificates. Some of them were kind of funny and amusing at the same time. Danny Ray quickly reminded me that we were supposed to be on our way to choir rehearsal in case I had forgotten and that we were already late.

"Go ahead, man. I think I'm going to hang out here for a while with Anthony, so I'll catch up with you later."

He was hesitant at first, but soon he gave me a dap and turned around and walked out the door, shaking his head! I knew I would be hearing about this later from my mother prosecutor as well as her two assistants and the rest of the family, but at the time, I didn't care. There was a huge pool table at the back of the pool hall, and it was crowded with men and women standing shoulder to shoulder all around it. The sound of so many voices talking at the same time sounded like the humming of a trillion bees!

Anthony said, "Come on, man, it's a dice game. Let's go back there."

I had never seen a dice game before so I said, "Sure, man. Why not?"

# Charlie Soft

We walked to the back, and the first thing I noticed was a tall well-dressed man that seemed to be in control of everything that was going on around the pool table. He looked straight at me, as if he knew me from somewhere, and smiled! He motioned for me to come to the front of the table, and those butterflies came flying in again because I just knew he was not talking to me right here, right now! He said to the people who were betting around the table, "Ladies and gentlemen, we have a new player coming to the table, so for those who are not betting at this time, let the young man through, please."

My heart dropped because this was something I didn't expect. Anthony shoved me in my back, pushing me to the front of the table. "That's Charlie Soft, Ray Ray, so go, man!" I had no idea who this man was, but my feet started moving toward him as people cleared the way for me to come to the front of the dice game that was in progress.

Charlie asked, "What color dice do you prefer, young man?"

"Mr. Charlie, I have never played this game before, and I sure don't have any money to do so," I replied.

"What's your name, young man?"

"Ray Ray, sir."

Everyone laughed out loud, and I was standing there, feeling like I had just said something wrong.

"Well, Ray Ray, today is your lucky day because you don't have to worry about that today, so come on up to the table. People call me Charlie Soft, Ray Ray, not sir, okay?"

"Okay, Mr. Soft." And the crowd laughed again. I couldn't help it because I was always taught to respect my elders, and he was definitely older than I was because I was only seventeen!

"All I need you to do, Ray Ray, is pick up your favorite color of dice and roll them out across the table, and I'm going to do the rest. You will learn as you go how to play this game. It's a fast-paced game that's played for real money, Ray Ray, so I need you to pay close attention! I have a good feeling about you, son, and I'm very seldom wrong."

I looked at the dice sitting on the table, and there were two different colors—red and green. Anthony tapped me on the arm and said, "Get the red ones, Ray Ray."

Charlie cleared his throat to get my attention and said, "Ray Ray, never be a follower. Always follow your own mind."

Right away, I picked up on what he was saying and grabbed the green ones. I rolled them out across the long pool table, and they stopped on point 6. Charlie took a long stick with a curve at the end and pulled the green dice in front of him. I didn't know it at the time I was throwing the dice, but Charlie was the houseman, and this was his place and his game for the taking.

There was a very pretty lady sitting directly across from him, and her name was Ms. Kay. Believe me when I tell you that *pretty* was an understatement because the woman was ravishing! She had money stack so high that you could barely see those forty double D headlights she was sporting, if you get my meaning. She was not like the average lady I had ever seen before for more reasons than one. She had a necklace that hung from her neck that read "Assorted Flavors" in diamonds, and that heightened my senses big-time for some reason! She was slim in the right places, but she had more curves than the roller coaster at Disneyland! She caught me staring at her, so she reached in her Burberry bag and pulled out a small bottle of Maison Francis perfume and sprayed herself while, at the same time, winking at me. Now the only reason I remember the name of that perfume was my sisters talking about how much it cost. It was a 400-dollar bottle of perfume according to my sisters, and only high-maintenance women wore it.

Then Charlie Soft asked her, "Are you betting anything on point 6 or you going to just keep smiling at Ray Ray?"

I glanced down at those forty double Ds and smiled at her, and she said to Charlie, "He is cute but a little too young and green for me right now, but I think there's something about him. So I'll bet this on his hand." She threw six-hundred-dollar bills in front of Charlie and said, "Bet this on the cute young man."

Charlie responded by saying just one word: "Bet!"

*Why did she call me green?* was my first thought.

Charlie winked at me and threw me the dice again and said, "Do your thing, Ray Ray." I looked at him for some kind of instructions on what I was supposed to do as far as winning money for him, but he didn't give me a clue. Instead, he flashed that million-dollar smile and said, "Roll the dice, son."

I picked them up again and threw them down the long pool table again, and they stopped on the point of 9. The table was elbow to elbow, and everyone was betting a hundred miles an hour with multiple people at the same time. But Charlie and Ms. Kay seemed to only be betting at each other for the time being, and if I didn't know any better, they seemed to have a thing at some point or maybe even now, with the way they sometimes looked at each other!

I was starting to like this game, and people were betting real money like it was monopoly money. Ms. Kay bet nine hundred dollars more on the point of 9, and it didn't take me very long to figure out she was betting on every number that I rolled out on the green dice like it was nothing! I continued to roll the dice across that long pool table, and the more I did, the more comfortable I became with this game. Even though I didn't understand the whole betting process yet, curiosity had planted a seed in my brain that was sure to grow!

People were saying funny little metaphors that I had never heard before, and most of them had a mystery behind them. For instance, if someone was betting in the point of 9, they would say things like "Here comes little old Nina from Pasadena." And I was standing there, looking for a little old lady named Nina from Pasadena to come right through that pool hall door. (That's why Ms. Kay called me green, I guess.) "Come on 8, don't be late" was another that comes to mind, but there were more than I could even remember. I had only been going to church and school for the better part of my life, and now there I was in the back of that pool hall, shooting dice and looking at more cash than I had ever seen in my life. And I was only seventeen years old! My first thought was *I got to learn this!*

I continued to roll the dice across that long table until they stopped on 7! Seven, in this case, was a loss for someone that was betting the dice to pass, like Ms. Kay for instance. But Charlie was betting the dice didn't pass, so that made him a winner. He reached over and picked up thirty-one-hundred-dollar bills from the craps table and looked me straight in my eyes and winked at me, as if I'd done something right! But how could that be? Then it hit me! Charlie wasn't betting on me per se; he was betting with the odds of the dice. I had learned a lot about ratios and probabilities from school, and it was starting to look like that was Charlie's strategy in a craps game! My curiosity shot through the roof at that point, and I knew then that this was a man that was different than most!

"New shooter," Charlie said, so I backed away from the table. I was just a little confused but more curios than anything. "Ray Ray, don't leave just yet because I have something for you. My lady friend will show you where my office is, so just wait there, son. I'll only be a minute."

Right on cue, Charlie's office door opened, and someone beckoned me to come into the office. Now don't get me wrong, Ms. Kay was pretty, but this woman was in a class of her own. This woman was what men call drop-dead gorgeous! Anthony and I started walking that way and she stopped us and said, "Just you, Ray Ray!"

Anthony put the "Oh, damn" look on his face and backed up to let me go in by myself. As I entered the office, I couldn't help but notice a big picture of Dr. Martin Luther King on the wall. Charlie stepped in and asked me, "Do you know who that is, Ray Ray?"

"Of course I do, Charlie."

"Well, tell me about him then."

"He was a Baptist minister and activist who became the most visible, outspoken person and leader in the civil rights movement and was assassinated on April 4, 1968!"

"I'm impressed, Ray Ray, because too many of our youth don't know their history like they should about our people's struggle to make it in this sometimes-unjust world that we still live in today!"

"Charlie, I would have to have been living in a cave to not know who this great man was and the dream that he had for our country and all people, no matter what color or creed. He was definitely a king, Charlie, and apparently, someone disliked him for it—someone that didn't want to accept change in the world. And it is very unfortunate that there are still people living in the world today that still think that way! Charlie, did you know that there still are states that don't even acknowledge the great doctor's birthday?"

"Yes, I know, and that is a prime example of how change is still a long way off. Ray Ray, you definitely seem to be a smart young man, but you need to make better choices when it comes to you calling someone your friend."

"What do you mean by that, Charlie?"

"Are you still going to school, Ray Ray?"

"Yes, I am, Charlie, and besides, my mother wouldn't have it any other way."

"So what is your favorite thing about school, Ray Ray?"

"Well, lately, Charlie, school hasn't been that interesting since I stopped playing sports and my girl left me."

"Well, the girl thing will solve itself with time, but I'm curious about why you stopped playing sports."

"Actually, I broke my leg and lost my starting position, and one thing lead to another, to say the least."

"Ray Ray, you're still young, so it will be easy for you to bounce back if you're as smart as you seem to be."

"Never really thought about it much, but my mother does be on me about it."

"Sounds like a smart woman, Ray Ray, and I'm glad to hear that! Your boy who you came in here with doesn't have anything going for himself, so what's the connection between you two? In other words, why do you hang around with him?"

"Really, I don't, Charlie. He's just a boy I knew from grade school, and he just happened to be standing outside the pool hall when I passed by."

"You need to surround yourself with positive people who have ambition to win in life, Ray Ray, but even those people need paying attention to for more reasons than one! Is that too deep for you, son, or do you get what I'm saying to you?"

"Yeah, Charlie, I think I do."

"Have something in common with who you hang out with. Winning at whatever you do takes dedication and, most of all, awareness, no matter what your craft may be. You have to stay sharp at all times. Do you drink alcohol, Ray Ray, or do any other kind of drug?"

"Of course not, Charlie! I'm only seventeen years old. I'm telling you my mother is by the book when it comes to her children, and when I say by the book, I mean the Bible book!"

"There's nothing wrong with that, Ray Ray, because we all have to believe in something. Now your boy Anthony doesn't believe that fat meat is greasy, and that's why I don't even try to teach him anything! The alcohol wouldn't let him hear me anyway! One thing you got to understand right now, Ray Ray, is that fast money can be a downfall for some people if you don't know what to do with it. The worst thing you can do is pick up a drug habit. Everyone has some form of stress that appears in their life, but doing hard drugs just makes it less stressful as long as the high lasts. When that high wears off, that problem multiplies many times over! And when the money becomes slow, and trust me, it will, Ray Ray, because drugs will knock you off your game and put you in a whole different lane with no brakes. You hear what I'm telling you, son?"

"Loud and clear, sir."

Charlie reached in his pocket and took out two hundred-dollar bills and gave them to me, and now I was really confused!

"Charlie, why are you giving me this money?"

"I'm not giving it to you, Ray Ray. I'm going to make you earn it by answering this question. If you get it right, I will double it right here, right now! If you get it wrong though, you walk out of here with nothing, and you will owe me two hundred dollars to be worked off by coming in and helping me clean on the weekends."

Right away, I started thinking about those Jordans I saw in the mall the last time I was there, but at the same time, I did not want to owe him anything because my mother was not going for me coming in on weekends and cleaning up no pool hall! But the new Jordans would look great on my feet, so I said, "Okay, Charlie, what's the question?"

"Why did I not bet on you when I called you up to the table to roll the dice?"

"Because you were betting on the ratios' odds instead of me; I'm assuming this game is all about mathematics rather than just being lucky!"

Charlie stared at me for a second before he reached into his pocket again and pulled out two more hundred-dollar bills and said, "That's the way to double your money, Ray Ray, and you're absolutely right. You see, I knew Ms. Kay would bet on you because she believes in luck, not percentages. The object of any competitive game is to know your opponent, and I know Ms. Kay very well! Even if she is winning, she won't be for very long because luck will only take you so far before it runs out. Now in the back of my mind, I know all I have to do is keep her playing and the odds will eventually catch up to her. You were a face that she never saw before, and she believes that a first timer like you would have beginner's luck!"

I had never in my life had someone let me earn money just like that, so as you could imagine, I was shocked and, at the same time, intrigued. The seed was growing like it had been sprayed with Miracle-Gro water. "Hey, Charlie, as much as I would like to sit here and learn more about life from your eyes, I have to get home because my mother thinks I'm somewhere else right now, I think!"

"What do you mean you think, Ray Ray? Did you lie to your mother?"

"No, Charlie, I didn't lie to her. I just didn't tell her I was coming here! It's a long story, Charlie, and I don't have time to explain it to you right now."

"Okay, Ray Ray. See you next time."

Anthony was still waiting for me, and the boy had a million questions about what Charlie and I talked about. I was definitely not going to tell him what Charlie thought about him because I didn't want to hurt his feelings, so I told him I was still trying to figure it out myself on the way out the door. It was cold outside, and I had to get home fast. As I started walking toward home, Danny Ray drove up, so we quickly jumped in the car with him to get some heat and go through the first interrogation, sort of like a warm-up for what was to come.

The first thing Danny asked me was "Ray Ray, I know you haven't been here the whole time, have you?" I reached in my pocket and pulled out four hundred dollars, and his eyes just lit up with curiosity. "Ray Ray, where did you get all that money? I mean, I just dropped you off for a couple of hours, and you have already turned into a professional gambler?"

"Man, it's a long story, and I'm still processing it all myself!"

# Facing a Missed Choir Rehearsal

"Was my mother looking for me at choir rehearsal?"

"Yes, and she's probably going to use that same money right there to bury us both when she finds out where you got it from!"

Then Anthony said, "Hey, Ray Ray, if that money is going to get you in trouble, you can always give it to me."

I looked at Anthony and reached into my pocket again and peeled of a C-note and gave it to him because it seemed like the right thing to do since he was the one that brought me in there in the first place.

Then Danny Ray said, "Hey, Ray Ray, man, you already know I had to make up a lie when I saw her, right?"

"Well, enlighten me so we can be on the same page when we walk in the door."

"Hey, Ray Ray, I didn't say the lie worked. I just said I had to make up one!"

Then Anthony said, "Maybe you should give me the rest too, Ray Ray, before Danny sends you off to meet your maker!"

"Don't push it, Anthony, or I'll take that C-note back."

"Hey, Danny, this is my stop right here, so you can pull over and let me out right here if you don't mind."

"Yeah, that's what I thought, boy. Get out of here, and don't spend that money on alcohol."

"Oh, Ray Ray, I didn't tell you?"

"Tell me what, Anthony?"

"I don't even drink anymore. I only smoke pot now." Everyone in the car laughed before we pulled the car over to let him out.

"Now, Danny, what story did you tell my mother?"

"I mean, before I could even think of who you might be playing ball with, she started rolling her eyes back in her head and walked off toward the front of the church. She seemed to be praying that everything was all right with you. At least, that's what I thought! But when rehearsal was over, she let me know that she was mostly praying for me because if our stories don't match up when she catches up with you, she is going to punish me first for telling her a lie! Ray Ray, I'm kind of scared. And you should be, so let's make sure our stories match because if they don't, it's going to be all bad, brother."

For some reason, I thought about those railroad tracks when I was only five years old, and I thought this pool hall thing might just rank up there with that level of discipline. My mother did not accept any kind of lie or her kids missing out on any church function of any kind unless you have a legitimate excuse, which pretty much falls under the almost-dead or dead type of excuse. You have to understand something about my mother—she not only spanked her own kids but other parents' kids who she knew too. Then she would take you home and explain to your parents what you did, and most of the time, that would lead to maybe a second beat down!

Then Danny said, "Before I could even think of a name of one of the guys who you might be playing ball with, those assistant prosecutors that you call your sisters were rolling their eyes at me and making all kinds of ugly faces. Your mother didn't even let me finish before she walked away, speaking in a very scary, low voice!"

My mother is Ms. Johnson, and all the parents and kids in the neighborhood know her and respect her. For example, one day there was an after-school fight going on, and the kids were all crowded around, watching, including me too. The city bus came rolling down the street toward us and stopped right in front of the loud cheering crowd. My mother came walking off that bus, and when those kids turned around and noticed it was Ms. Johnson, there was an immediate pause in the action! The fight stopped immediately because everyone knew the deal with my mother and wanted no part of being disciplined by her at all.

Now keep that thought in mind. What story would you tell? I know that you hear me referring to my mom as a prosecutor, and there is a very good reason for that! If you have ever watched the TV show called *Law & Order* with Mr. McCoy, well, she was a female version of him to the tenth power! In other words, she was a master at getting to the truth. And it had better not take you a long time to get there either or there would be consequences! Danny Ray was against the truth because he had already gotten caught off guard and put a lie out there for me! But I assured him that I would carry my own weight about being in the pool hall, and it wouldn't come back on him at all.

"Yeah, I hear you talking, Ray Ray, but just maybe you're forgetting one thing, man! I was the one who drove you there, and she is going to want to know why I would do something like that! I already know she is going to ask me why I didn't just keep driving to the church for choir rehearsal, and that's the one that I don't have an answer for, man!"

"I will tell her I insisted that you stop so I could speak to an old school friend."

"I don't know about that, Ray Ray, but I do know that if we get caught in a lie, we're not going to like the outcome."

I only live right around the corner from that pool hall, but it seemed like it took forever to get home. It was probably because we could have walked faster than Danny Ray was willing to drive that car and for good reasons! When we pulled up, two of my sisters were already outside discussing the story Danny had tried telling my mother. I tapped Danny Ray on the shoulder and said, "The assistant prosecutors are here, so this might be all bad because we already know they have put their two cents in with their own theory of what they think might have happened."

Dee had a baby diaper behind her back and raised it up when Danny and I approached the porch. She and my other sister Bobbie thought that was still a funny thing to say, even though I was seventeen years old now.

My heart was beating fast, and I was sure Danny's was too, so we both took a deep breath and said, "Let's do this because there's no turning back now, man, unless we run away."

My mother used to tell all her children that when they thought their life was off track, just go and have a talk with God, and I was thinking now might be a good time to call that number. Now remember that I told you earlier that there was always the calm before the storm with my mother, so we were definitely expecting bad weather because after all, I had been in the pool hall, learning how to gamble!

My mother had a little Chihuahua dog named Dominic, and when Danny and I walked in the house, the first thing that caught our attention was that little dog sitting on my mother's lap while she pretended to read the paper. (But she was definitely waiting on me!) Now Dominic wasn't your ordinary dog because she had been taught how to bow her head and pray when she saw my mother doing it or heard really loud noise. So when we walked in, I thought I would break the ice with a "How you doing today, Mom?" (Bad idea.)

"Don't you patronize me, Ray Ray! Why were you not at choir rehearsal?" (There went the calm.)

"Mom, I'm not going to even make an attempt to lie to you because of two good reasons! One, I'm not good at it, and two, they don't make baby diapers that will fit a seventeen-year-old that I know of."

Mom said, "Oh, is that supposed to be funny?"

"Well, not if you don't think so!" I said. "I went and hung out at that pool hall around the corner."

She pulled her glasses down on her nose and asked me why I would do a thing like that.

"Mom, to tell you the truth, I've always been curious about what goes on in there. I saw one of my school friends standing outside when Danny rode by on our way to rehearsal, so I made Danny Ray turn around and stop there."

Dominic, the little dog, merely bowed her head and started praying. I tried to stay focused on my mom's demeanor, but that dog was funny. Danny nudged me and whispered, "Even the dog knows we are dead!"

"So let me get this straight, Ray Ray. You went inside that pool hall because you are curious about gambling?"

"I don't know if it was the gambling because I had no idea that they even did that when I went in there."

"Ray Ray, I have a million questions for you right now, but I don't even know where to start right now, so I'm going to tell you boys a story!"

# My Uncle Grady

She leaned back in her chair and said, "Ray Ray, my brother, your uncle, was a gambler. His name was Grady, but everybody called him One Shot! [Now I had heard his name mentioned before but never in that context.] He earned that name because if you left him so much as one shot on the pool table or the craps table, the game would be his at the end for sure! He was killed the same year you were born, so he never got to meet you. They say he was killed by a jealous man because the jealous man had a promiscuous wife who flirted with Grady every time she got a chance. No one was ever arrested for his death, as far as we know, and I don't think the police put up much effort to find his killer. You see, Grady was not only a very good gambler. He also was a ladies' man with a charming personality and the kind of charisma that most men only wish they could have.

"He was never married, but they say he has kids living in New York—a son named Brain and a daughter named Melissa. Although Melissa was his granddaughter, he raised her like his own. I know for a fact that he sent money there every month for as long as I can remember. I never met them before, and he never, ever, ever talked about them. I think whatever happened between him and those kids and their mom was painful for him, so I never pushed that conversation on him. A lot of people say you look just like him, and I think you do too.

"Most black people didn't have an abundance of nice things back then, at least none we knew, but your uncle did. And that made some people dislike him, but it made even more admire him. He was a different kind of man, to say the least, and he looked out for his family too! Sometimes, he would just pay Mom and Dad's bills up for a whole year at a time without them even knowing it. I always took care of all the bills, so they never knew! I would just save their own bill money and give it back to them if they needed it. Your Uncle Grady put that plan together, and it worked like a charm! Grady would grant a favor to get one back in return, and that made him seem like the prince of the city with the keys to everyone's front door. Whatever the year was, your uncle drove an automobile in the same year, and every time he appeared, he made a fashion statement, with mostly tailor-fitted apparel. He would dress in the most elegant of men's wear that sometimes weren't even out in stores yet."

"One Shot didn't really see color the way some people do. He saw personality, especially when it came to the ladies. He had this friend named Paul, and Paul had this little rhyme he used to say that I thought was kind of funny, especially the way he said it. 'My name is Paul, and I try them all' or something like that. It was a long time ago."

"I used to tell my brother that he needed to settle down with one woman, but it just wasn't in him like most men. Or maybe the right one just never came along. I don't know! Grady didn't trust many people, man or woman, and I think that's why he never got married. Trust was a very big thing to him, and he had to feel that about you to even let you in his circle. He used to say that he would rather have trust over love any day. Trust trumps love every time because without trust, how can you possibly have love? I think he made a very strong point when you really think about it."

One Shot made so much money that he ran out of places to hide it. He used to have me get him jelly jars, and he would dig deep holes in the ground at night and bury those jars with nothing but cash inside. He didn't really like the idea of someone else holding on to his money, so he definitely didn't trust banks! He liked his money where he could pick it up and count it whenever he felt like it, and he definitely could not do that with someone else holding on to his money! Still to this day, we don't know where some of those jars are buried. The reason that he gave me the money is because my parents wouldn't accept it from him because they thought it would just encourage him to do what he did. They didn't approve of his lifestyle, to say the least, because that wasn't something that was in the Bible, and they were all about the good book. I had a job, so they were in the blind when I gave them money a little at a time, and that kept the light turned down low on Grady giving me money to hold for them.

My mother and father worked very hard to just put food on the table for their kids, and that drove One Shot crazy because to him, they were only existing instead of living. But we both agreed that the slavery days were responsible for the way some things are still today. Grady thought those generations of slavery had done so much damage to our people who broken genes had been passed down generations after generations to our people, and that damage could never repair itself. And the powers that be weren't giving out any help, only Band-Aids to patch a very big problem! He thought, 'How could that happen when the drugs that flood our communities don't originate from our communities?' There was a higher power that was responsible for this act of 'genocide' that was not being held accountable at all! We didn't agree on many things, but that is one of the things that we did!

One of the things that was admiring to myself was that Grady was not afraid to talk about what most people were scared to talk about. [Racism!] He himself didn't see anything wrong with interracial couples, and he dated women of all races and didn't care what anybody thought about it. But he did see a big problem with making someone else rich off his hard work like that, because to him it was just updated slavery, and with the way some things are, I can't disagree!

# About Slim

"Grady dated this girl once who went by the name of Slim, and if I might add, she deservedly earned that name. She was about six feet tall with the slim body of a goddess. Slim was also very attractive as well as smart. In fact, they were so in sync that, most of the time she knew what he wanted before he did. That's just one of the things that he really liked about her, and that added to the many things that made her so unique over the rest."

"Your uncle was more of a nighttime kind of guy, so daylight caught him often getting ready for bed. He met her in a nightclub that he frequently went to from time to time. Now your uncle had a lot of ladies. But this one in particular, he liked a little bit more, and everybody knew it. You know, Ray Ray, one thing I never did understand about the women that he dated was, they all knew about one another, and yet they didn't seem to mind, as long as they got their own face time with him. But Slim was his favorite, and I think if things would have gone a different way with her, he would have settled down and married her.

"Grady was a traveling man, and a lot of his time was spent in other places, doing other things with other people. And over a period of time, that took its toll on her. Slim started hanging out with the wrong crowd, and that's where she took the wrong turn in life. She started using hard drugs to try to fill that empty spot that One Shot left in her heart when he was away, and if you add that with the wrong type of friends, there is no happy ending to the end of that story! That led them to that fork in the road that separates even the strongest of couples. By the time he noticed how bad her problem was, it was too late. The deceitfulness and lies that come with every junkie tore them apart like a cotton shirt getting snagged on a barbed wire fence."

"Wow, Mom, that's deep!"

"Yes, Ray Ray, everyone has their breaking point, and One Shot had seen enough. Instead of hanging around and watching her go down like the Titanic, he packed his bag and left everyone and everything behind to try to get that image of her slowly bewildering body out of his brain. It took its toll on him though because he had an itch for her that was hard to scratch, and each time that he would take her back, she would tell him that she was done with the drugs. But each time, that story would be just like the rest that he had heard so many times before! It would break him down like a double-barreled shotgun when he had to face that it was just another lie, just like the last fifty times! She had his heart though, so he kept trying to save her, even though he knew he was fighting a war instead of just a battle!

"One day, he was in the middle of a very high-stake pool game when a close friend interrupted the game to whisper something in Grady's ear. After receiving this news, his concentration flew out the window, and he ended up losing the most cash he had ever lost at one time! Ten grand was the purse on that particular night, and after that, he stopped gambling for a long time because his concentration just wasn't there anymore! The guy who had whispered something in his ear that night had told him that Slim had been found in her bathroom, overdosed on the floor, with her cocaine pipe lying on the floor beside her and her eyes wide open! He blamed her some, but he blamed the people who let these drugs come into our country without persecution a whole lot more!

"Grady had more pride than any man I have ever known, and I'm not saying that just because the man was my brother. One Shot was just not going to work nobody's job that was going to be telling him what to do and where to be every day! My dad used to say that One Shot was just cut from a different cloth, and he had no problem with that because people are going to be who they are no matter what! Nobody is the same in this world, and people will always have difference of opinions. That's just how it is. Grady had shaped his way of thinking from what he had experienced in his life, and he just couldn't acknowledge anyone having power over him like that after seeing his people enslaved for hundreds of years and his woman lying on the floor with her eyes wide open, looking to God for a way out. Working a job for low wages was just out of the question for him, as far as he was concerned. It seemed like the only options, as far as a good job, were working in some place that was either too hot or too cold, and he was not feeling it either! His people had gone through too much, and they were not even mentioned in early history books. From the things his people had gone through already, he just couldn't see that!

"I loved my brother dearly and still miss him very much, even to this very day. Son, you have to understand something about your Uncle Grady and me. We both grew up in an a era where you could drive by the cotton fields and see black people picking cotton, and Grady never got that image out of his head. It haunted him. Times are different now, and I wish Grady was around to see some of the progress his people have made, even though we still have a long way to go! Son, I've been noticing since you were born into this world that you have a lot of your uncle's characteristics, but I pray every night that you don't follow his same path because it's the wrong road to travel on, Ray Ray!"

Danny and I just sat there, stunned and silent because this was not what either of us expected to be hearing right about now! I attempted to break the awkward silence by reaching in my pocket and pulling out the three hundred-dollar bills I had left that Charlie had given me after that learning episode from the pool hall. "Mother, it may already be too late because I can see Uncle Grady's point, and I kind of feel the same way as far as just existing instead of enjoying life in a profitable manner."

"Ray Ray, I know you're very smart for your age, and you catch on pretty fast to just about anything. So here is something you better catch on to real fast, son. You're only seventeen years old, and if you want to make it to being eighteen, you better get that idea out of your head right here, right now! God and family first and school second, son, and just maybe you need to see about getting back into sports because I like coming to see my son participate in sports. Mad Skills, you're so good at whatever sport you want to play, and even I know that!"

I smiled at my mom and looked down at Dominic, and she had gotten in the praying position again. I took that as a sign that I just might be found comatose if she ever found out I was back in that pool hall again. She didn't take the money, even though I knew she needed it. So I went to my room and put the money in my sock drawer, and Danny and I made a quick exit out of there.

The next morning, I got up earlier than usual for school because I was up thinking about a lot of things from the night before. Mostly the part about how Uncle Grady didn't trust too many people, man or woman. I thought about how Stacey and I had come to our fork in the road and couldn't help but wonder if Uncle Grady had been through something similar with Slim. Charlie had also said, "Never hang out with people whom you have absolutely nothing in common with." And I had to wonder if there was some kind of a connection there too. That made a lot of sense to me even at seventeen years old! But why would he care? I mean, I didn't know this man and had never even seen him before, so why would he just pick me out of a crowd like that without knowing who I was?

I wasn't playing basketball at school anymore, so school just wasn't as interesting as this pool hall right now. I still went to all my classes because most of my teachers went to church with my mother on Sundays, and they would be most eager to give her a progress report in their Sunday conversations. Sometimes, I would be in a daze, thinking about Stacey in her little girlish giggle in some of my classes except one—music! My music teacher had a cockeye, so I could never really tell who she was looking at most of the time. She would be looking one way but could see on the opposite side. That was scary as well as confusing. I figured, why take a chance of acting out when she may or may not have been paying attention to me? Besides, I had always liked music, and pretty much up until now, gospel music was all I knew, except the occasional tunes I would hear on the radio.

When I got home from school that day, my mother was still at work as she usually was at that time of the day. So I took two hundred dollars and put it where I knew she would find it because that was my mom, and I didn't need a better reason than that. I turned the radio on, and there was that song again that I had heard at the pool hall jukebox that day when I was in there ("What's Going On"). I immediately started thinking about Charlie Soft and that craps game that occurred that day, and I knew in the back of my mind that seed that Charlie had planted was growing!

# Back to the Pool Hall

I put my books in my room, and out the door I went! It was a short walk, and I was at the front glass of that pool hall door before I knew it. This time I was all by myself, no Anthony or Danny Ray. But I wasn't nervous, so I pushed the door open and walked inside like I had been doing it for years. I like the kind of music that fits my lifestyle or, at least, that I relate to in some kind of way, but I also am a big jazz lover too. "Day Dreaming" by Aretha Franklin was playing on the jukebox this time, and it seemed to be tailored fit for the state of mind I was in at the time for sure because I had been daydreaming about Stacey all day.

The first person I recognized was Charlie Soft, standing at the back of the pool hall, running the craps game. He had not seen me yet, and my stomach, all of a sudden, started turning with butterflies. I didn't know why, but I became nervous all of a sudden! Charlie must have sensed me being there because he looked over his shoulder and saw me standing there like a deer stuck in the headlights. He motioned for me to come where he was, and I took off toward that direction, not knowing what was in store for me this time! Charlie was a well-dressed, soft-spoken man, and I couldn't help but wonder if that was where the name Soft came from—his voice!

Remembering what my mother had said about my Uncle Grady, the charisma part seemed to be established in Charlie as well. The guy never spoke loudly, and I didn't know if the girl who let me in his office was his wife or not, but she was the most beautiful woman I had ever seen in my young life from head to toe! Yes, there was definitely something going on in this place, and I liked it. I mean, the woman was way past beautiful. *Radiant* would be the more proper terminology because everything was in place from top to bottom! Now I know I only met this guy one time, but he was becoming very interesting. And now, since my mother had filled me in on my uncle One Shot, my curiosity level went through the roof! For the first time, I realized I was on the other side of those tracks that I came from back in Texas!

I made my way to the front of that long green pool table, and people were elbow to elbow just like before, betting that cash like it fell off a tree or something.

"Hey, Ray Ray, it's good to see you again. What's going on, little man?"

"Oh, nothing much Mr. Charlie. You know, same old soup, just reheated." The whole room laughed and snickered because everyone just called him Charlie.

"Well, Ray Ray, come around to the front of the table because I'm going to need you to help me out some."

I had no idea what this man wanted or why he wanted me to do whatever it was, but my curiosity wanted to find out! I held my head high and started making my way toward him. I literally bumped into those forty double Ds that Ms. Kay was highlighting with that low-cut top, and it definitely made me pause for a second before she grabbed my hand with her very soft ones and asked how I was doing today. I kind of blushed a little and said, "Fine, and thank you for asking."

"Ray Ray, if you really want to thank me, how about making me some money on the craps table tonight?" She took a seat directly across from Charlie and winked at me as she sat. Then she reached off into those double Ds and pulled out a roll of cash, and for some reason, I winked back at that point.

Then Charlie said, "Let's go in my office, Ray Ray. I need to have a conversation with you real quick!"

# Learning How to Run the Craps Game

Now I didn't know if it was curiosity or desire, maybe a little of both, because I wanted to know what was really going on. We stepped into his office, and he got straight to the point of what he wanted me to do! "Ray Ray, I have a really important pool game to play in one hour, and I'm going to need you to learn real fast how to be the houseman of a craps game because I can't be in two places at the same time."

"You're kidding with me right now, right?"

"No, I'm not, Ray Ray, and all you have to do is pay attention to every bet inside the box because the side bets are not your responsibility unless there is some kind of misunderstanding. Then you have to be something like a referee enforcing the game. But you're a natural, and I have about an hour to walk you through what I need you to do!"

"Charlie, whoa man, slow down! What makes you think I can do this with an hour walk-through?"

"Intuition and probabilities, Ray Ray; didn't you already win money off me with the probabilities?"

Now if it was any doubt in my mind that I could do it, he just erased it with that remark for sure! The guy was better than just good; he was a natural people person, and I caught myself admiring that too!

"Ray Ray, this is going to be easy like Sunday morning son, so let's go because I don't have much time before my guy shows up. Ray Ray, there are numbers on the dice that are called bar points, and they are the numbers 4, 5, 9, 10."

"Wait a minute, Charlie. What does that mean exactly?"

"It means that if someone is betting the dice pass and the dice miss by throwing a 7, with a 6 and a 1 showing, he draws his money back! He don't win nothing, but he don't lose anything either! Now if somebody is not betting on the bar on those same points, he or she loses if the dice miss with any kind of 7!"

"Well, what about the points 6 or 8?"

"They are not bar points, so for any kind of 7, he or she loses if they are betting the dice pass. Also, you have to cut three dollars out of the pot in the box on 6 or 8 every time the dice catch either point."

"So what are you going to be doing in an hour anyway if I can't remember all this that fast!"

"I'm going to be playing pool, best out of five freeze out, and the bet is for high stakes, Ray Ray. That's why I need you. I need you to get this, Ray Ray, before my guy comes in to play pool, so pay attention to everything I do and say. I know that you have a million questions going through your head right now, but now is not the time, Ray Ray."

I was still confused about the pool game freeze out and what that really meant. Now I was assuming it had nothing to do with takeout, pizza, or nothing, although I was a little hungry at the time. Charlie and I walked out of his office and went straight back to the craps game. Only this time, I had the dice rack that he used to rake the dice in for all the shooters. I was filled with mixed emotions for a minute, but Charlie was standing right there, telling me to just pay attention and let the game come to me! Now at the time, I didn't have a clue what that even meant, but I was sure about to find out quickly!

"Hey, Charlie, it's been a long time since I've seen you let somebody run your game or go in your office, so is that your son or something?"

"Why yes, it is, Ms. Kay. You mean to tell me you did not know that?"

I was shocked by his response, but I just winked at him and asked, "What do you want me to do, Pops?"

"After the dice roll and come to a stop, I need you to call out the number it stops on out loud so everybody can hear it before you let them roll again, and then mark the point with the other pair of dice that you keep right in front of you at all times. I also need you to take two dollars out of the pot every time he or she passes three times."

"Sure, Charlie, I can do that" was my response.

"So let the game begin," Charlie said.

The first person to roll the dice went by the name of Red. You see, everyone had some type of nickname, so I just assumed Red maybe got his from mostly the red apparel he wore most of the time. Or maybe it was the red foreign Mercedes-Benz he drove in his worldly travel he did from day to day. I'm not sure. But whatever it was, his money was green, and that's all that really matters when it comes to gambling, I guess!

# Meeting China

On the other side of him, there was a young woman that I didn't see the last time I was in there, and everyone called her China! She had slanted eyes, so I knew right away where the nickname China came from. She was very petite and about five feet and six inches tall and had a pair of thighs that were easy on the eyes, if you know what I'm saying. She had a Colgate smile, and those water balloons with the low-cut top weren't half bad either. They jiggled every time she took a step, just like a real water balloon would, and my eyes followed every bounce of every ounce for a good minute before I noticed I was starting to drool a little. Now you would have had to be living on the moon or something to never have heard a man say these words, "Man, the woman was so fine I would drink her bathwater!" Well, I'm going to put it like this—I'm getting thirsty right now just thinking about her!

China wasn't really gambling at the time; she was mostly just hanging out, it seemed. And later on, I would find out why. She smiled at me and said, "So you're Ray Ray?"

I saw her tongue ring, and my imagination took off because a woman with a tongue ring kind of made me feel a certain kind of way. That's all I'm saying! "Yes, I'm Ray Ray, and how did you know that's my name?"

"My mother told me about you."

"Oh yeah, so who is your mother?"

She pointed at Ms. Kay and said, "There she is right there, Ray Ray. You didn't know?"

It was believable to me because they almost looked like twins around the breast area, so she had me convinced! Charlie started laughing because she was no more Ms. Kay's daughter than I was his son, so the joke was on me. There were several other people at the table that I didn't know yet, but I had the feeling that would change soon enough. For a second, my mind drifted off, thinking about how hard my mother worked every day just to make ends meet, and these people were betting money like it wasn't real. I was thinking, *whatever type of job they are working must be different than the job that my mother has for sure.*

Red peeled off five hundred-dollar bills and tossed them to me since now I was the houseman running the game. Now Red was a very interesting character, to say the least. According to Anthony, he had many ladies, and they all knew about one another. "Hey, Ray Ray, can you even count that much money? Because I don't need any mistakes made on my money, rookie!"

"Red, if the dice pass for you, then I will throw you back one thousand dollars, but if you want more than that, then you're going to have to bet more than that. Is that good enough for you, or do you need a calculator to figure it out?"

China smiled with delight and said, "You keep impressing me like that and I'm going to have to give you a call if you're not too scared to give me your number!"

Then I did Charlie's wink and said, "Someone throw me a pen, please!"

Charlie was quick to do so, and he smiled at me while doing it. I wrote my number down and held my hand out to give it to her. She was a little older than I was, but I was up for the challenge. She was the first girl whom I had even locked eyes with like that since Stacey left, and with the way her eyes sparkled at me, she seemed to be feeling me too. Not only did China have slanted green eyes, she also had a slim waist and was very cute in the face and smelled nice too, and I liked that. I have always been athletic and always admired a woman that kept herself in shape. China had that Coke-bottle-shape thing going on, and that turned me on big-time! Stacey and I used to make that top priority, and when we were not making out, we were working out.

Those were two things I liked about her, but I was not going to go down the memory lane about Stacey because I had China up and personal right here, right now.

She was giving me that "I feel ya" look, and I was definitely giving it right back to her. She took the number and said, "I'll be calling you very soon, Ray Ray!"

"Not soon enough," I replied.

You know how sometimes you can just feel someone staring at you? I noticed that Red was paying close attention to what was coming out of our conversation, and I thought that was kind of odd! Charlie cleared his throat to get my attention back on the game, and for the first time, I noticed that China had a slight resemblance to Charlie. I don't know. Maybe I was just tripping!

"Okay, Ray Ray, she has your number, so let's get this game moving along and get Red a fade."

Ms. Kay did just that when she also threw up five hundred dollars to bet against Red and said, "Let him roll!"

Red shot the green ones and set the craps table on fire! With every number he caught, he took just a couple of rolls at it before that number was sitting pretty in the middle of the craps table. By the time he finished passing on Ms. Kay, her forty double Ds had been reduced to a C cup at least. The game went strong until the guy who Charlie had been waiting for showed up with a pool cue with the name Jaws inscribed in the side of it.

# Here Comes Teddy

Charlie looked at me and said, "Hold it down just like you been doing, Ray Ray. It's show time for me, so keep the game going if you can."

I heard somebody say, "Hey, there's Stay Ready Teddy, who always stays ready." I looked over at him, and he also was a very well-groomed man that looked like he was good at his craft because the man looked like money! He was about six feet tall with black-and-gold dreads hanging down way past his shoulders, and I thought to myself, *this guy is simply just cool, and there is no other way to describe it!*

I had lost track of time, so I glanced up at the clock that was on the wall. I had already been in there way too long, but there was way too much going on right now for me to even think about leaving right now! Some of the big gamblers from the pool table fell back from playing craps to go watch the pool game between Charlie and Teddy. I could tell this was going to be an exciting competition just by the reaction of everyone there. Charlie went up to Teddy and shook his hand, and you could just tell by their body language that they both had mutual respect for each other. And you could just feel the anticipation of what was to come. Charlie made an exit after that and went to his office to retrieve his own pool cue and his good-luck charm, his fine-ass woman who went by the name of Chanel! The word around the pool hall was that she could recognize a man's shoes before she could his face because she wouldn't even make eye contact with another man that would try to flirt with her out of respect for Charlie.

I had the craps game running like a well-oiled machine my first time out the gate, and I was somewhat surprised myself! But soon that pool game between Charlie and Teddy consumed the craps game because these were two top pool players, and it was about to go down like four flat tires right here, right now! Charlie told me to take everything off the table and put it in his office and come pay attention. Maybe I just might learn something.

"It's been a long time, my friend. How have you been?" he asked Teddy.

"I can't complain, Charlie. What about you?"

"Still on the learning channel, my man, still learning every day."

"Still being modest, huh, Charlie? That's what I love about you, man. You're one of the best pool players nationwide, and yet you're still learning. Ain't that about a bitch! You are always a gentleman first before you do your thing, and I admire that about you, Charlie. I really do. But it's not going to save you today because it's going to be a flip side to how things went the last time, my brother!"

"Well, Teddy, one thing about you telling that story is, you can tell it any way that you want to and nobody would know the difference. So name your game, man."

"Nine-ball, Charlie, five-game freeze out, just like before. But this time, I'm breaking first."

"Now, Teddy, you know how the game is played."

"Well, last time, I didn't get but one shot, so I thought you might be in a courteous mood and let me break first."

"Oh, I am in a considerate mood. We can bet as much as you want to bet, but we are still going to have to flip the coin just like before because you're way too good for me to just let you break first."

By now everyone was watching, including me. China came and stood right beside me, and we locked eyes again. But this time, I reached for her hand, and she accepted the reach with a smile. For the first time, I noticed that those green eyes had a twinkle in them, and I was assuming that the sparkle was for me. When I looked deep into her green eyes, I could still see Red's reflection staring at us, so now I was starting to think something. But she never even looked at him once, so I let it go for now!

Teddy won the coin toss and stepped into position for the nine-ball break. China looked up at me and asked why the name Jaws was inscribed on his pool stick. Now I knew that this was not her first rodeo, but I answered her anyway. "I guess that stick eats amateur pool players alive, but I'm guessing Charlie is no amateur by a long shot."

"Your right, Ray Ray, he's not. I have seen him play many times, and it depends on how big the bet is whether he wins or loses." Then she winked at me and pulled me close and whispered in my ear, "Charlie wins when he is supposed to and never before!"

"China, what exactly does that mean?"

"It's a long story right now, Ray Ray, and this is neither the place nor the time, so we will have a conversation later about this, among other things."

"China, I was thinking the same thing. How did you know?"

"I'm a little psychic, Ray Ray. You didn't know?"

"I do now!" We both laughed, and then I leaned in and kissed her on the cheek before we both turned our attention back to the pool game.

Teddy hit that nine-ball break with furious thunder, and that cue ball jumped back after hitting that pack of balls like it had a string on it and returned and made contact with that pack of balls again, sinking three balls with ease. The onlookers started making bets on who they thought was going to win the set, but Charlie seemed just as relaxed as ever with his good-luck charm, Chanel, right at his side, doing what she did best—being a distraction for Charlie's opponent! There was cigarette smoke all in the air while the gamblers placed their bets. But whatever kind of perfume that Chanel was wearing negated all that, right along with that radiant look that she had on display. I heard later on that she was a cross mix between Portuguese and Puerto Rican, and you could just tell that she was just like fine wine that only was going to get better with time. Teddy smiled with the utmost confidence after winking at her and walked around the table, looking for his next shot.

China squeezed my hand firmly with eagerness, as if what Chanel was doing excited her, and that made me curious as to why. But I just spaced it off for the moment. Usually, the pool hall was humming like bees, but you could hear a pin drop right about now. And everyone was watching Jaws eat up those pool balls like an old game of Pac-Man! The jukebox was playing "I'll Be Around" by the Spinners. Charlie definitely didn't look like he was about to go anywhere, so the song just kind of fit the moment. In fact, he and Chanel were having such a casual conversation that it didn't even seem like there was a pool game going on at the moment.

But Teddy hadn't missed a shot yet, and he was making that cue ball do some fancy dancing around that table, and Jaws' appetite seemed to be growing hungrier for Charlie's stake as the game went on. You see, a lot of guys think they can play the game of pool very well because they can shoot pretty straight, but if you can't control that cue ball and make it go where you want it to go; you better not get on the table with either of these guys! Teddy zipped through that first game like it was nothing, without Charlie even getting one shot! Charlie didn't appear to be even a little agitated! (It was like he knew something.) Teddy broke into the second game with the same confidence as the first game and pretty much got him the same results too, because he ended the second game more quickly than the first one without Charlie ever getting a shot!

Now you know Teddy was feeling it right about now, and he was talking smack and letting it be known that he was the best while he ordered up a drink! It was the third game now, and Charlie started chalking up his pool cue. People started to whisper something, as if they all knew that that drink was a very bad idea while playing against a guy of Charlie's caliber. Teddy was two games up, so he thought there was no way he could lose now! I wasn't sure at the time, but I think people were starting to bet on Charlie. Even Ms. Kay placed a five-thousand-dollar bet on Charlie, and I couldn't understand why, especially since Teddy was two games up already!

Teddy looked at Charlie and said, "I know what you're thinking, but I can drink ten of these and you still wouldn't come back at this point, man, because all I need to do is win one more game, which I can do with my eyes closed. I don't know why you are chalking that pool cue like this drink is supposed to knock me off my game or something.

I'll tell you what, Charlie, you can go ahead and have a seat with that beautiful woman that you have right there and watch how I end this show."

Chanel stood up and walked over to him like a model walking the runway with all that junk in her trunk following close behind her! She got close enough to almost touch his nose with her own before she whispered in his ear! "Can I refresh your drink for you, Teddy?"

"Why yes, you can, pretty lady," Teddy said.

She pivoted like she was on the Paris runway for superstar models and took all that she was dragging in that beautiful wagon back to the bar to refresh Teddy's drink! Teddy dropped his pool cue to watch that wagon. I couldn't blame him though because, man, what a wagon it was! She looked over her right shoulder to look back at Charlie for a brief second, and at that point, Charlie gave her that wink that only she knew what meant. She turned back toward Teddy and slowly walked back over to him and bent down to pick up his pool cue for him while showing off those two cantaloupes that she had in the back pocket of those painted-on jeans that must have been painted on by the great Picasso himself! Even I knew that had to be a lot of pressure on him. That had to be a lot of pressure for any man and probably for some women too if they wished to play on that team.

It was after that that Teddy's accuracy started to fade and Charlie got a break. Teddy was facing a very difficult shot and a hard decision at the same time because he had left himself out of position for the next shot! After walking around the table about four times, he decided to play it safe by leaving Charlie an even more difficult shot than he had himself! Charlie got up and surveyed the table for a second, then he looked at Chanel and said, "It's only geometry, baby!" She raised her champagne glass in agreement while smiling the whole while.

Teddy's light switch got turned on with what Charlie had just said! You could tell when he slapped his knee very hard and sucked in a deep breath and said, "Damn, Charlie, I didn't even think about the angle that you're getting ready to take, but I see it now! Just don't miss, Charlie!"

"I don't plan to, Teddy. Why don't you have Chanel get you another drink? You just might need one after this shot."

With that being said, Chanel scooped up Teddy's glass and walk off toward the bar again, and Teddy was following those fresh cantaloupes she had in her back pockets all the way to the bar again! Right away, I noticed that Charlie and Chanel were a team, and I have to admit, that fascinated me some. Charlie wasn't the trash-talking type like some. Instead, he was modest and smooth and always showed class, and that stood out to me for some reason also. When Chanel returned from the bar, she gave him the most seductive look that would make any man week in the knees! She looked Teddy right in the eye with a very provocative look for a good minute before setting the drink down on his table. And, readers, I got to tell you that drink could have easily been placed right on top of that wagon that she was dragging as well.

The room got quiet, like she was on stage and the billiard room was her audience, and everyone was paying close attention to the role that she played. Then China whispered in my ear, "Did you catch that, Ray Ray?"

I whispered back, "Yes, I did."

Charlie got into position and ran that cue ball three rails with high-top English and kissed the nine ball in, and the funny thing about that shot was, I didn't think nobody even saw that shot coming except him. Not even Teddy saw that shot coming! He had this surprised look all over his face after that shot was made, and I was sure in his mind he was starting to realize this game was over with! Charlie buzzed through those next two games with combinations, making two balls at once sometimes. I mean, the man had skills!

China was still leaning on my shoulder, and I was kind of caught up in absorbing the warmth of her body, because God knows it was putting out heat. I looked over her head, and I glanced up at the clock. I should have been home two hours ago at least, but there was still too much going on for me to leave. I had to though if I wanted to live to be eighteen years old because I had already been warned by my mom! I bent down and kissed China on her forehead and tried to make an exit for the front door, but she grabbed me around my waist with amazing strength for a woman and asked where I was running off to so fast. I told her straight up, "It's a school night, and I got to get home."

She tightened her grip and took my right hand and placed it right on her ass and whispered in my ear, "But the night is so young, Ray Ray, and you don't know what you will be missing out on if you leave now."

"You're probably right, China, but if I don't hurry up and get home, I won't miss out on that fresh can of whoop ass that my mom will open."

China thought that was funny, but I was dead serious. I looked up to see Teddy and Charlie going into his office, and I could hear Teddy asking Charlie, "One Shot taught you that three-rail shot, didn't he?"

*One Shot? Is that what I just heard?*

Now, readers, as you can imagine, I had red flags popping up in my mind like popcorn right there, right now! But I needed to get home, so I broke away from China and made for the exit for the door. Please believe me when I tell you that it was not as easy as it sounds, breaking away from her with the warmth of her body draped all over me as I backed away, going toward the front door!

On the way home, I couldn't help thinking about what I had heard Teddy ask Charlie about my uncle One Shot! Could this be true? Did he know my uncle Grady? Is this why he picked me out of the crowd as soon as I walked in the door for the first time?

# Facing Mother Prosecutor

By the time I got to the house, all the front porch lights seemed brighter than usual, and that was probably because I didn't even want any light on me right about now at all! I just wanted to sneak in without seeing my mom because I had just come home from that pool hall, and I knew making it to being eighteen years old might have been hanging in the balance on that one! I reached for the door, and it opened up quickly with my mother standing right in the doorway with her little dog, Dominic! I panicked and said, "Oh, shit!"

"Ray Ray, I know you didn't just say what I think you said, boy! Where have you been? Do you know what time it is?"

I looked down at Dominic, and she was in the praying position already. *God, I sure hope your line isn't busy because I'm about to be calling you* is what I was thinking!

"Ray, I know you have not been back to that pool hall after I told you not to go there anymore."

I couldn't even make eye contact with her. Instead, I just dropped my head and tried to walk by her, getting on up in that house. "I know, Mother, but I was bored and was only going to stay for a minute. But one thing led to another, and I think I just met someone that knew my uncle Grady!"

My mother stared at me with a look that I just knew wasn't going to let me make it to becoming eighteen years old. I was dead! "Ray Ray, come on in this house and have a seat because I think it's about time we have another talk, especially if that person you met is Charlie Soft!"

Now, readers, as you might imagine, I was ecstatic and shocked at the same time because how could she know Charlie Soft? I mean, that's like an oxymoron or something, isn't it? I mean, my mother was like a woman that went back and forth to church on a regular basis! Charlie hadn't struck me as the kind of guy that attended church on Sundays, but then I thought, *what do I know? How can she know a man like Charlie Soft?* Then the *how* came to light.

"Ray Ray, what does the word *apprentice* mean to you?"

"A person who is learning a trade from a skilled employer. Mom, why do you ask me that?"

"Because, Ray Ray, that's exactly what Charlie Soft was to your Uncle Grady, and he taught Charlie everything he knows about gambling and much more. You see, Grady believed that the whole world was playing some type of game just to feed their ego. He told Charlie that sometimes, you just have to play the game with the uniform that you're issued. The only thing is to know what uniform you have been issued. Charlie learned that very fast because shooting pool was just a natural thing to him, and he took to that game like a fish takes to water! My brother Grady took Charlie into his home when Charlie really had no one to turn to when life got too hard for him. Charlie really didn't have the kind of parents that you have, Ray Ray, and he was just a lost soul without any kind of direction in life until Grady taught him how to bet. One Shot used to say that Charlie was lost in the sauce."

"What did he mean by that, Mother?"

"It meant Charlie never had a chance, Ray Ray, because of the way he was raised or wasn't raised, however you want to look at it. He was just wondering around in life with no purpose, but your uncle gave him the purpose that he was fit for. And if you watched him play pool tonight, then you know what I'm talking about. What, you thought it was just a coincidence that Charlie picked you out the moment he saw you walk into that pool hall?"

"Mom, I don't know what I thought, but I can assure you that never crossed my mind until I started walking home just now!"

"Well, what happened tonight Ray that made you realize he knew One Shot?"

"A pool game that I watched him play with a guy named Teddy. Everyone said he always stayed ready."

"So watching him play pool led you to thinking that he knew your uncle?"

"No, Mom. It's what Teddy asked Charlie after that game that got me thinking that somehow he knew Uncle Grady."

"Go ahead, son. What did he say?"

"Well, Charlie made a very difficult shot on Teddy, and after the game, Teddy asked Charlie if One Shot taught him that shot!"

"What did Charlie say, Ray?"

"I didn't hear how he responded because I was trying to get out of there because I knew it was getting late."

"Okay, Ray, here's what I want you to do the next time you're in that pool hall."

"What? Go back?"

"I want you to go back into that devil's den and tell Mr. Charlie Soft that I want to talk to him, and I'm sure he won't be surprised at all. In fact, I think he will be expecting it from you! Now it's late, so I need you to go to bed because you have to get up for school in the morning."

"But, Mom, you got my mind all filled with curiosity, so at least give me some small details on their relationship!"

"I just did, Ray Ray. Now go to bed, and we will finish this conversation tomorrow! Okay, Ray Ray, I'll tell you one story that your father told me because he used to run with them both back in the day before he started dating me."

# A Story about One Shot

"Mom, Dad knew Charlie too?"

"Yes, your dad used to gamble too, but he stopped when he married me and started having a family because the risks were just too high for a man with a family. Anyway, Ray, Charlie was in Minnesota, playing pool at seventeen years old when he should have been attending school. But nevertheless, he was playing for very high stakes, and he had the owner of the club backing all bets. But when it came time to split the money down, he was only willing to give Charlie 10 percent of the purse because he was only a teenager, and that was unacceptable to him. But Charlie stayed cool and calm and collected, and he made a long-distance call to One Shot and laid out a plan that would be a cinch on breaking the owner out of all the cash he won off Charlie's talent.

"One Shot drove all night without any kind of sleep, but he was pulling into St. Paul, Minnesota, in the early morning to accompany Charlie in a deed that had to be done in Charlie's eyes. Charlie had been beating all the locals without even displaying all his skills, so he knew the club owner would be betting on him. And the sky was the limit. The very next night, Charlie went without One Shot to secure the plan. About an hour after Charlie was doing his thing, in walks One Shot with his breath smelling like liquor, and your Uncle Grady never drank alcohol before a game. He acted as if he didn't even know Charlie and went straight to the restroom. When he came out, he took a seat to watch the action as he surveyed the club.

"At the end of the set that Charlie was playing with another guy, One Shot called out for the winner of that set. The club owner looked at One Shot with some curiosity because he had never seen One Shot before. In fact, the only other person that knew Grady was your father, and he gave no indication that he knew either of them. Your father always watched Grady's and Charlie's backs, especially when the stakes were high, and there was a very good reason for that. He also carried the money and sometimes brought them money if they needed him to, and they never had the slightest doubt that it would get there."

"Mom, why are you just now telling me this stuff?"

"Son, I wouldn't be telling you this at all if you had never walked in that pool hall and met Charlie Soft! But Charlie was your uncle's best friend until he passed on, and that kind of makes him family. Anyway, you wanted to hear a story, so be quiet and listen 'cause you have to get up for school and I have to get up for work. The guy Charlie was playing went by the name of Drew, and he was no mediocre guy by a long shot, because when you are the best, you also attract the best players. I'm sure Charlie will tell you that if he hasn't already. It's like what they say about New York. If you can make it there, you can make it anywhere!

"They were back and forth for two sets, until the seventh game in a nine-ball freeze out, but in the end, Charlie rose to the occasion like he always did when the stakes were high. One Shot walked over to the pool rack to get a pool cue out of the pool rack and said, 'I guess it's my game now, so I'll rack!' The club owner looked Grady up and down after One Shot stumbled a bit with his drunken act! Your father smiled because he had seen Grady and Charlie pull this act for high stakes way too often, so he did everything in his power not to give away the plot. But the club owner was a seasoned veteran and wasn't going to just jump in the deep water without a life jacket, so he lowered the stakes just to see what One Shot had.

"In the first set, One Shot would shoot balls straight in as expected, but he wasn't playing for position for his next shot. The club owner noticed that, and by the time Charlie had won the first two sets with ease, the club owner got that itch to raise the stakes just like Charlie knew he would. At the beginning of the third set, the club owner raised the stakes to double or nothing, and One Shot played just good enough to beat Charlie. But he made it seem like a tough game for the both of them. The club owner didn't like the way the game turned out, so he upped his bet even bigger this time around. And the plot thickened! Charlie and One Shot battled back and forth, making the club owner's patience get the best of him, and that's what they were counting on.

"'How you feel about one last game for ten grand, Mr. Grady?'

"'Well, I just don't walk around with that kind of money in my pocket, sir, but just maybe there is alternative that we can agree on.'

"'Well, I'm all ears, Mr. Grady, so what is your proposal?'

"'I don't have ten thousand cash, but I do have the pink slip to that fine, astonishing automobile sitting outside. We can play this last game for the worth of that automobile if you're up for that.'

"'Let me walk outside and take a look at it because I could use another car as long as it got a clean title, Mr. Grady!'

"Norman was the club owner's name, if I remember correctly, but anyway, he stepped outside to see that new dark-gray Mercedes-Benz. His mouth just dropped open because like I said before, most black people didn't have an abundance of nice things, and this car was, by far, reaching way past his wildest expectations! Norman walked back inside the pool hall and got on his phone, and as he hung it up, he called Charlie over to him and said, 'Win this game, and we split everything down the middle, fifty-fifty this time, so are you ready, Charlie?'

"Grady ordered a drink just to make Norman think he would have some kind of edge, even though it was just club soda, but Norman didn't know that! Charlie knew Norman would never split fifty-fifty with him, so he went along with the plan that he and One Shot laid out to separate Norman from the money that he never intended to split with him anyway.

"Now the bet had changed to fifty grand instead of ten, and it was show time! They flipped a coin for the break, and One Shot won the coin toss and the break. Your father took a seat right beside Norman to watch his every move 'cause after all, this game was for very high stakes, and he wanted to make sure that Norman was on the up and up about everything. One Shot walked up to the front of the table and got in position to break the nine-ball pack, but just before he did, Norman stood up and changed the game from nine-ball to last pocket on a straight eight-ball game. Your father just smiled to himself because it really didn't matter what game he changed to. He had no chance of getting out of there with that money, and your father knew that! Charlie winked at Norman as if he had done a good thing for doing that because in Norman's mind that was what Charlie was best at."

"Mother, how is the last pocket game played?"

"According to your father, the eight ball on the table has to be placed in the same pocket that your last ball went, and that's why it's called last pocket! Anyway, One Shot ran the table, all except his last two balls, without Charlie even picking up his pool cue! Norman was overwhelmed with One Shot's ability to run the table so easily because he had never seen a pool player with those kinds of skills except Charlie! Then it happened. One Shot missed his cue on his next shot, and now it was Charlie's turn to shoot. And he made the best of it. Charlie ran all his balls down to the eight ball that was already sitting right on the edge of the side pocket! Norman smiled with delight because he knew this game was over, and he would have the pink slip to a brand-new dark-gray Mercedes-Benz at Grady's expense!

"But Charlie had a trick up his sleeve. He was not going to let the club owner off the hook, so he used high-top English instead of low-top English, and that white cue ball ran right behind that eight ball straight in the pocket behind the eight ball, and game over! One Shot won the game by default is what your father explained to me. Now the club owner had just witnessed a mystical experience that he would always remember because the loss of fifty grand would haunt him forever!

"Now, Ray Ray, it is way past your bedtime and mine too, so love you and good night!"

"Wait, Mom, did the club owner pay the money?"

"Yes, he sure did! It was either pay or deal with your father, so he chose to pay."

"So, Mom, Dad was like a henchman or something?"

"Let's just say he was a faithful follower of his financial advisers. Anyway, that's the way your father described it."

"Really, Mom, he went with that?"

"He sure did, and yes, I thought it was kind of funny too when I heard him describe it. And the way your father told the story, Charlie scratched on the cue ball on purpose because he only ran all those balls off to make the club owner think he was going to win. He felt like he owed him some anguish for the way he had treated him on the previous splits on the money! You see, Charlie could have stopped the cue ball from rolling into that pocket behind his ball by simply using low English on the cue ball, but he used high top on purpose."

"Mother, I was just going to ask you if Charlie did that on purpose. So now I know, and I have to tell you, I like it!"

"Boy, if you don't get your butt in that bed, it's going to be lights-out with the lights still on. You see where I'm going with this, Ray Ray?" That was the calm before the storm.

# My Brothers

"Okay, Mother, I'll see you in the morning." I turned and started to walk down the hallway toward my bedroom that I shared with my older brothers Arthur Ray and Johnny, and they were sound asleep already, or so I thought anyway!

Now Johnny was a mama's boy and the sharpest dresser of the family. He worked in a men's clothing store, so he kept fresh clothing apparel that I used to sneak into from time to time! I would always get caught though because he was so neat that he could always tell that they were hung different when I tried to hang them back the way he had them! He would never say anything about it until I asked to borrow a shirt or something. Then he would let me know that he knew that I had been borrowing his clothes from time to time by making this little remark! "Oh, now you want to ask me?" I would always respond by acting like I didn't know what he was talking about. "Ray Ray, don't play crazy because there is still a mustard stain at the bottom of my blue shirt that you're going to pay for when you become employed somewhere!"

Johnny always gave in to whatever I wanted, but he always had to talk a little smack first. Johnny was also the choir director at our church, so singing in the church choir was something that most of the family had to participate in every Sunday, whether they liked it or not! It was cool though because we used to go out of town on chartered buses, and that had its perks too because some of those church girls used to flirt around with Danny Ray and me on the long bus rides out of town. That was cool! I actually like singing gospel music, and I later started my own choir called Young, Gifted, and Black. It didn't last long though because between basketball practice and that pool hall, I just lost interest!

Now Arthur Ray was just the opposite of Johnny in more ways than one. He also was athletic and had the body to prove it. He was all-city champion in wrestling and was the number one fullback in football in the state! The family used to listen to the high school football games on the radio when their team played out of town, but you can rest assured that we were at all the home games whenever there was one! There was already talk of Arthur Ray at the NFL level by many people as far back as junior high school. Once he was diagnosed with epilepsy, his dreams just floated away. That made him start drinking, which led to other things that went wrong in his life. I was not at all making excuses for my brother's fork in the road because we all have our own trials and tribulations down that road called life!

I tried to ease into the bed without waking my brothers, but they seemed to just be waiting on me to come home because they sat up in their bed as soon as I came in the room.

"So where have you been this late?" Johnny asked.

"It's a long story, big brother, and I don't have time to explain it all because I have to get up early!"

"Didn't you already know that before you hung out at that pool hall?"

"Well, if you already knew where I was, then why are you asking?"

"Just wanted to see what you were going to say, little brother, that's all."

"You heard mother talking to me a while ago, didn't you?"

"Yeah, I did, One Shot Junior, and what I remember about Uncle Grady was all good when he hung out with Dad. That's who you're going to end up like if you keep going to that pool hall."

"I don't know, Johnny. Uncle Grady didn't seem like a bad person according to Mom."

"No, he wasn't, but he wasn't your average guy either. Now stop making all that noise, and go to bed!"

I laughed and said, "You are the one asking all the questions, but you're telling me to stop making all the noise?"

He smiled and turned over and turned his light off and said, "Oh yeah, next time you borrow one of my shirts, could you please take it off before you eat your mustard sandwich?"

"Oh, so now I'm just eating straight mustard sandwiches?"

He didn't even respond, but I could hear him laughing to himself under the covers. Then Arthur Ray said, "Well, at least it's not syrup because you know the boy can eat a whole bottle of syrup with just one biscuit."

Then Johnny rolled over one more time to say, "Yes, syrup is hard to keep in this house even if there is only one biscuit left." Then we all laughed about that on our way to sleep.

The next morning, I woke up to Arthur Ray calling me by the name of Biscuit to wake me up for school. That seemed to still be funny to him and Johnny. I thought I was running late when I heard my mother calling out my name! "Ray Ray, the phone is for you." I had no idea who could be calling me so early in the morning, but I was definitely curious! I quickly put some pants on and ran to the phone to see who this was because I had never gotten a telephone call from anyone this early in the morning unless it was Stacey! So of course, she came to mind. My mother had this smirk on her face, like she was not liking this call before school at all, but she handed it to me anyway!

It was China, and I had completely forgotten about our little encounter yesterday, but obviously, she hadn't. "Good Morning, Ray Ray. How are you doing?"

"Now that I hear your voice, I'm good, China, and why are you up so early?"

She replied, "Ray Ray, I have a job to go to, so will I see you at the pool hall later this evening?"

"Yes, China, you will if you're going to be there!"

"I sure will, Ray Ray, so I'll talk to you then."

As soon as I hung up the phone and turned around, my brother Arthur Ray was standing there with condoms in his hand, smiling at me. "I think you're probably going to need these at some point, so take a few." I quickly snatched them out of his hand and shoved them in my pocket before my mother could see them. I ran out the door, already late for school, thinking about confronting Charlie about knowing my uncle Grady and not saying one word to me about it!

# Getting Back on the Team

My first class was algebra. I liked it 'cause it was challenging, and I always like being challenged, even at a young age! After first period, I had gym, so I had the thought of getting back on the basketball team for the first time in a long time. As soon as I walked into gym, I locked eyes with my old basketball coach with that thought in mind. "Hey, Coach, how about letting me try out for the basketball team again?"

"Well, Ray Ray, what has gotten into you?"

"I don't know, Coach. I've just been thinking about it a lot lately."

"How's your knee, son?"

"Well, I've been playing pickup games sometimes, and I'm undefeated in one-on-one. So I think I'm ready to give it a try."

"You have not been competing against all girls, have you, Ray Ray?"

"Coach, I see you still have that sense of humor, but I'll tell you what. Put me on the court with your best guard, and if he beats me, then I'll hang it up!"

"Ray Ray, you know I'm not going to do that because this is a team sport. But be here after school, and we will see if you really do have mad skills."

"I will definitely be here after school, Coach, and you can count on that."

I showed up for practice, and you could hear a pin drop with the silence of my arrival with the other players. Yes, it was kind of awkward at first, but I just went up to everybody and greeted them like I was happy to get another chance to play. Coach Wilson was the head coach and knew how to do his job very well, and he had three championship trophies in five years to prove it. I went to the locker room to change, and when I came out, the coach had a little surprise for me.

"Ray Ray, before you get on my court to play, you're going to have to show me what kind of condition your body is in before you just walk back on the team. I know you're good, but it's not about that today, son. It's about conditioning, so I'm going to need to see how your knee is. So this is what I'm going to need you to do. Run black line, black line to see what kind of shape you're in before we get to practicing with the team!"

Now I was not expecting that, but if that was what I had to do to get back, then bring it on! I was in shape but not that kind of shape, and that black line, black line kicked my butt like I was in a UFC match. At one point, I almost threw up, but I fought right through it like a champ until I finally caught my second wind. Then I was good. The rest of the team was playing a scrimmage game, so I thought after I finished doing my cardio Coach Wilson would let me scrimmage with the team. But boy was I wrong!

"Ray, I'm going to need you to go take a shower, and I will see you tomorrow. We will be doing black line, black line again until I think your cardio is in order to step onto my court."

It was not at all what I had wanted to hear, but if that was the test I had to pass to get back out there, then bring it! After all, it was just another challenge, and I liked being challenged! Then I thought, *My mom is probably wondering why I'm not home from school yet*, so I asked Coach to let me use the phone in his office to call my mom to let her know what was going on so she wouldn't run black line, black line on my behind! She was glad that I had made getting back on the team a goal again 'cause she really didn't want me hanging out at that pool hall anyway!

"Hey, Ray, some girl just called here and said to make sure I tell you that she called."

"Mom, was it Stacey?"

"Now, Ray Ray, you know that I know Stacey's voice, but this girl sounded more like a woman rather than a girl your age."

Then I thought it must have been China from the pool hall, so I asked, "Mom, was that China who called?"

And she replied, "Yes. Ray, where do you know this girl from? Because she didn't sound like she was at school or nothing. I heard music playing in the background, and it was not gospel music either. Ray Ray, I need you to not stay out late tonight because of school tomorrow, son. I will be working late, so go home!"

"Okay, I'm catching the late bus, but I'll be home soon, Mom."

On the way home, I had to pass by that pool hall, but I kept pushing it because I was not about to lie to my mother. As soon as I stepped inside the house, I could hear Danny Ray and my sister Bobbie playing the dart game downstairs. I walked back to my room to put my books away and change out of my school clothes when I heard the phone ringing. I picked it up, and it was China! "Hey, China, what's going on?"

"Ray Ray, I thought you were coming to the pool hall."

"Well, I was, China, but I had a long day today. I'm kind of tired because I went to basketball practice today. Plus, I promised my mother I would come straight home."

"Are you home now?"

"Come on, China, isn't that where you just called me at?"

She laughed and said, "Exactly!"

"What do you mean by exactly?"

"Well, Ray Ray, you did go straight home, I'm assuming, so she didn't say you couldn't leave once you got there, did she?"

"China, I see where you are going with this, but I'm not coming out tonight."

"That's fine, Ray Ray, so how about you tell me your address? I will come to see you!"

I gave her my address and went downstairs to play darts with Danny and Bobbie until China arrived. They were arguing about whose turn it was to throw the next set of darts, so I just sat back on the bed, laughing at them. Danny Ray had taken Bobbie's turn, and she was not even trying to hear what he was talking about unless he was giving her turn back. After a while, Bobbie just went to the dartboard and took

Danny's darts out before he could even add up his points. Danny got a little frustrated and threw a dart at the dartboard, and it missed that board by a mile and struck Bobbie right in the side temple of her head. She fell to the floor like she had just been shot! I jumped up off the bed and ran to my sister's aid while looking back at Danny Ray's reaction at the same time! He was standing there with this look of shock on his face while at the same time covering his mouth like he was just as shocked as everyone else.

The dart didn't even break her skin, but you couldn't tell that by her reaction because she fell like an overripe apple falling from the tree! I mean, the girl was lying there with her eyes closed like she was dead or something until Danny ran over and knelt down to see how serious her injury was. And that was possibly the worst thing he could have done at that particular time because she rolled over and punched him right in his nose. Blood shot out from his nose like a water faucet! She jumped to her feet like one of those ninjas that you see on TV and stretched like she was ready for whatever was about to happen next! Danny quickly retreated, like he wanted no part of that ninja, and I couldn't blame him, not even a little bit, because the girl was terrifying to say the least! He ran all the way upstairs and straight out the door down the street to his house, holding his nose and crying like a little girl, and I started laughing so hard that tears came to my eyes! Bobbie turned and looked at me as if she was saying to me, "You want some? Because I have plenty more where that came from."

I heard a horn blowing outside, so I assumed it was China out in the driveway, waiting on me, so I took that as my way out from this ninja who was still in ninja mode. When I got outside, China had this confused look on her face because she had seen Danny Ray running out the door right past her car! I went outside and sat in the car with her, and by the way, she had a very nice car!

"Ray Ray who was that who just ran past my car; I think he was bleeding. Was he all right?"

"Yes, I think so, but I really don't know because he was just attacked by a ninja!"

"A ninja? Ray Ray, what are you talking about?"

"Oh, it's nothing; just that my sister got a hold of him over a dart game."

"So you're saying your sister is a ninja?"

"Well, she was tonight, and let's go before she comes out, wondering where I am."

So she pulled out of the driveway, still with a confused look on her face, shaking her head.

"China, let's get straight to the point. What are you trying to do? I mean, what's the catch here?"

"Ray Ray, I know your bloodline, and I know more about you than I let on."

"How's that, China?"

"Charlie Soft. How do you think?"

"Whoa, you mean to tell me Charlie knows who I am and never told me?"

"What, he never told you?"

"No, not even a little bit, but my mother told me a story about my uncle Grady and him. But he has never even mentioned anything about him to me!"

"Well, I'm sorry to let the cat out of the bag, Ray Ray, but don't let him know we even had this conversation. Anyway, at the moment, I want to talk about us!"

"Okay, let's do that, China, because you are quite an interesting lady yourself that I know nothing about!"

"Well, Ray Ray, that is a conversation I don't want to have in the car, so can we go to my place for a minute?"

"China, I have the kind of mother who can beat me home, so it cannot be an all-night thing, even though I wouldn't mind it."

She put the car in reverse, and away we went across the tracks to her spot! On the drive over, I couldn't help but notice her perfect, silky smooth skin and how well-groomed she was from head to toe. She had long silky black hair with light-brown highlights, and she had light-brown skin. And I was thinking, *somebody pinch me so I can wake up because I must be dreaming right now!*

We pulled up to her place, and I was quite amused on the location and how nice the inside smelled once I got in. (As you might have already guessed by now, I have a thing for a nice fragrance.) Looking at her neighborhood, I could not help but notice how much nicer things were on the other side of those railroad tracks. Once inside, she put on some soft music, and I would never forget it because it was the first time I had ever heard jazz so smooth. It was a tune by Richard Elliot called "This Could Be Real." Right away, I was thinking for the first time since Stacey that *this just might be real between China and I. I mean, so far, I like everything about her.* "China, you seem to know so much about me already, so tell me a little bit about you."

"Well, Ray Ray, where do you want me to start?"

"How about at the beginning, let's try that out first."

"Okay, Ray Ray, you're funny and I like that. I am what people call a trust fund kid because my family is wealthy, but I have been on my own for quite some time now without their help."

"China, how can you afford to gamble every day in such high-stake games the way that you do?"

"I don't gamble as much as you might think, but when I do, I only play when the stakes are high. You bet big, and you win big. That's how I roll! I also did other things back in the day, and I did it just long enough to open my own business, which is now a real estate business. And sometimes, that is a very lucrative business. I have always liked to gamble since I was fifteen years old."

"China, how old are you now?"

"I'm twenty-two years old right now. Ray Ray, I'm almost five years older than you, so do you see that being a problem?"

"Not at all, China, but as beautiful as you are, I just know that you have a man somewhere!"

"That is very nice of you to say, Ray Ray. You're making me blush! I used to, Ray Ray, but he was killed in a car wreck eleven months ago, and I have been single ever since."

"Wow, I'm sorry to for your loss, and I also have been down that road before of losing a loved one."

"So what was her name, Ray Ray?"

"How do you know it was a girl?"

"The way you looked when you said it."

"Well, you can't go by that alone because I also have lost my father just not too long ago, and that is still a loss I struggle with from time to time. What about your parents, China? Do you still have both of them?"

She answered like she had been caught off guard before she said, "Yes, I do, Ray Ray, and I know what you're thinking. I have no idea what kind of hurt losing a father has brought on you, right?"

"You're absolutely right, China, and guess what? You have won the grand prize finale." Then I leaned over to give her a kiss, as if that was the prize that she had just won.

She smooched my face when I was just about to make contact and said, "Don't change the subject. What was her name?"

"Does that really matter now, China? I'm here with you right now, so don't take me down memory lane because I don't like going down that street!"

"Ray Ray, you still care about her, don't you?"

"To tell you the truth, China, I still think about her sometimes. But that's only natural, I guess, since I still have that empty spot in my heart."

"Yes, it is, Ray Ray, because I still think about my late boyfriend too, and I like that you told me the truth about it because most guys would have straight up lied in my face just to get between my legs."

"China, how do you know what most guys would do?"

"Ray Ray, I'm not going to start off lying to you. I have dated a few guys, but I guess I'm just too picky because I never went past one date with not one of them." Then she smiled and said, "So I'm almost a virgin now, if you get my meaning!"

My imagination took off, but I regained focus to say, "China, I can relate because I haven't been with anyone since Stacey myself, and if there's one thing you can count on from me, it's the truth about whatever it is because I expect the same thing in return. A fair exchange has never been a robbery, so let's not rob each other, please!"

"No, it's not, Ray Ray, and I can see that you're different than most guys already. And I like that."

"So where do we go from here, China?"

"To the top, if you're not afraid of heights! I want to see where this goes, Ray Ray, if you want that too."

"More than you know, China, so how about we kick this in cruise control and enjoy the ride?" I pulled her to me and kissed her like I needed to, and I think she needed to also because after that kiss, she held on to me until the song ended on her stereo.

After that, she looked at me straight in my eyes and said, "Stay right here tonight with me, Ray Ray. It's not because I want you to. It's because I need you to!" She pushed me down on the couch and took off my shoes and asked me to give her a minute, and then she disappeared back to her bedroom with my shoes in hand! Before she turned that corner to go into that room, she looked back at me with a smile that I hadn't seen since Stacey and I were together intimately! I have to admit, going home was the last thing on my mind at this time because it was about to go down right here, right now!

I sat on the couch, pretending to read the latest edition of a sports magazine, and it seemed like forever before she called out my name to come back in her bedroom. But when she did, I almost sprinted back to that bedroom with great anticipation of what was to come. "Ray Ray, it's been a while, so take your time and do it right because I want this to be a night that we both remember for the rest of our lives." She had the lights turned down very low, but I could still see every curve in her body that she had to offer. Her slanted green eyes twinkled like stars in the sky when I got undressed, and shortly after that, the foreplay turned into tenplay. Just like she wanted, I took my time to make her reach the top of that mountain she so eagerly wanted to climb with me!

After I did my thing, we both dozed off for about an hour, and then I woke up to the sound of the shower running. I glanced up at the clock on the wall and saw it was four o'clock in the morning, and I jumped up and reached for my clothes when she called out my name again to come jump in the shower with her. I gladly accepted the offer once again because I was still a little backed up, so I took the opportunity to get caught up.

After we got dressed, I asked her to drop me off at my house so I could get dressed for school. She said, "Ray Ray, your days of riding the school bus are over with." And then she threw a set of car keys to me!

"China, what's going on?"

"Ray Ray, I can't have a man of mine riding a school bus, can I?" Now I was only seventeen years old, so all this was blowing my cap back right now! "You can drive yourself to school now because I have another car parked right next to mine. So you can take that one, and I will see you later tonight."

Of course, I was speechless as you might imagine because things were going a hundred miles an hour, and I hadn't had time to process it all just yet! She knew that she was taking me really fast, and I think she kind of enjoyed doing so! She walked up to me and said, "Ray Ray, just go with the flow of what's happening right now and roll with it, papi!"

At that point, she didn't need to say anything else because calling me papi was my sweet spot, so that just sealed the deal with me, if that was what she was trying to do! She held my hand and kissed me on the lips ever so sensually, and I pushed her back before I had her marching back to her bedroom again for round 3! She laughed and called me a scaredy cat and walked out the door, leaving me standing there like I lived there too. I followed close behind, noticing all that junk that girl had in her trunk while locking the door behind me.

At that point right there, I came to the conclusion that I wasn't going to just admire the good life; I was going to live it as well! To all the nine-to-five people out there in this big old world, I say more power to you, but for us people who come from the other side of the tracks, I say keep your head up and find something that you're good at and do it. It's that simple; just do it!

The car was a large black Audi sedan with white interior, and I jumped in it and chucked the deuces up before driving off to my house to get what I needed for school! I turned the radio on once I figured out how to work her stereo system. A tune by the great late Curtis Mayfield was playing on the radio ("Give Me Your Love"), and of course, that seemed to fit the moment right about now because I thought China had just given me hers. I was seventeen years old, and I had the keys to a beautiful woman's car and house, and what a nice house it was. I was on cloud nine right about now, and I had a feeling going through me like never before. I was thinking, *not bad for a guy that's from across the other side of the tracks!*

I pulled up in front of my house in China's car at about 5:30 a.m., and my big brother Arthur Ray was coming out of the house, getting ready to ride off to work. He paused for a minute to notice me pulling up in a seemingly new car that he knew didn't belong to me! I looked him straight in his eyes and responded to a question that was written all over his face while at the same time running right past him because I was already running late! "Yes, it's a ladies car." I shrugged my shoulders and ran into the house to get changed for school.

I heard him saying as I entered the house, "I hope you can do better than that when Mom comes home!"

"Yeah, I hope so too!"

My sisters were up, so I got grilled over and over about the car while trying to get dressed for school. I was trying to get out the door before Mom got home because I knew whatever questions she had for me had to get answered on the spot! Once I got to school in that car, the gossip started, and I was the talk of first period. There were girls and guys acknowledging me who never paid attention to me before, and I have to admit, it felt good! By the time lunchtime came around, girls from all over the school were trying to give me their number, but I had China. I didn't need another number!

I was feeling the need for some learning that school couldn't give me. I went and jumped in that little sporty Audi and headed straight for the pool hall! It was still early, so the crowd was lighter than before. But I parked and went inside anyway. Charlie was in his office, so I walked to the open door and stepped inside to confront him about knowing who I was and also my uncle Grady. He was doing some paperwork when I walked in, but he quickly looked up and saw me standing there. This time, he had a shocked look on his face because he knew I knew what I knew and that it was time for him to explain! I started the conversation off by asking him who One Shot was to him.

"Well, Ray Ray, I'm assuming with the way you ask me that you already know something about our relationship already. Close the door, son, and take a seat because this may take a while. Ray Ray, I'm assuming your mother has spoken to you about me."

"Charlie, your assumption would be right, and I want to know why you never told me. And how did you know that I was Uncle Grady's nephew?"

"You look just like him, Ray Ray. And when you walked in, I thought you were his kid honestly because as many young ladies as he entertained, well, he just never said no. I just felt like I had to get to know you because of who Grady was to me. Besides, I really didn't know that you were his nephew. But I did know you had to be some kind of kin to him, and if you were going to be coming around, I would have to make sure that you didn't end up being anyone's mark."

"Well, Charlie, I told my mother everything, and she wants to see you soon."

"I knew that was coming next, Ray Ray, and I will take time out to go visit with Ms. Johnson soon."

"So you know her, don't you, Charlie?"

"I know she is One Shot's sister, and that's all I really need to know. I knew she had kids, but I've never seen you before you walked in that pool hall. Yes, I do, Ray Ray, and I know I am going to get an earful for letting you even come in here, not even mentioning the part about teaching you how to run a craps game when you're still in school! By the way, Ray Ray, why are you not in school right now?"

"Charlie, let's just say my curiosity about you got the best of me! Let's just go with that!"

"So how did you get here, Ray Ray? It's too early for the school bus!"

"Well, that's a whole different story, Charlie, but you seem to be very good at putting two and two together, so go for it."

He got up from his chair and walked to the front of the pool hall glass and surveyed the parking lot before he came to the right conclusion of how I arrived there. "Ray Ray, you spent the night with China, didn't you?"

All I could do was smile because at that point, I was thinking about just how wonderful a night it was. "Yes, I did, Charlie, and I enjoyed every minute of it too."

Charlie showed no emotion to what I said, but he did voice his opinion of her. "China is a good girl at heart, and as far as I know, she has never been with another guy but the one that she just recently lost. So be good to her, Ray Ray, because she has a fragile heart right now."

"I'm still young, Charlie, so I don't know a hell of a lot about women because I have only been intimate with one girl, and she broke my heart in pieces when she left."

"Ray Ray, you're still young, and that will happen from time to time until you find the right one. So don't sweat it because it's just one of those things that people go through. I will tell you from my own experiences what I have learned about choosing the right mate. It can't be just about sex that keeps you together because sex only goes so far. The anticipation of sex may draw you together, but it will never keep you together because the more truthful conversation is going to come after sex. It's the conversation that comes after sex that determines whether you stay together or not! That will be the more honest conversation that you will ever have because the sexual anticipation will be over and it will be out of the way for you to see what you have in common. Do you get the meaning of what I'm telling you, son?"

"Yeah, I think I do, Charlie. I think I do! Think with my big head instead of my small one."

"That is a very good analogy, Ray Ray. I couldn't have said it any better myself."

"How about your lady, Chanel; How did y'all hook up, and how did you know that she was the right one for you?"

"Good question, Ray Ray. Chanel and I met when I was broke on my ass and didn't have anything but a plan to get money, and that was the deciding factor for me. Like the song says, 'Everybody loves the sunshine, but can you stand the rain?' If a lady is willing to stick it out with you while it's raining, then that's the woman for you, hands down!

Ray Ray, you will run into a lot of women that only want you for what you can do for them. Chanel knew I didn't have much but a plan, but she believed in me, and here we are! She is more than just my lady. She is my friend also. I love making her smile because when she is happy, I'm happy, and it's very important that you both are feeling the same way, Ray Ray. We both have a lot in common, and that is the key to a long-lasting relationship!"

"I thought I had that with Stacey, but I was wrong."

"Well, I think you will find that with China because she is a lot like Chanel! She don't fuck around. When she is with you, she is with you 100 percent, and you don't have to worry about her recklessly eyeballing darkness as long as she sees the light in you."

"How do you know that, Charlie? Are they friends?"

"Yes, they are, Ray Ray, and they are probably talking about you right now since you spent the night with China and you are showing up in her car. Are you going back to school, Ray Ray, or you hanging out for a while?"

"I think I will hang out for a while with you, Charlie. Maybe you can show me that three-rail shot you made on Teddy yesterday again."

"I can show you all the shot's your uncle Grady showed me if you think you want to learn, Ray Ray, but it will not come overnight!"

# The Seed Grows

As we played pool, Charlie taught me to line up every ball by the spot that drives the ball into the pocket that I would aim at, and the rest was just common sense. "Ray Ray, there are people from all walks of life that love to gamble. Some are good, and some bad. Most of them don't even know how to gamble. They just like the thrill of it! Gambling is based on ratios and percentages not luck. And the sooner you learn that, the better you will become at it, Ray Ray, and that is what your uncle One Shot taught me. You don't even gamble with the person really. You are percentage gambling only and in your head, and in time, you will learn that if you are anything like your uncle."

Before I knew it, school was letting out because the school buses where rolling by. "Oh, snap! Basketball practice! Later, Charlie, I have to go back to school for basketball practice."

"Okay, Mad Skills, see you later."

I looked back at him with a little bit of shock because he knew that name, but nevertheless, I had to get out that door. So I jumped in that Audi and rolled out of there like a popular race car movie. I pulled up to the school in a matter of minutes and ran all the way to the gym, gasping for air when I entered the gym.

Coach Wilson was standing there, pointing to his watch, as if he was showing me how late I was. "Ray Ray, I'm glad to see you're taking your cardio very seriously." And the team thought that was kind of funny in a sarcastic kind of way. I ran into the locker room to get dressed, and when I came out, the teams were already playing a scrimmage game.

So I went and stood beside Coach Wilson to see what he had in store for me, especially since I was a little late. "Okay, Ray Ray, let's see what you got. Take over the point guard spot for Jason, and let's push that ball down the court."

I ran to the court to show my mad skills, but that full court had me gassed almost immediately. My shots were coming up way short because I just didn't have the lung power that I thought I did, and I even got my pocket picked twice by Jason, and that had never happened to me before because I had handles on a basketball like I had a string on it. Since my wind was short, I couldn't keep up with the fast pace of a scrimmage game, so I knew right then and there that I had to get in better shape, even though Coach said I did what he expected and that my performance wasn't that bad.

I went to the locker room and took a shower and dapped the rest of the team on the way out the gym. I jumped in that Audi once again and zoomed to the house because I still hadn't seen my mother yet, and I needed to link up with her before I went back to that pool hall. As soon as I pulled up in front of my house, my brother Arthur Ray was coming out of the house with this confused look on his face. "So what the hell is really going on, Ray Ray; whose car is that, little brother?"

"It's my girlfriend's, I think."

"Okay, you just said you think. Did I hear you right?"

"Well, I met her in the pool hall, and we just kind of clicked ever since then."

"Pool hall? Yeah, that sounds like the kind of girl that you want to tell Mom about for sure! Does Mom know about your clicking?"

"Not yet, but she is about to find out, I guess, huh?"

Arthur Ray pointed to Charlie's car parked across the street and said, "I think she may already be ahead of you on the clicking, little brother. Did you use the condoms last night, Ray Ray? I know there was some sticking going on with your clicking last night, little brother."

"Man, I completely forgot about them in the heat of the moment."

"Heat of the moment? Ain't that some shit? Boy, you haven't felt heat yet! Being a seventeen-year-old father will burn your ass off. Do you want to be walking around with a burned-off ass? Not a good look,

I'm telling you, lil brother. You're asking for trouble all the way around! I don't care if she has your ass inferno hot next time. You better stop long enough to strap that jimmy on! Ray Ray, you're still a teenager, so don't tie yourself down like that until you're ready."

"I hear you, Arthur Ray, loud and clear!" I dapped him and walked inside, waving my way past the assistant prosecutors to face off with the head prosecutor (my mother)! She was sitting in her favorite chair with her trusted friend, Dominic, the little praying Chihuahua!

"Ray Ray, whose car is that you are driving, son?"

"Mother, I have something like a new girlfriend now, I guess."

She turned to Charlie and asked him, "Do you know about this?"

Charlie just shrugged his shoulders like he knew nothing.

"You know what, Ray Ray, I don't even want to know right now, but I do want to talk to you and Charlie about that pool hall."

I looked over at Charlie, and the conversation began.

# Mom and Charlie Talk

"Now, Charlie, I know you let Ray Ray in that pool hall because he reminds you of your mentor, One Shot. But here's the thing, Charlie. He's not One Shot, and you need to acknowledge that!"

"I know, Ms. Johnson, but when I saw him for the first time, I thought he was Grady all over again or his son or something. And I just had to meet him to see. I never even mentioned One Shot to him, but I'm sure China, his new girlfriend, did."

"Oh, China is his new girlfriend?"

I looked Charlie in the eye with a very surprised look because I never even told him anything about that conversation that China and I had, so how did he know and why was my mother acting like she knew who China was? How could China know anything about One Shot? She wasn't much older than I was. Something wasn't quite right here!

Then my mom said, "Charlie, I know how these things work, and since you let him go in that place, he is your responsibility every time he goes in that devil's den. I don't even want him going in there, period, but I know my son. When he is curious about something, there is no end to his curiosity until he gets it out of his system, so don't you let anything happen to him, Charlie. And another thing, Charlie, if he goes in there during school hours, you better run his tail out of there and call me."

"Yes, Ms. Johnson. I will make sure of that. You have my word on that."

After that little speech from my mother, I felt like I kind of had her blessing on the pool hall because she knew the seed had been planted as much as I did! The next few weeks went by pretty fast, and my schedule was starting to drain me because I was burning the candle from both ends. School and basketball practice took up most of my time, but on the weekends, it was the pool hall and a whole lot of China! I was still driving her car, and most of the time, I would just crash at her place instead of going all the way home across the tracks! My older brothers and sisters really had no problem with it, especially my brothers, because our bedroom was too small a room anyway for three boys, and now there was more room for their things with me being at China's house a lot now.

I had been practicing with the team now for almost three weeks. We had one practice last Thursday before a Friday game, and I had worked my way back to a starting point guard. I was excited about that. I had told everyone I knew to come see Mad Skills put on a show. I mean, we had some boys who were ready to bring the noise, and my teammates could ball. I was in practice going hard to the glass to snag a rebound, and I came down on one of my teammate's feet and snapped my ankle, breaking two bones at the same time! At first, I thought it was just a bad sprain, so I jumped up to try to walk it off, but I kept falling down. My teammates ran over to aid me, and I heard one of them say, "Damn, Ray Ray, you just broke your shit, man!" I looked down at my ankle, and all I could see was blood and my two bones sticking out the side of my ankle. And then the pain awakened with a fury!

The ambulance came, and the paramedics jumped out and did their thing. But just like that, my basketball career was out the window. Man, I went into depression for a while because being on crutches is no joke, but I have to admit that China was there with me through the whole process. I think it was at that point that I let my guard down with her and just let it happen! I literally moved out of my mom's house and moved in with China, and that was really when I knew that I cared about her for real! While my leg was healing, China would take me to the movies or the grocery store whenever she knew I needed to get out of the house for a minute. She also took me to all my rehab appointments, and that rehab stuff was no joke! She even took me to the pool hall to visit with Charlie sometimes, and that was the determining factor that made me not return to high school.

I was eighteen years old now, and that fork in the road was coming up in plain view now. I had learned how to bet on the craps table and the card table and wasn't that bad at nine ball on the pool table either, so I was keeping a nice bankroll in my pocket every day. Charlie was now my mentor, and I was absorbing the game like a dry sponge and had the cash to show for it. So when I got to that fork in the road, I made a hard right onto Easy-Money Street!

China was still doing her thing, so life was good enough for me to start helping others that were less fortunate than I was, starting with the guys I grew up with who were standing in front of that liquor store every day, waiting on a drink. I used to go to the grocery store after a good win and have China make a bunch of sandwiches and pass them out to those who were hungry, along with a few dollars. China used to ask why I gave them money when I already knew they were just going to drink it up or buy drugs with it. I told her, "I'm not God, and I can't judge them for what they do with the money after I give it to them. It just seems like the right thing to do. I don't know what they have been through in their life, and maybe they need to do what they do to just cope with whatever went wrong in their life. My parents always told me to always look out for another human being if you can because God sees everything, and he is the one you have to stand before when you leave this world. Besides, China, I know most of those guys, and it just feels right to me."

Two years later, I was twenty years old, and China and I were still together. I had enough money now to ask my mother to quit her job because she was getting older and she needed to rest. I used to come by when she was asleep and just put money in her purse or put it in an envelope and put it right where I knew she would get it every time—in her Bible! Charlie finally brought me in on the business side of things by buying up cheap homes and making them after-hours casinos. "We're going to need people we can trust because once this catches on; we might need some jelly jars too." Charlie laughed. So with that idea in mind, I started picking the brains of everyone I came in contact with because after all, we were gonna need sharp people on board!

I started to take my pool-playing skills outside of the pool hall. Sometimes, it was at strip clubs and just about anywhere that had a pool table. Going to play pool at the strip clubs was kind of interesting because everyone in there was also about living today instead of twenty years from now, and I sure could relate to that big-time!

Most of the girls were hot and sold a fantasy to every guy who came through that door, but that didn't bother me at all because they all knew I was cut from a different cloth. Most wanted to join my team that they had heard so much about. I was on the same page of being a hustler myself, so I gave some of them my number to call me when there was big cash in there. When I won from the information that they gave me, I would always give them a cut, and that made them respect me as well as admire me very much. China was my girl though, and I didn't mess around on her. I let those stripper chicks know that if they wanted to be on my team, they had to bring something to the table that I could use financially. Otherwise, see you, wouldn't want to be you.

I also kept a dice board in my trunk so that when I went to the park where the ball players hung out, it would be Mad Skills time. Oh, I could still play ball with just your average guys, but I was far away from NBA level. After every basketball game, a dice game or a card game followed, and that was what I was really there for anyway! In thirty days, I had thirty racks put to the side to put with Charlie's money to put his idea in full effect. But Charlie said we would need payoff money too, in case we were ever shaken down by the crooked cops that ripped the drug dealers off whenever they got a chance to. The reason Charlie didn't like the drug game was because there were too many risks, and he also saw that as genocide on God's people, which I still agree with until this very day. You see, Charlie didn't want to tear people down as much as he wanted to educate them to pulling themselves up. He saw gambling as a competition. If you thought you could do something better than he could, to him that meant one thing—a bet!

As I got older, I also got wiser about a lot of things because life just makes you like that. I had a gift for reading people just from what they talked about and the body language they displayed. Charlie said we were going to need at least ten people we could trust because we would have about thirty that we couldn't! "Okay, Charlie, I'll play along. Why would we have people around our business that we can't trust?"

"Ray Ray, who will the people who we can trust have to feed us to show us they're trustworthy themselves? That will make the people we can trust be very loyal or get exposed for not being trustworthy at all. Trustworthy people are the people who we will keep around for a long time to come. You understand what I'm telling you?"

"Yeah, I do, Charlie. If we have a trustworthy staff, we can estimate our cash flow better! Anyway, that's what I'm hearing."

"That's what I admire about you, Ray Ray. You are exactly right, and I can tell you think a lot like me when I was about your age."

"Is that what One Shot saw in you, Charlie? Reasonable thinking on your part?"

"I like to think so, but your uncle wasn't the "pat you on your back and tell you good job" kind of guy. In fact, when you did something right, he acted as if you were supposed to anyway. Once I was playing a game of pool with this guy who was much better than I was. But he had a weakness—he tried to make every shot he looked at without playing defense. So I had to figure out how to leave him a difficult shot in order to get me an easy one. When I finally beat the guy, One Shot's only words were, 'It's about time!' But I will tell you this, Ray Ray, because he is gone now! This after-hours casino spot that we're about to get cracking was all your uncle's plan, but he never got the chance. So this is personal for me, Ray Ray, very personal!"

I went home that night with my uncle's idea in my head, so I could hardly wait to see China! She was a real estate agent, so getting those houses wouldn't be a problem. Anyway, that was what I was thinking!

# Stacey's Back!

As soon as I walked in the house, China had her favorite song playing—
"The Closer I Get to You"—and when she was in that kind of mood,
I was in for an early evening is all I'm saying! Fellows, if you got a girl
that you really intend to hold on to, just play this song after dinner,
and I guarantee that you will have a happy ending to your night. And
if you play it again in the morning when she comes out of the shower
smelling all good and sporting those thighs that will make your nature
rise, you just might get another "Hello, good morning" before she goes
out that door or she just might call in and use some of that PTO! I'm
just saying, shit happens!

I leaned over to kiss her, and she pulled back from me. I had no
idea why, but I knew I was about to find out. She pointed to a letter
sitting on the table with my name on it, and from the way she pointed
that finger, I knew it wasn't a bill! I walked over and picked it up, and
the return sender's name on that mail was Stacey! Now I was looking at
this brand-new shredder we hadn't used yet, and my first thought was
*Now would be a good time to use this.* But that would just make China
suspicious, like I was hiding something, and I would just deal with it
later when she was nowhere around. So what did I do? I'll tell what I
did. I sat right down beside her and opened it and read it out loud so
she could hear it too because after all, I did care about this girl. And
up until now, I had never kept any secrets from her, and I thought she
never kept any from me.

As soon as I got to the part that said she was in town at her mother's house, China's whole demeanor and face expression changed, so now I was thinking, *maybe this wasn't such a good idea.* China was quick on the draw with the question! "So is this the girl you were in love with before I came along, Ray Ray?"

Then for just a second, I asked myself, *Why do we do this to ourselves? Ask questions that we know we don't want the real answer to!* But I responded with "China, that was then, and this is now. And the past is just that, the past! I'm down with you now, and I love you and will tell that to anyone that act like they don't know." I really did care about her, but I was young. I didn't know if I really wanted to go that far to calling it love now that Stacey's letter made it to my house. I mean, I had no reason not to love her because this girl was the complete package and we just clicked from day 1. But Stacey had been with me when my father passed, so there was that.

China was not only beautiful; she was smart, book smart, with a touch of street as well, and she had a very unique look. I mean, the girl had a tongue ring and slanted eyes that lit up every morning when she opened her eyes to look at me. That always made me look right back in those beautiful eyes and smile at her for seconds at a time. That was the glue in our relationship, so now I guess I was getting ready to find out if it was Gorilla Glue or not!

"Ray Ray, I don't mean to seem insecure, but I just lost someone I loved very much. And I can't see myself losing you so soon because I don't want to start all over again!"

"China, I'm not going anywhere, but I can show you much better than I can tell you. So get dressed because we are going for a little ride."

"Where are we going, Ray Ray?"

"To Stacey's house right now, so I can prove to you you're my lady. And I don't want anyone else to think different, including Stacey! It's time you know that and her too, so let's roll!"

She kind of hesitated at first, but I knew she wanted our relationship to be validated, and this was the only sure way to do it in my mind, even though I didn't really know if I was over Stacey yet to tell you the truth. I dialed Stacey's number and put the call on speaker because I didn't want any doubt in her mind that she was my only girl. Stacey's phone rang about three times before she picked up, and when she did, I went right into it, getting straight to the point. "Hey, Stacey, this is Ray Ray. I got your letter, and I'm just wondering how you got this address!"

She replied with "Come on, Ray Ray, you know it wasn't that hard because your family still loves me, and I'm hoping you do too."

I thought to myself, *Man, she is not playing fair at all.*

"I know I left you hanging with no real explanation, and that's why I want a chance to sit down and explain to you what happened to us."

I was looking in China's eyes during the whole conversation with Stacey to let her know that I was right here and that no matter what Stacey said, I was right here. I knew I needed to do what I had to do because at that point, I didn't know if this was Gorilla Glue or honey! "Stacey, are you at your mother's house right now?"

"Yes, I am, Ray Ray. Are you coming over now?"

"I sure am, Stacey, because what we need to talk about just can't wait!"

"Oh, Ray Ray, I can't wait to see you because it has been at least two years, give or take."

"Yeah, something like that. But I'm on the way right now, so the wait won't be very long."

China and I jumped in her pearl-white Benz and jumped on the highway with me behind the wheel, and I put the pedal to the metal in that fine automobile. China reached in her purse and pulled out a fat joint and lit it up and cranked the stereo up to level 10, and it sounded like a live concert inside that brand-new Benz. She was bumping that Ty Dolla $ign—"I still fuck with you!" I felt like she was sending me a message through the music, like she was going to be with me no matter what this was about. I smiled with delight and put the *puff puff* pass down! I had never indulged before that day, but it seemed like such a good time to link with my girl that I didn't even hesitate the slightest bit. It made me feel mellow and very cool, and I liked it.

Then I thought about what Charlie might say if he knew I had smoked some pot. Just as I was thinking this, China turned the music down and said, "Charlie smokes too, so don't feel like you're doing something he doesn't do. But you didn't hear that from me!" I didn't say anything at the time, but I sure did wonder how she knew that! Right then, I knew I wasn't with a normal girl. I mean, she was really the complete package! I mean, how could she know what I was thinking?

We pulled up in front of Stacey's house with the mellow-eye look because that pot was some kush, and it did what it came to do (calm my nerves because even God knew they needed calming!). Stacey came out with a really confused look on her face because she saw China in the car, and I really couldn't blame her because I knew she never saw this coming. I jumped out of the car open casket clean because that was how I rolled each and every day. I asked her how she had been all these years before I hit her with what she knew was coming. "Stacey, I'm going to keep it real because that's how I do, and I'm sure you remember that already."

"I do, Ray Ray, and that's one of the things I've always admired about you."

"Well, you couldn't have admired it that much the way you just left me hanging like that!"

"I guess I had that coming, Ray Ray, but at least let me explain what happened and why."

Now Stacey was still Stacey, and I could tell that life had been treating her very well because she was looking more radiant than she was before! Fellas, you ever notice that your ex always looks better when you haven't seen her for a long time? Even though I cared very much for China, Stacey was still stunning to say the least! A part of me wanted to hear Stacey's explanation of what happened and why it happened. But I turned to glance at China right in her eyes, and those eyes brought me back to reality! Right before Stacey started to tell me her explanation for why she left, I motioned for China to get out of the car and join me by my side so she could see nothing had changed between us. She was still the woman who had been there for the last two years. On top of that, I knew China really did love me. I knew she was giving me the best that she had, and I knew in my heart that she was my soul mate. But I would be lying if I didn't think for a slight second, *sure would be nice to have them both!* (Be careful of what you ask for.)

I grabbed China by her hand and pulled her to me with my focus and attention directed straight in her slanted green eyes, and I kissed her like it was the beginning of our honeymoon. I came up for air just long enough to look Stacey in her eyes and say, "China, this is Stacey, and Stacey, this is China, my rock and foundation and the love of my life!"

"Nice to meet you, Stacey," China said. She reached her hand out to shake Stacey's hand, but Stacey declined on the handshake with a head nod and turned and walked back in her mother's house with a tear running down her cheek! China and I jumped back in the car and drove off like neither one of us saw the tear that was rolling down her cheek before she turned and walked back in the house.

Now, readers, you know when something like that happens the conversation on the ride home is not one for at least five minutes! I tried to break the awkward silence by asking China if she wanted to go out to eat. (Wait for it 'cause it's coming.)

"Ray Ray, you know that girl is still in love with you, don't you? So how do you feel about that?"

Now I'm sure I don't have to tell you that that was a mind-blowing question that I was not prepared for at all because no matter what answer I gave, it was not gonna be the right answer. (Then it came.)

"Ray Ray, I can see she is still in love with you, so my question to you is, do you still have some kind of feeling for her?"

Now like I already stated, no matter how I would respond, it was not going to be a right response, so whatever was going to happen next had to be more action than just words! So I put the pedal to the metal and drove that pearl-white Mercedes-Benz straight to the jewelry store and hopped out without giving her time to even ask me why I stopped there.

# Amanda Simmons

I walked in the store and went up to the counter, and the salesman was an older guy who gave me the vibe that he just wanted to sell me any ring, not the right ring. So I immediately surveyed the jewelry store for a young female because I knew she would be more suited for the job that I needed right here, right now! I glanced at her name tag, and it read Amanda Simmons. So I called her over and asked her what ring she would accept from her boyfriend and be overwhelmed with if her man brought it home to ask her to marry her. She looked up at me with a flirtatious smile while handing me her business card. I don't know why, but I gladly accepted it and put it in my inside jacket pocket! She pulled a tray of rings out for me to look at, and I informed her that this ring had to say to the woman on the receiving end that "since I found you, things have been so right that I have no problem at all with going down that road with you as my lifelong friend, my partner, and my wife!" She looked in my eyes, smiling so long that I had to clear my throat to bring her back to the matter at hand, which was China, not her.

"Oh, mister, I'm so sorry. It's just that you sound so sincere about her, and I don't hear things like that from most men that I have ran across or who come in here."

"Amanda, if you don't believe in many things, you damn sure can believe that a woman is as close to a superhero as any man can get, and I'm going to take advantage of that. By the way, my name is Ray, not sir, so what ring do you recommend for this special occasion?"

"Well, Ray, for what you're trying to say, I think this ring will be perfect for her."

I asked her to take it out of the case and put it on because she seemed to have good taste. I had her wrap it up in a box in China's favorite color, which was the same as mine (blue). Then I walked out to the passenger side and asked her to drive.

# Letting China Know

I opened the door while she hopped out and walked around the car to the driver's side, looking straight in my eyes the whole time. When she pulled away from the curb, I didn't waste any time on what I wanted to say to her! "China, you have been there for me since day 1, and I know when you got someone like you, you hold on to them. So this is my way of doing just that." I opened the box and took the sparkling two-karat ring out and told her to hold out her hand, and she gladly did with tears rolling down her face at the same time. "China, there is no doubt in my mind about who I want to spend the rest of my life with, and it's been that way for a while now! So I'm asking you, do you feel the same way?"

"Of course I do, Ray Ray, and it's always been that way for me too! I've known that for a very long time now, and my answer is yes, Ray Ray, if you're asking me to be the woman who you spend the rest of your life with."

"That I am, China that I am."

"Okay, Ray Ray, but here is the thing. I don't want to be husband and wife. That's too formal for us, and you know it, Ray Ray. I want to be your lifelong partner for life."

At this point, it really didn't matter to me if that had a significant meaning to it or not. I just wanted the problem solved, so I responded with "You know I can hear you right? [That always made her laugh when I said that.] That's exactly what I'm asking, China, so you're saying you will stay a little while?"

"No, that's not what I'm saying at all, Ray Ray. I'm saying till death do me apart from you, and even then, I will hunt your ass!"

We both laughed at that and put our lips together one more time while she was still driving! She quickly hit her turn signal light to pull to the side of the road so we could enjoy it just a little longer! People passing by honked their horns and stuff, but we kept right on doing what we were doing until we felt satisfied. You ever heard that song "Do It ('Til You're Satisfied)"? Well, we did!

But I wasn't going to let the enthusiasm end there, so I suggested we take a little break from everything and go rent a room at a ski lodge in Colorado and go skiing for the weekend. She welcomed the idea, so I picked up my cell and called Charlie and told him the good news. He congratulated us and told us to stop by and see him before we departed. I told him we would definitely do that, but it probably would be tomorrow because we were going out to celebrate our engagement. He said he understood and that he would see us both tomorrow! We raced home to change clothes for the night's event and surfed the internet for what was happening around the town and came up with this jazz concert.

It was off the chain. There were multiple artists there, but the artist who stuck out the most in my opinion was Ms. Erykah Badu! She put it down for about an hour or better and then walked off the stage with the band still grooving, and readers, I'm telling you they were doing just that (grooving)! And just when you thought the show was about to come to an end, Ms. Badu walked back out on the stage with a whole different outfit on and rocked it again even harder! The sister was worth every penny we spent that night and more because she put it down until she was ready to stop, and that took a while! I have been to many concerts since then, but Ms. Badu was, by far, the best I have ever seen!

We sipped champagne all night long and then went out for lobster tails, and after that, I looked up to the sky and thanked God for bringing China into my life because in my mind, it didn't get any better than this! The next morning, we went to the airport to catch our flight for Colorado, and she slept almost the whole flight there, right on my shoulder. I enjoyed watching her sleep peacefully. The night before we went skiing, we didn't sleep that much and you don't have to be the brightest crayon in the box to figure out why! This woman really did turn me on mentally and sexually, which is something that is very rare these days. Plus, she had a tongue ring that really turned me on, and whenever she wanted me to come to bed early, all she had to do was stick her tongue out at me! That damn ring was just like kryptonite and made me week. That's all I'm saying.

China was very sexy and could have had any guy she wanted, and the fact that she wanted me made me feel special. She knew both sides of the tracks—the gambling side and the college side—and that made her very unique and rare in many people's eyes, mine included. She had things on lock with her real estate business and pretty much left the gambling up to me now because the more property that she sold, the more time she spent at her office, so she didn't have time like she had before we were together. I didn't mind though because absence does make the heart grow fonder, so when we did have a quiet evening at home, we enjoyed it a little more, I think. I later had learned that her late boyfriend was into lucrative cash-making ideas himself, so I just assumed that China liked bad boys, sort of speaking.

Things were good that whole weekend, but China and I both knew there was an elephant in the room, and that elephant was Stacey! I knew that conversation was going to pop up sooner or later, but I was going to leave that elephant at the zoo for now! You see, I had made a vow with China long ago that there would never be any secrets between us, and I knew that she would be paying very close attention to that vow now, knowing Stacey was in town!

# Reassuring China

The very next morning, I rolled over to reach for her, and she was already up, taking a shower. I thought that was kind of odd because out of the whole two years we had been together, she had always woke me up if I was still asleep when she woke up first. Nevertheless, I jumped up and went into the bathroom to ask if she was okay, and she smiled and stuck that tongue ring out at me and asked, "Why wouldn't I be?"

Now this is kind of confusing because she did just stuck the tongue ring out, but at the same time, she went to the shower without waking me up. I'm just saying I would have gone for just a simple yes, but I guess that would have been just too easy! I knew if I took this conversation any further, I would be entering the danger zone, and I wasn't about to do that. So I opened the glass on the shower and walked in just like I was in my birthday suit. She had her back to me when I approached her, so I grabbed the bottom of her long hair and rolled it up slowly in my hand until it became so tight that she could only move the way I directed her to!

Now we were both very athletic, so being resistant was kind of like role-playing for us. Sometimes, our role-play before the main event was like a UFC match with some furniture moving going on, and we both loved it! I had a hair lock on her head, so that head had to do whatever I commanded it to! She tried to sweep my legs from under me, but I saw it coming because I know all her moves, especially since I taught her most of them. I sidestepped the leg sweep and spun her around by her hair, pinned her with my weight, looked her straight in her eyes, and said to her, "China, I need you to trust me because without trust, we really have nothing, and I need to know we have something special."

She placed her arms around my neck and said, "Ray Ray, I knew that at some point, our relationship would be in question on my part because I'm older than you and Stacey is more your age!"

"China, you talk like you're old or something, girl. Your breath still smells like Similac milk. What are you talking about?"

"It's not only that, Ray Ray. I saw her with my own eyes, and I must admit the girl is beautiful! Ray Ray, we just can't turn our feelings off like running water coming out of a faucet or something. Feelings just don't run like that. So tell me the truth, Ray Ray. Do you really want to marry me?"

"China, you have a very short memory! Do you remember when I told you how I knew I loved you? Remember that?"

"You said I was the last person or thing that you thought about before you closed your eyes at night and the first person or thing you thought about when you opened your eyes."

"Yeah, I told Stacey the same thing before, and at the time, I meant every word of it. So yes, I had those same feelings for her too, but I wasn't about to tell her that. Wait a minute now! That Bentley coupé is the first and last thing I think about."

Then she said something I would say to make her laugh, "You know I can hear you, right?"

I had to smile because to hear her mocking me was funny. "China, nothing has changed with the way I feel about you, so you have to just shake off anything else that's going on in that pretty face of yours. I am not going anywhere, and you should not only know that, you should also feel that from the tip-top of your pretty little head to the bottom of those well-manicured feet."

She seemed to snap out of her delusional state of mind for a minute, so I took advantage of that opportunity to call Charlie and tell him I would be coming by soon to catch up on whatever it was I missed when I was away!

# My Sister Gladys

As soon as I got to Charlie's place, he had this look of concern written all over his face like he was daydreaming or something! "What is it Charlie?" I quickly asked.

"Ray Ray, you been by your mother's house yet?"

"No, should I be there right now?"

"Yes, Ray Ray, I think you should go there right now. It's about your sister Gladys!"

"What happened with my sister, Charlie? Don't antagonize me like that, man!"

"Let me grab a jacket, Ray Ray, and I'll tell you on the ride over to your mother's house. But you're not going to like it!"

We jumped in Charlie's car because with the news that was about to be unleashed on me, he didn't want me driving when I heard it. "Someone broke into your sister's house and took advantage of her while she was sleeping in her bed."

Now Charlie had a reputation for making a hard blow soft, but I knew right away that someone had raped my older sister who was in a wheelchair! I looked at him with red in my eyes and said, "Drive this car faster, man, faster!"

We pulled up at my mother's house, and I jumped out before the car even stopped rolling to get this news that I didn't want to use. Gladys was still in the hospital, so the family had to tell me all the details. After they were finished, we all went to the hospital to visit her. The police were there too, asking my sister a million questions, as you can imagine, but they were getting nowhere because Gladys never saw his face, only heard his voice. After the cops left, Charlie and I hung around for a while to promise her we would not rest until we caught up with him and make it right for her.

Gladys was the sister who always had a good domino or card game going on, and sometimes, she would let me bring marks over to her house for me to relieve them of that cash that they carried around in their pocket. After a good day of gambling, I would always go buy her bierocks from the little restaurant around the corner because they were her favorite when she was hungry.

My three older brothers were furious, but Arthur Ray and I were seeing red because Gladys would not harm a fly, plus she was in a wheelchair. She had to be literally placed on the toilet seat just to use the restroom, and she didn't feel good about people helping her do that. Her daughters did that most of the time, but sometimes, they just didn't have the strength to accomplish such a difficult task. So I used to come in and act like it was no big deal, just something that had to be done. Even though I was the youngest of the family, I think it hit me the hardest because I spent more time with her than most of the other family, but for good reason. They had jobs and went to work every day.

Charlie and I eventually made it down to the pool hall and set up for the events that would be occurring later on that night. I had left my cell in the car when I was at the hospital. China had called several times, so I figured I should call her back and let her know what had happened to Gladys. She said she was going to the hospital right away, but that wasn't anything I didn't expect because China spent many hours at Gladys's house too, keeping her company with all the games she liked to play. I told her it would probably be better tomorrow because she was resting when I left, and she agreed but wanted me to take her. "Sure, China, and I'm sure she will be glad to see you too."

The craps game went on till early morning, so by the time Charlie and I closed up, daylight had caught up with me again. I was tired when I got home, and China was coming down the stairs like she was late for work. I kissed her on the way up to the house and told her we would meet at the hospital at lunchtime to visit with Gladys. She said, "Baby, you look tired, so I'll call you at 11:00 to wake you up. So make sure you hear your phone."

"Bet, baby girl, I will. Have a good day at work." I went inside and took a shower and went straight to bed.

# Stacey Wants What She Wants

The phone started ringing about 10:00 a.m., and I reached for it without even looking at the caller ID. And it was not China! "Hello," I said, and there were crickets for a moment. And then I heard a voice I knew all too well (Stacey)!

"Ray Ray, this is a very awkward moment for you, I'm sure, because it's one for me too, but you just have to give me a chance to explain to you what happened because it's important to me. And I think it may be to you too."

"Stacey, it doesn't really matter at this point because in case you have forgotten, I'm with China now, and that's the only thing that matters to me right now."

"Only one way to find out Ray Ray, link up with me by yourself, and then tell me that!

Now I didn't know why I didn't just hang up the phone instead of asking where she was calling me from because I knew her mom's number, and this sure wasn't it. "I have a bartending job downtown from one to ten, so I'll be expecting you before my shift is over tonight."

"Stacey, I can't do that, so don't expect me to! I don't want to mislead you in any way, and that's exactly what that will do. So you forget about me and move on with your life because I already did!"

"I still love you, Ray Ray" was the next thing that came out of her mouth, and those were dangerous words if she really meant it.

I hung up the phone and tried to fall back asleep, but that was an eye-opening phone call, so how could I go back to sleep after that?

China would be calling soon, so I just got on up and jumped in the shower. But on the way from coming out of the shower, I noticed something different about our bathroom! China and I had taken pictures together on the ski trip, and they were all placed strategically around the bathroom. I kind of just stood there for a minute, looking and admiring China's arrangement because she must have put a lot of thought into this ongoing project. There were more pictures that were still in the package that was still sitting on the wash sink. I was still standing there, admiring the arrangement, when I heard my cell ringing again, and this time, it was China!

"Ray Ray, you sound awake already. Did you get some sleep, baby?"

"Not much. I guess what happened to my sister is still heavy on my mind."

"Well, you want me to come pick you up, or do you just want to meet me there?"

"I'll meet you at lunch, China, so I'll see you then, baby."

"Okay, Ray Ray, and while you're at it, why don't you stop at that little restaurant she likes and pick her up some bierocks? I'm sure she will enjoy that."

"Bet, China. That's a very good idea. See you there at lunch!"

Now, readers, I know what you're thinking. Why wasn't I honest with China, and why didn't I tell her about the phone call? I have the perfect answer for you, even though it may be more of a question! Are you crazy? I wasn't about to open that can of worms because I didn't need to be questioned about how I felt about that again! Nope, nope, nope, not going to do it.

When I got there, China was already there, waiting in her car for me, so I quickly parked my car and jumped in her car to chat it up with her before we went in to visit with Gladys. "Ray Ray, are you good?"

"I don't know if I'm good, China, until I talk to my sister first and hear what happened firsthand from her mouth!"

"Hey, Ray Ray, Charlie called and told me the plan about the houses you're going to need to get the plan off the ground."

"Oh yeah, I completely forgot about it when I heard about my sister!"

"Well, I have already gotten started on the paperwork, and I will let you know something as soon as I get any word on the properties that I looked at!"

"Thanks, baby, I appreciate that very much."

We walked in together and got on the elevator to go up to my sister's room. She was sitting up in her bed and looking at the TV when we walked in, but her focus quickly shifted to China and me when we both walked into that room. We both went over to give her big hugs, and shortly after that, I wanted to know what the hell happened and if she had any idea who the guy was!

She look me straight in my eyes and told me just like this, "Lil brother, if I knew anything, I would have told the cops because I'm scared to even go back home."

"Don't you even worry about that, sis. You're not going back there ever!"

We hung around there until my sister felt a little better, then I jumped in my car and went straight to the pool hall because it was time to go to work! China went home to get some rest because 5:00 a.m. comes early, even when you do go to bed on time. Halfway through the night, just when my mind started to be at ease from all the activities that had been going on, Stacey walked through the pool hall door, looking like an international model!

# Stacey Is Different

I mean, nothing was out of place anywhere on her body as far as I could tell because I looked her up and down from head to toe twice before I could even say one word! Now I can't even lie. My mind went straight down memory lane, and no one else was on that street except Stacey and me! That was until I heard Charlie say two words! "That's trouble!"

Then I heard one of the guys say, "If that's trouble, then that's the kind of trouble I want to be in!"

Now I don't have to tell you, readers, that my blood pressure went off the charts when I looked into this beautiful woman's eyes, and I'm pretty sure hers did also! She motioned for me to come that way, and for some strange reason, my feet just started walking that way. "What are you doing here, Stacey?"

"Ray Ray, if you really have to ask me that, then you're not as sharp as you think you are! Ray Ray, you're going to let me explain what happened one way or another, so we can do it right here or wherever you feel comfortable. It really doesn't matter to me! And then if you can look at me straight in my eyes and tell me it's really over between us, I'll walk away and never look back, but you're at least going to let me get this weight off my shoulders!"

A part of me just wanted to walk right past her and walk out that door! But I didn't! Her heart wanted closure, and just maybe mine did too. Maybe she would just put our past relationship in the past once and for all if I gave her that chance. I looked over at Charlie, and he pointed toward his office, as if he were saying, "Ray Ray, you're going to need some privacy on his one, son!" As soon as he did that, an image of China popped up in my head that made me a little dizzy. After all, this was my ex, and I had years with this woman! I motioned for her to follow me into Charlie's office, and she did that little Betty Rubble (Flintstone) laugh that always made me smile, and then she walked in front of me into Charlie's office.

As soon as I turned around from locking the door, she tilted her head and bit down on that pinky finger, and I knew I was in trouble! She flashed that serious look on me and said these words: "Ray Ray, lately I don't know what to do because I know I put you through a lot, but the truth is I don't want anybody else but you. I know I have broken the trust barrier with you, but I'm willing to do whatever it is you need me to do to gain that trust back, including be the other woman, if that is what it's going to take."

"Stacey, what do you mean by that exactly?"

"I mean, I don't care about your other woman. I just want you to not shut me out!"

Now, readers, let me describe to you what I was looking at when she said that. I was looking at a woman who had that athletic body that looked like it was made by Mattel and who had the brain to match, and she always wore that perfume that smelled similar to flowers but was much more sensual!

"Stacey, could you get to the point of what happened and why you just left me hanging without no kind of warning or anything! Let's talk about that because I don't have all night."

"Well, Ray Ray, I let my parents get inside my head. They were saying you were going nowhere with your life and that I needed to think about my future ahead. They knew you had broken your leg and given up on sports, so I knew the only way to please them was to date someone that they would approve of. After all, they were paying for everything. Even though I never stopped loving you, my dad told me to just cut my ties with you altogether because that was the only way to move forward with my life, so I did. But now I see that it was one of the biggest mistakes I have ever made in my young life. And I'm sure I will make more the older I get, but at least let me try to fix this one, Ray!"

"Stacey, you have crossed a bridge that you can't come back across because China and I will be married soon, and that will make me the happiest man in the world."

"So when is the date, Ray Ray?"

"We haven't made one yet, but it's up to me when it happens."

Now, readers, the average woman would have taken that answer and moved on, but there was nothing average about Stacey! I could look in her eyes and tell she was not giving up by any means. She had her head tilted to the side, biting down on her pinky's fingernail as she always did when she had to have some type of answer to whatever question she would ask. Yes, I knew that look way too well because that was the move that always made me give in to her.

Just then, my cell started to ring. I looked at the caller ID and saw it was China calling, so I looked at Stacey and told her I had to take this call. She did the little Betty Ruble laugh and said, "Go ahead, Ray Ray. Take it. I'll wait!"

I opened the door to Charlie's office and walked out the door for some privacy, but at the same time, I felt butterflies entering my stomach right along with sweat beading up on my forehead that was visible to anyone looking, including Charlie! So I walked right past him and the whole pool hall crowd and jumped into my car before I answered China's call! The first thing she asked me was if I was having fun with Stacey! Wow. How could she know that I was talking to her that fast? I mean, it couldn't have been more than five minutes of face time between Stacey, so how could she know that fast about my social activities with this woman? "China, it's not what you're thinking, and I'll be home in ten to tell you all about it." There was a long silence on the phone, followed by a hang up! All I could say was "Oh, damn."

I was getting ready to go through interrogation like never before. I hadn't even told her about Stacey calling me earlier, and I knew that would come out when she asked if I had been completely honest about how I really felt about Stacey! I sat there for a minute, thinking about what I was about to go through once I got home and how I was not ready for the stress that was going to come with it!

As I was sitting there, pondering the situation, Stacey came out of the pool hall and waved bye to me with a girlish smirk on her face and jumped in her car, as if she were going to pull off. But she backed her car out of one parking spot just to pull up right beside me and let her window down and motioned for me to let mine down too. Even though I had never admitted it to China or myself, I still had feelings for this woman, and Stacey knew it all too well! I dropped my window just low enough to see what she wanted, and she didn't waste any time getting to my weak spot. "Ray, you look like you could use a friend right now, so you wanna come to my place and talk?"

"Stacey, you stay with your mom, so what do you mean by me coming to your place?"

"Ray Ray, you have seen my place on TV many times, and they always tell you that they will leave the light on for you. It's called the Motel 6!"

I have to admit, she was funny sometimes, and she could still make me smile. But I had to focus on the matter at hand! I shook my head no and let my window up and backed out of my parking spot and burned rubber in that new Audi sedan. I was going to just think for a minute because after all, Stacey and I had a lot of history, and I needed that history to stay just that! I picked up my cell and called Charlie for some advice because Lord knows I needed some right now.

"I kinda thought you might be calling, Ray Ray. Where are you at, son?"

"Rolling on that one-way street called confusion. You ever been on that street, Charlie?"

"Yes, I have, son, many times over, and you need to make a U-turn before you wind up being in a crash, dummy!"

"Hey, Charlie, could you look outside and tell me if Stacey's car is still there?"

"Lil brother, you got bigger problems than that because China and Stacey are both outside at this very moment."

"What?"

"Yeah, man, you heard me correctly. They both are here!"

"Well, Charlie, don't just leave me in suspense. What are they doing?"

"They seem to be talking, but I don't know what about."

"Charlie, are you trying to be funny or something? Because it's only one thing they could be talking about, and that's me."

"Hey, Ray Ray, don't mess up our plan by acting like your uncle Grady. We need those spots that only China can provide to make that real money, man! I think you need to get down here and get on top of whatever is going on."

So I down-shifted that Audi and made that U-turn like the police in a high-speed chase after he had just gotten an emergency officer down call over his radio! When I arrived at the pool hall, neither one of them was sitting in their cars, so I quickly parked and went inside. What I saw made my jaw drop! They were both at the back pool table, playing pool together and having a casual conversation, and I just stood there, frozen! I didn't know how to react, so I did the only thing that could be done! I approached the pool table with caution and looked them both in their eyes and asked, "What the hell is going on here?"

It was like they had rehearsed what they were going to say when I asked that, and they both responded right on cue with the same answer. "Girl talk, Ray Ray, so can you give us a minute?" I turned around to see what Charlie's reaction would be to all this because I just felt like he knew something! It seemed that all eyes were on me and the whole pool hall was watching and I was on stage, whether I wanted to be or not!

When I finally locked eyes with Charlie, he was holding up his office key for me again, and I took that as a sign that I needed to take myself off stage and get some privacy before this went any further, because after all, this could be the calm before the storm. If that were the case, I wanted to get some kind of shelter before the storm came. I walked over to Charlie and plucked the key out of his hand and headed straight to the back pool table in the eye of the brewing storm! (Anyway, that was what I was thinking.) "Ladies, can you both follow me into my office?"

They both looked at me with a smile and said, "Sure, papi, lead the way."

This was the last place in the world that I wanted a catfight to jump off, so I made sure they both took a seat as soon as they entered the office because I was assuming it's hard to throw blows if you're sitting down. Now both of these ladies were smart and classy, but what was going on right here, right now was way beyond both of them. And I was just a little confused, as you might be right now as well.

China spoke first, "Stacey says she still loves you, Ray Ray, and probably always will, and so do I! What do you think about that, Ray Ray, and what are you prepared to do about it?"

I looked Stacey in her eyes with a very concerned look and answered China's question. "Stacey and I have already had this conversation, and I don't know why she is coming to you with it."

"Ray Ray, didn't you tell me that you and Charlie will need people who you can trust when these house casinos start up?"

"Yes, China, but what has that got to do with Stacey?"

"Well, I think she will be good for the business, and I think you can trust her. Plus, she works at a very high-class bar, so she can bring some high rollers from that extravagant club that she works in. Ray Ray, we all have feelings, but this is not what this is about. This is about getting what we all want and being a team to get it!"

"China, what in the world is going on with you? What are you getting at?"

"Ray Ray, I'm thinking of us being a team rather than adversaries if this is going to be about getting that big money. I would feel better if we all were on the same page. That way, you don't have to lie to me about something I already know. Stacey has already let me know how she feels about you. She is not going anywhere, and neither am I, Ray Ray!"

Then Stacey spoke, "Ray Ray, this is how this is going to go! You're going to have two spots because we all don't have to live together to be a team. Don't either one of us want to hear what you do with the other one intimately because that's just something we're not going to do. When you're with her, then you're with her, but when you're with me, you're with me. And that's the rule we want to live by!"

"Wait a minute. How long have you ladies been talking? This is all going way too fast for me right now! China, have you forgotten that we're supposed to be married soon?"

"No, Ray Ray, but I also know why you proposed to me. It's because I seemed to be insecure when I knew Stacey was back in town, but there is something about me I never told you during our two years together, and that is an intimate conversation that we will have later when we're alone. I can let you know this already though, Ray Ray. I like the ring, and I'm not giving it back."

Stacey stood up and said, "Ray Ray, that's my cue, so call me later after you and China have that conversation. Then it will be our turn to have our own private and personal conversation as well." Then she grabbed my hand and kissed me on my cheek and walked out the office door with swag I had never seen before!

She closed the door behind her, and I was standing there, looking at China with a million questions going through my head all at once. But I could ask only one at a time, and the main question that I asked China first was "What the hell just happened here?"

# Flip Side

"Ray Ray, I have to go close on those houses that you and Charlie want, so I'll get at you when I'm done!" She gathered her belongings and kissed me on the opposite cheek that Stacey had kissed me on and walked out the door with the confidence of a championship boxer! I was standing there, thinking, *either I'm the luckiest man in the world or I just got punked!*

Before I could reach for the door handle, Charlie came through that same door so fast that we almost bumped heads. "Ray Ray, please tell me that we are good on our plan for the casinos."

"Charlie, if I got this all right, which I sure hope I do, I think we're better than just good, man! Charlie, I got this feeling that you know more than what you are portraying to know about China, and I think it's time you come clean about everything you think I don't know about this woman!"

"Ray Ray, I've known China way before you, and whatever it is you think you don't know has got to come from her, not me, son."

"So, Charlie, you know I listen like a counselor, right? You just implied there is an unread chapter in China's life."

"Ray Ray, I think there is an unread chapter in both ladies' lives that you're going to find very intriguing to say the least, Mad Skills. Now let's see if you got any of your uncle's traits, because I've seen him in the very same predicament, and he came out shining like a rock star. Sometimes, Ray Ray, curiosity makes you smarter, and I know you have a lot of that right now. So go take care of your business, and I'll see you later."

He was right about one thing for sure. My curiosity level was at its highest peak, and I wanted to know everything there was to know about both ladies. Right then, I started to wonder if this was how my uncle Grady got started off dating more than one woman at a time! I still didn't drink and had only smoked pot once before with China, but on that particular night, I felt the need to light one up.

On the way to my car, I saw Red pulling up, and I wondered why he had paid so much attention to China and my conversation. But I wasn't about to mention it to him because I wanted to see if he would do it first! I went up to his car and asked him for a joint. He told me to jump in and kick back and he would take care of the rest. I opened his car door with some tunes of Marvin Gaye coming out of those Bose speakers, so I jumped in and took a few pulls off the blunt with him.

"Hey, Ray Ray, I heard China is your girl now. How does Charlie feel about that?"

"What do mean by that, Red?"

He kind of stared at me for a second before he looked away and said, "Man, I was just tripping. Forget that I even said anything."

I just spaced it off because I had enough on my plate right now! I jumped in my own whip and turned on my own tunes and put the pedal to the metal and smashed out! I picked up my cell and called Stacey, and it seemed like the phone didn't even ring before I heard her little Betty Ruble giggle. "Hey, papi, are you close?"

"I'm five minutes away, and I have an abundance of questions, as I'm sure you can imagine."

"Okay, Ray Ray, I'll see you in five!"

When I got there, she was sitting on the porch like a schoolgirl waiting on the bus. I motioned for her to get in the car, and this time, I wasn't nervous but overwhelmed with curiosity. As soon as she took a seat in my car—which, by the way, was really China's car—I got right to the point. "Stacey, I don't know what you said to China to get her to accept whatever it is you're selling, but I need to know before I go talk to her."

"Ray Ray, I'm appalled at your dismay. What makes you think I'm the one doing the selling?"

"So you're saying China put all of this together?"

"Ray Ray, that's a conversation you're going to have to have with her. I'm sitting here right now to let you know what happened when I went away to college."

"I got that part already. Your parents, right?"

"Yes, but the two years I was gone wasn't all college, Ray Ray."

"What do you mean by that, Stacey?"

"Well, after I broke up with the guy I was with, I started waiting tables at underground poker games to support myself. My parents stopped supporting me after I broke up with Brad because to them, Brad was as good as it was going to get for me. He was on his way to being a doctor in a few years, and that's all they noticed about him. In fact, that's all they really cared about. Ray Ray, he used to abuse me in more ways than one when he drank alcohol, so one day, I just packed up and left when he was away on one of his so-called business trips. Anyways, I wasn't going to beg my parents for money, so word of mouth led me to the underground poker games to become a cocktail waitress. The money was great, but it kept me up all night. And that led me to falling behind with my grades. It was so far that it became impossible for me to catch up. During those long poker nights, I would see people from all walks of life come through there from time to time, so guess who one of those people was?"

"Stacey, I have no idea, but it must be someone I know for you to ask that question."

"You're absolutely right, Ray Ray, China!"

"So you knew China before now?"

"Well, I never got a chance to meet her, but we definitely locked eyes a few times."

"Well, don't keep me in suspense. What guy was she with, Stacey?"

"What makes you think it was a guy, Ray Ray?"

"Wait, Stacey, are you saying China is a lesbian?"

"Not at all, Ray Ray. Calm down a little, man." She could tell all my wheels were turning, and I was starting to think that she was doing it on purpose. "Your wife-to-be was a madam and had many ladies of the night who answered to her!"

You know how some people say "Man, you have to get up pretty early in the morning to get something past me"? Well, right about now, I was just now rolling over to open my eyes from a long night of good, hard sleep, and Stacey was already at the breakfast table, eating Frosted Flakes. So how is that for getting up early? I'm just saying. "Stacey, you're highly mistaken because China is into commercial real estate, and on top of that, I would know something like that, don't you think?"

"Yes, she is now, but how do you think she got the money to start?"

"Stacey, and you know all of this how?"

Just then, Stacey took her cell out and dialed China's number, and I was shocked that she even knew her number. She put the phone on speaker so I could hear what was being said! China didn't even say hello. Instead, she asked Stacey, "Did you tell him yet?"

"I did, China, and you're on speaker phone, so he hears you."

"Ray Ray, I'm on my way home right now, so why don't you meet me there when you're done there and I will explain this from *A* to *Z*?"

I looked over at Stacey and told her, "I guess I will be in touch with you later, but right now, I have some business to tend to."

She leaned her head back and bit her little fingernail and said, "Take your time, Ray Ray. I'll be here when you get back."

Now usually I got the pedal to the metal on that Audi, but this time, it seemed like I was cruising to arrive at a bruising because I didn't see how this conversation was going be a good one. One of my favorite tunes came over the radio ("What You See Is What You Get"), so I cranked the volume on those Bose speakers and put the pedal to the metal and got on the freeway to get me home in light speed! I parked the car, and as I was walking up those steps, Charlie's name popped up in my mind because I was wondering just how much of this story he knew about. After all, he did imply that there was something about both ladies that I would find intriguing.

I walked in the house, expecting China to be sitting on the couch, but she was nowhere to be found in the living room. So I went back to the first bedroom, and she was at her little desk and on her laptop.

I reached over slowly and gently closed the top of the laptop to get her full attention!

She looked at me with a look I had never seen before, but it was understandable because we were about to go into uncharted territories— to this little place called Trust Island! She didn't want to make eye contact, but she knew she had to. So she looked at me and asked, "Do you really want me to start from the beginning, Ray Ray?"

"Yes, China, I do."

"Okay, you want to hear it. Here it goes! I used to be one of Red's girls, and I learned all I could from him and broke off on my own."

"Wait a minute," I said.

"Don't interrupt me, Ray Ray. Let me get out what I've been holding in for almost two years!"

"Bet. Go ahead and finish," I said.

"As I was saying, I used to be one of Red's girls a long time ago. I never loved him, but I did admire what he did. I was mostly interested in what made him tick and what made him think like he did, and women still flocked to him. You know what they say, a woman don't want a man that another woman don't want."

"Wait! Stop right there! Who said that?"

"Ms. Kay, my play mother, kind of."

"Wait, what do you mean kind of?"

"Well, it was Ms. Kay that got me away from Red and helped me learn the business from a woman's perspective."

"You mean, Ms. Kay was a madam too?"

"Yes, and she taught me that whatever a person decides to do, just be good at it. And I'll tell you this about me right here, right now. I was very good at it! Nobody is the same, and it's okay to be yourself and do you! People are always going to be judgmental and hate. That's just the way it goes, and the only defense for people like that is to not let them in your circle. It's that simple! I really learned that at a very young age from Charlie. Ms. Kay just drove it home! Have you ever been around someone while just watching TV or something and they say something like 'I don't even like that actor or maybe that ball player'? They don't even actually know that actor or that ball player, but they say they don't like them. Those are the haters showing you who they are identifying themselves to you as haters, so pay attention, Ray Ray!"

"China, I never really thought about it like that, but I do see your point."

"Everyone has some kind of secret that they'd rather not share with just anyone because if it got out to the public, certain people might feel different about them. So they do the obvious—they fake it to make it! They can't take that chance, so they keep it bundled up for as long as possible and sometimes until it drives them over the edge. My dad used to say that sometimes you have to do wrong to position yourself to do right."

"Your dad told you that, China?"

"Yes, my dad is also my best friend, and he always keeps it 100 percent with me. And that's why I look at things the way that I do. Do you see how light-skinned Ms. Kay is? Her grandmother was a descendant of former slave owners, and being light-skinned reminds her of the rape and torture that her ancestors had to endure during their time on this earth. That's why she has a thing for dark skin, and you see how dark-skinned Charlie is."

"Hold on right there, China. Are you insinuating that there is something between those two?"

She just looked at me and smiled. "Anyway, the reason I never told you is, I didn't want to take the risk of losing you. I mean, I did lose my boyfriend in a car wreck. I didn't lie to you about that, Ray Ray. I did lie to you about other things though! I'm not a trust fund baby like I said. In fact, Charlie is my father, and when he went away to the penitentiary, Ms. Kay looked out for me."

"Wait, Charlie is your father?"

"Yes, he is, Ray Ray."

"Shit, I knew you resemble him, but I had no idea he was your father! Wait, he wasn't mad at Ms. Kay for making you a lady of the night?"

"Ray Ray, nobody made me do anything! What I did was by choice, not by force. Plus, Charlie and Ms. Kay was an item at one time."

"What do you mean by that, China?"

"Charlie used to be a gentleman of leisure, Ray Ray. He had ladies, and Ms. Kay was one of his best ladies of the night! Once Charlie came home, I put him on his feet by giving him some money that Ms. Kay had given me to hold for him. After that, I invested in real estate and never looked back to those days."

"Wait a minute, Charlie is your father? Why did he never tell me, and why do you call him Charlie?"

"Because my dad lives in the underworld, and he doesn't want his life associated with mine for security purposes. And I'm sure he has his reasons for thinking that way."

"You know, now I know why Charlie was always a step ahead of some of the things I did, even some of the conversations I had with you. Even Red knew something because he tried to tell me earlier tonight! How could you and Charlie keep this kind of information quiet like this for almost two years, China, and why are you telling me this now?"

"Ray Ray, everything we do in the dark eventually comes to the light, and it's just that time because of what we are about to do."

"Wait, you really don't have a problem with Stacey?"

"Of course not. I'm used to just about anything. My previous lifestyle should tell you that. Sometimes, Ray Ray, you just got to take everything in and go with what works. The Super Bowl is not won by one man. It's done by a team. And we are going to win the Super Bowl, Ray Ray, for Charlie and his best friend, your uncle Grady, better known as One Shot!"

"You know about my uncle One Shot too?"

"Only what Charlie has told me about him."

"What about Stacey?"

"What about her, Ray Ray?"

"I mean, are you really okay with me being with her intimately?"

"What did I tell you earlier, Ray Ray? A woman doesn't want a man that another woman doesn't find attractive and want for herself. In fact, it makes me kind of hot for you, papi, but I don't want to hear about it unless I ask, Ray Ray."

"Wait, what did you just say?"

"I was just playing, Ray Ray, calm down. Charlie knows about all of this and doesn't have a problem with it."

"Problem?" I kind of sat it up.

"Ray Ray, here is the address for a house that you can get for Stacey, because if she is going to be with you, she can't have her family snooping around and watching her every move now, can she?"

"Sounds like you have done this before, the way you're so smooth and calm about the whole thing."

"This is not my first rodeo, Ray Ray. Placing people where they need to be is kind of my forte, but the rest is on you and Charlie."

I picked up my cell to call Charlie and ask him a million questions, but China grabbed my phone and turned the power off. "Not tonight, papi. Tonight is my night."

Needless to say, the night continued with more questions than being intimate because I was still processing all of what I just heard, and before I knew it, she was asleep on my shoulder. The next morning, she took the day off because she wanted to see Charlie's reaction when we both walk in the pool hall together, and so did I!

# All About Charlie

The next morning, China and I got up early and went out across the tracks to the hospital to visit with my big sister Gladys to get updated on what was going on. We were stopped at the front desk by one of the nurses and told that the family checked her out about an hour ago. "Not a problem," I said. China and I jumped back in the car and drove straight to mother's house, but I was still a little puzzled about this whole thing. But my sister's situation was more important at the time, so I kept those thoughts to myself for the time being.

As soon as we turned on the block, we saw Charlie's car was already parked in the driveway. China and I parked the car and went inside to find out what was going on. My sister was back in my mother's bedroom, watching TV with some more family members, so I motioned for Charlie to come outside with me to have a little talk. I had a very strong desire to learn a lot of things considering the circumstances, wouldn't you think?

"Ray Ray, I know you have a lot of questions, but I can only answer one at a time. So calm down and start from the top or the bottom, whichever one you prefer."

I took a deep breath and asked, "Is China really your daughter, Charlie?"

"Yes, she is, Ray Ray, and I know you're going to ask me why I didn't tell you after all this time. So let me get the elephant out of the room, so to speak. Ray Ray, China's been a very fragile young lady ever since she lost her mother."

# China's Real Mother

"In the two years you have been with her, I'm willing to bet that she has never even mentioned her once!"

"You would definitely win that bet, Charlie, because she has never, ever brought her up one time, at least not the mother whom you speak of."

"There's a reason for that, Ray Ray. It's just too damn painful to her!"

"Charlie, tell me about China's real mother, if you please, sir!"

"Okay, Ray Ray, you want to hear about her? China's mother was a very attractive Filipino woman that I met in Waikiki, Hawaii. Back in the day, that taught me many things, and not all of them were good."

"What do you mean by that, Charlie?"

"Well, let's just say the way that she made her money bit me in the ass later on. Her name was Jasmine, but I just called her Jazz because she was every bit the jazziest woman I had ever seen in my young life. And that is where China's slanted eyes come from."

"Well, Charlie, I kind of figured that because you damn sure don't have slanted eyes, brother."

"Ray Ray, you going to let me tell the story or you going to be a critic?"

"I'm sorry, Charlie. I couldn't help it, but go ahead."

"She was about five-nine and walked with the grace of a queen. In fact, she was just that to me. I mean, she was definitely a head turner, and she had my nose open like the freeway at three in the morning in a very small town. She had the same slanted eyes that China has right now. Just like you, Ray Ray, there was something about her that was most unusual and very unique! She had that exotic look that you don't see on the women that I was exposed to growing up, and I think that was a very attractive feature that drew me like mosquitoes to a bright light. Most relationships always start off good because you're not really dating that person at the beginning. You're actually dating his or her agent. That's the person who is going to say everything right and do everything right until you have bought into their sales pitch!

"Anyway, Grady and I were hustling craps in Hawaii, and I ran across her selling lingerie out at the mall from a small little shop that her parents owned. I was never afraid of the word *no*, and she was just going to have to tell me no if she wasn't feeling me because I was going to ask her out for a date. Sometimes, when a woman says no, her eyes and smile will definitely say yes, and that's what I'm shooting for—the yes! She accepted, but only if she got to choose the place. I agreed and left her my number, and she called later on that night to set up our date for tomorrow at the downtown library. I'm only thirty years old, but I knew then that if you exchange numbers with a woman and she calls you before you call her, there is already something about you that she likes.

"I read a lot, and I had your uncle for advice on the ladies. So I thought I could have a conversation with anyone about anything no matter what background they came from! At the time, she was about twenty-six and was way more advanced than I was in almost everything except gambling. I was not an indecisive young man at all because I knew what I wanted when I wanted it, and I wanted her!

"When I got to the library, she was standing on row 3, looking at marketing books, and right away, she earned some cool points off me because I knew a lil bit about it. I have always liked beautiful women, and this woman was way beyond that. She was exotic, so she got a lot of cool points for that too. Grady and I were staying in New Jersey then, and we had to be home in a week. So if this was going to go anywhere, I needed to go ahead and shift this into high gear! I asked her if she had ever been to New York, and she replied, 'No, but I've always wanted to go, Charlie.'

"'Well, today is your lucky day because I'm ready to take you home with me right now!'

"She flashed the flirtatious smile and said, 'Charlie, if you get me to go home to New York with you, it will be more of your lucky day than mine, don't you think?'

"I looked at that Coke-bottle, model shape of hers and smiled and replied, 'I'm going to have to agree with you on that, Jazz, because I see myself very happy already just by you being in my company.'

"'Aha, a sweet talker. I like that! I just hope you're not all talk if I do decide to visit the Big Apple one day.'

"I grabbed her hand very softly and pulled her close enough to whisper in her ear, 'There's only one way to find out, Jazz, so should I book the flight now or later?' Her English was very good for her to be a full-blooded Filipino, and I was very impressed. We talked for a while, and then she went to the front to check out the books that she had picked out. And I was more impressed when she talked in her natural Filipino language to the guy behind the counter. We walked out of the mall together and agreed to keep in touch while I was there in town. I went to my hotel room to get ready for the night's event of gambling on the island of Hawaii at the underground clubs, and they had many for it to be such a small island. I took a shower and lay across my king-size bed to watch a little TV, but it wasn't long before the TV end up watching me because I went out like a light.

"I awakened at three twenty-five in the morning, and I remember that exact time so well because I rolled over and saw my message light blinking on my hotel phone after looking at the clock first. I checked the message, and Jazz had called four hours ago! I sat up in my bed and called the number that she had given me earlier back, but no one answered the phone. I called Grady's room to see if he was rolling with me tonight because sometimes we just did our own thing, especially if there was a lady involved. He didn't answer, so I got dressed and went and jumped in my rented red Corvette and put in my Prince CD and headed out to the hottest gambling spot in the town called the Jewelry Store.

"Even though it didn't look like any jewelry store I had ever seen, it got its name by loaning people cash on their jewelry if they had a bad night at the craps table or the card table! There were no door admissions, but you did have to have stacks of cash or a high-dollar piece of jewelry on to even get in the VIP section. That's how it got its name, the Jewelry Store! They had a special room upstairs for the high rollers. If you were not in a certain tax bracket, you would not even know that upstairs even existed! But sometimes, it's not what you know as much as it is who you know, and your uncle Grady and I knew everyone that gambled at a high level. I had been in the town for a few days now, so I knew some of the high rollers already. So getting in wasn't a problem.

"They played a billiard game called snooker a lot in Hawaii, and the tables seem much bigger and the pockets are much smaller than the ones we play eight-ball on here. After you have played on the snooker table for a while, the pockets on a regular-sized pool table seem wide as basketball rims, and you should be able to run the table with ease. Anyway, I was about two hundred up when I saw the silhouette shape of a woman in the far distance that looked way too familiar. I could only see her backside, but man, what a backside it was. I gathered up my chips and went toward the cash-out window where she was standing, and sure enough, when that silhouette image walked into the light, it turned out to be Jazz in the flesh! We locked eyes, and to make a long story short, China was conceived that night."

"Charlie, I don't want the short version because that short version don't have Ms. Kay in it!"

He smiled and asked, "How much did my daughter tell you?"

"Obviously more than you're telling me right now, Charlie, and I want to know everything, man, because you have kept me in the dark long enough!"

"Yeah, Ray Ray, you're right, but I'm going to only give you the quick version for now."

"Bet, Charlie, I'll take what I can get right now."

"Ms. Kay was after Jazz got me sent upstate to the penitentiary."

"Wait, hold on, Charlie. Let's go back to Jasmine. How did she get you sent upstate?"

"Well, Ray Ray, Jasmine was into a lot of things that I didn't know about until it was too late. Grady tried to tell me that she was moving drugs, but at the time, I didn't see anything that would make me believe something like that because she never did anything around me! I liked this woman, so it's very possible I didn't want to see. Jasmine introduced me to cocaine so I could stay up for days, hustling and getting that money. And I picked up a habit that I didn't even realize I had until I started losing noticeable weight. She had so much at her disposal that I didn't even know that I had a problem until it became a problem for me to stay focused on getting money the gambling way. Staying up for days made my game decline instead of me being the championship caliber player that I really was. I had a lion on my back that stayed hungry, and I was running out of cocaine to feed the hungry beast!"

"What did my uncle say when he found out, Charlie?"

"One Shot dropped me like a bad habit and left me alone to find out what he already knew. The outcome of messing with drugs always turns out bad! No matter if you're selling them or using them, it always turns out bad! You see, Ray Ray, when you have a drug habit, you're always the last one to see it because you like getting high so much that you tell yourself each and every day that lie that all junkies tell themselves! 'I'm not that bad. I only get high on the weekends.' When the truth of the matter is, you get high every chance you get on whatever is available with whoever you can! Drugs kill you in one way or another. That shit is a wicked motherfucker! Once people use it, they always abuse it, and just like a soul mate, they choose it. It kills your dreams and potentials, and you can try and quit, but it's just not that damn simple! It just keeps calling your name, and you'll do anything to get it because at this point, you have no shame. With fucking with drugs, in the end, it takes you down two paths, so take your pick. You can be judged by twelve or packed by six!

"One day, I got that one phone call that changed both our lives forever! We had two spots, one in Manhattan, New York, where we lived, and another in Brooklyn, where she did her business. The phone rang in our Manhattan apartment, and I picked it up high as hell, chewing on that invisible sandwich that I could never taste. Jazz told me she was in jail and that she needed me to make a trip to Brooklyn to move some things around and that it would be best for me not to ask why over the phone. I jumped up and drove to the spot to do what she asked me to do, looking in the rearview mirror all the way there. I got there and picked up what she needed and took it back to the New York apartment, only to have the cops follow me there.

"I got three years for trafficking drugs. She was a mule, and she received twenty-five years for conspiracy. All that time was just too much for her to handle, and they say she hung herself in her own cell. But I don't know if I believe that. Maybe she just knew too much . . . Anyway, while I did my short bit, Grady took China to live with him and his own kids right there in New York until I came home. He paid for everything so China could become the best student at school that she could be. Even though I had let him down big-time, he looked at me as if that had nothing to do with China, so he did things for her just as if she was his own kid, and I owe him big-time for that!

"China was almost sixteen years old when I went away, and she did that time with me. It was just as hard on her as it was on me! She knows what happened with her mother, but it's one of those things she has to be in the mood for to even talk about because it's just too hard for her! I didn't know anything about gambling of any kind until I met your uncle Grady, but what I did know was drugs was not the way I wanted to go! When I got out, he took me back under his wing and polished my game back up because I had become a little rusty during that prison bit. He showed me the difference of proposition betting instead of betting on luck because if you're going to know how to bet at the professional level, that is something that you have to learn fast! After he thought I was good enough, we hit the highway, hustling everything from craps to cards and pool.

"I left China with Grady's woman and kids while she was still young but far from dumb. Like they say, when the cat's away, the mouse will play! She started hanging out at the nightclubs on the weekends, right along with Grady's only granddaughter, Melissa, and that's where they both met Red!"

"Wait, Charlie, you mean the same Red that comes in the pool hall?"

"Yeah, Ray Ray, the very same one. So when Grady and I got wind of this, we packed our bags and headed home to see what the hell was going on! But when we arrived, they had both left town with Red, and we didn't have a clue where! Now Grady and I knew who Red was because we all ran in the same circles, just never in the same car! We searched high and low, looking for China and Melissa but weren't getting anywhere."

# Ms. Kay's Introduction

"One night, Grady and I decided to go to the Mike Tyson fight that was coming to town just to think about something else for a moment because that situation was eating up brain cells on both of us. We were on the second row of the Mike Tyson fight, so you know we spent a few racks to sit there. Iron Mike was about to enter the ring, so the crowd rose to their feet to see him walk in. As we were standing there, trying to catch a glimpse of Mike, some beautiful models walked in with escorts and went straight past us to the front row. These women didn't just walk, they were switching and swathing and had everybody watching, including me! They bounced with a slight glide, and you could just tell that they were on a whole different level than most women my young eyes had ever seen for sure! I was young, but I was far from dumb also. I knew these women were very high-maintenance, and I was somewhat amused! They had to be making a lot of cash to look like that! I mean these women were game changers, and they looked like they come straight out of a magazine.

"Grady smiled with delight because just like me, he noticed that these women were in a whole different category than most women that we knew. They all had some kind of short fur on their backs, but Ms. Kay had on that full-length white mink with a train on it that almost touched the ground with every step she took. Thanks to the escorts, the coat never touched the ground, so for that kind of attention, they had to be movie stars or something. Anyway, that's what I was thinking. I had never seen a madam before, although I had certainly heard about such women, but I had never had the pleasure to actually meet one.

"There were seven of them, and they all followed the one in the long white mink coat. She stayed on her cell phone like she was an international businesswoman making big money transactions. Not one usher, but five ushers parted the crowd like Moses parted the Red Sea to get these ladies to their high-dollar seats, so they had to be somebody important! I didn't know why, but on the path to those high-dollar seats, she turned and looked at me with one of those flirty looks while she gracefully walked to her seat with the other ladies right on her heels. They turned heads of everyone who they passed, and not only the men's but the women's heads as well! Ray Ray, here is something that you need to remember. A beautiful woman can always turn a man's head, but when she can turn a woman's head as well, she is in a whole 'nother atmosphere, known by many as drop-dead gorgeous!"

"Wait, Charlie, the girl was that fine?"

"Yeah, Ray Ray, the woman was so fine that she made most guys who tried to talk to her seem like they had Tourette's or something because all they could do was blurt out words like *shit, goddamn,* and *what the fuck!*"

"That's funny, Charlie, so let me guess, the woman that stayed on her cell the whole time was Ms. Kay, wasn't it?"

"Touché, Ray Ray! But I didn't know that at the time, so I kept an eye on her while watching the fight. And at the same time, she glanced periodically at me, flashing that flirty smile also. The fight didn't last that long because you know how Mike used to take care of his business in that ring, man!"

"Yeah, Charlie, Mike was no joke in that ring!"

"I think he wanted to give the crowd their money's worth that night because he played with the guy for about three rounds before he knocked his ass out cold, and the crowd erupted!"

"Aha, man, you talking about a gala affair."

"That night will stay with me forever, Ray Ray! Championship fights bring out people from all different kinds of backgrounds. There were all sorts of rich people there right along with some of the best ballers and players from all over the world, and the one thing we all had in common was being entertained. We all had money and loved to enjoy ourselves while spending it. Your uncle Grady and your dad were known by most, and it was for a good reason!"

"Yeah, Charlie, my mother told me that my dad used to run with my uncle back in the day."

"Run with him, Ray Ray? Shit, man, your mom was just being modest, man, because he was his enforcer! Everybody knew that, and if you were smart, you would not want a problem with your dad Willie. Anyway, even they didn't know who Ms. Kay was until that night. As we were all heading to the exit doors, I heard many people giving her props for being the queen of all madams across the country! Knowing that Red was a top player in the streets, I figured she might know how we could track him down and find China and Melissa. I approached her, not knowing exactly how to cut into her, but I had to find China and Melissa. So I was thinking I would cross that bridge when I got to it.

"I didn't even get close enough before the Madison Square Garden ushers cut me off! Ms. Kay was somebody important to all who knew her, and you could not just walk up and start chatting her up unless you were somebody as well. What I mean by that is you had to be in a certain tax bracket to get in her circle because her money was longer than train smoke. She was very aware of me trying to speak with her, and that got her attention also. So she told the escort to let me through. The crowd was still moving toward the exit doors, so I knew I had to get straight to the point of why I had to have a real conversation with her. When I got close enough for her to hear me, I said to her, 'Lady, I don't know you from Adam, but I sure would like to get the opportunity to know you.' She got off her phone and reached into her Burberry bag and handed me a business card and turned and tried to walk off, but I wasn't giving up that easy. I read the card, and it read, Ms. Kay Assorted Flavors. I caught up with her again and got her attention one more time. But this time, I was armed with China's and Melissa's pictures, and that made a big difference."

"Yeah, Charlie, I saw that necklace that read the same thing that card had written on it hanging around her neck at the craps game pool hall, and it definitely caught my attention."

"She took the card out of my hand and asked me for my name. 'Charlie!' I said. She looked me up and down before she wrote her personal cell number on the back of that same card and told me to call her soon.

"Kids learn what they see, whether it's good or bad, so I tried not to put my lifestyle out there for my kid to see. China was very smart and caught on very fast for her age, just like I did when I was around her age. When she was in college, I got a call from the dean himself! He told me that China was hustling the kids out of their money on the pool table, and if she wanted to continue attending school there, she needed to stop that immediately! I acted like I didn't know where she had learned something like that from while the whole time, I was smiling inside because China and I used to play pool for hours, and I could just imagine her kicking ass and taking names. The apple don't fall far from the tree, I guess, but that's the way I bonded with her, playing hours of pool together. And it made her almost as good as I was. She had bought her a brand-new car in her sophomore year in college, and I didn't pay for it either, so you know the girl had mad skills!"

(I kind of smiled at Charlie for that remark because I knew the mad skills remark was made in reference to me.)

"I called her and told her about the call I received from the dean. She said I didn't have to worry about her doing that anymore because she had switched to poker, and she would even let him win sometimes when he joined in. We both laughed, and I told her to be careful and that I loved her. She always responded with the same comeback: 'I love you more, Daddy!'

"I caught back up with Grady and told him I might have a lead on finding Red. I showed him the card, and he asked if I had called the number yet. 'Getting to it right now, man.' I took out my cell and dialed the personal number on the back. She answered with such a sensual voice that I almost forgot why I was calling her. 'Hey, this is Charlie. Can we link up?'

"She said, 'Hey is for horses, Charlie Soft!' Wow, I didn't know how she knew who I was that fast, but it felt like I was on the right track to finding China and Melissa!

"I let out a little chuckle with amusement while looking at Grady and told her, 'Now would be a good time.'

"'I'm at the Waldorf. Call me after you park your car, and I will make arrangements for you and One Shot to get to the penthouse area.' Then she hung up, and I was more fascinated with her even more now. And Grady could tell that too just by the way I stared straight ahead with a big smile on my face.

"'Hey, Charlie, focus! Well, what did she say?' I repeated what I was told by Ms. Kay, and One Shot put the pedal to the metal. Fifteen minutes later, Grady was throwing his keys to the valet who seemed to be expecting us.

"'Charlie, you and One Shot can just follow me to the penthouse elevator, and I will get you to where you need to be.'"

"Hey, Charlie, Ms. Kay also lived in New York too?"

"Ray Ray, let me fuck this cat, and if any of the kittens come out looking like you, I'm going to give you yours."

I thought that shit was funny as hell because what Charlie was implying was to let him finish the damn story. "Okay, Charlie, my bad, a brother was just asking a question. Carry on, please."

"Ms. Kay is what you call an international woman, to put it mildly. She has places and establishments all over. Anyway, One Shot looked at me with this curious look on his face, but all I could do was shrug my shoulders because I didn't have a clue how she knew who I was, let alone know who One Shot was that quickly! Anyway, we followed the valet guy to the elevator, and he took it up to the penthouse suite, where she was waiting in the penthouse lobby. She had a pink silk dress on that clung to every curve, and I took notice immediately because I love pink on a woman. I mean, she had enough curves to make any man dizzy while traveling on them, and I was no exception! She tipped the valet guy a C-note, and he thanked her and went back to work.

"'Gentlemen, I assume that you have lost someone that you think I can help you find. Am I in the neighborhood?'

"Grady's response was 'Lady, you're on the damn block, pulling up at the house!'

"'One Shot, my name is Ms. Kay, not lady from now on, okay?'

"'Didn't mean anything by it, Ms. Kay, my apologies.'

"'It's okay. What can I do for you, gentlemen?'

"Then I asked her, 'How do you know who we are, Ms. Kay?'

"'Come on now, Charlie. That's not really as important as you trying to find Red, is it?'

"'Well, obviously, you already know what we want, so can we just cut to the chase, please?'

"Then she said, 'Send the pictures to my phone, and call me tomorrow. I should know something by then.'

"'Ms. Kay, with all due respect, as fast as you found out who my friend and I were, something tells me you only need about five minutes.'

"She threw her hair to the side and said, 'Hmm, persistent! I like that about a man, Charlie, but what's in it for me?'

"'How much do you want for your services, Ms. Kay?'

"'Who said I wanted any money, gentlemen? I thought you and your friend were experts at reading people? Anyway, that's the word I got.'

"'Well, One Shot is getting a little old, and I'm still not quite there yet. So you're going to have to help us out a little.'

"'Well, what I want, Charlie is fair exchange, and we both know that fair exchange is not a robbery.'"

Now where had I heard that before?

"'So in other words, what I'm going to need from both of you is to owe me a favor for the one that I'm about to do for you.'

"'What kind of favor are we talking about, Ms. Kay?'

"'I don't know yet, but when the time comes for that favor, you have to honor it!'

"'Ms. Kay, with all due respect, I don't call bets in the blind, and neither does my friend! Let me put this out there so we are clear, Ms. Kay. We are not gangsters, and we don't fool around with drugs. So with that being said, what kind of favor would you expect from us?'

"'I assure you that it would be nothing of the sort, but it probably would be gambling related, and I believe that is right up both of your alleys.'

"Grady and I looked at each other and shrugged our shoulders and said, 'Bet!' Then we shook Ms. Kay's hand on the agreement.

"'All right then, let's go inside and make a few calls and see if we can get your daughters back to you!' Grady and I walked inside her penthouse, and the whole apartment was white with platinum trimming along the edges of her spiral stairwell that took you up to another even plusher white room. It was like we had just walked into a cloud with silver lining! Grady and I were very impressed because we both knew that to be living like this in New York City, you had to have serious cash flow coming in. We took a seat on her white couch as she drifted off to the master bedroom to make some calls.

"Grady said, 'Charlie, I don't know what this lady is into, but she is too mysterious for me, and she is making me kind of nervous.'

"When she returned, she had some news that we could use. 'Red is not a friend of mine. In fact, I'm his competition, but I do know him. He is one of the best of the best at what he does, and that makes him well respected by many. Both of your daughters are with him now, and they are both there by choice, not by force!'

"'I don't care,' Grady said. 'I want my granddaughter home right now!'

"'Well, you both know the law of the street, and FYI, every man has someone's daughter, even you guys. So let me see what I can do, and I will call you as soon as I know something.' Grady and I shook her hand, but when she shook my hand this time, she held on to it for a little while longer than Grady's, smiling that flirtatious smile again. So I knew she liked me some already. Then she called the valet guy back to lead us out the same way we came, and I walked out of there feeling like I knew we would meet again on a different matter in time.

"Grady and I went and played some pool to relax some because we both knew we couldn't go to sleep right away!

'Charlie, there's something about this women I don't like.'

"'What is that, One Shot, because frankly, I'm impressed!'

"'Nah, man, I'm telling you something isn't right about this woman. She knows things way too fast for me, and I can't figure out how she knows what she knows, but it's kind of scary. And I'll tell you something else. I don't like owing her a favor either! I mean, that's like giving up rolls in a craps game man, and you know we take rolls, not give them up!' Right then, Grady's cell rang, and Ms. Kay was on the other end. Now she was really starting to get scary because One Shot never even gave her his cell number.

"'Where are you, guys? I have some news for you, but not over the phone.'

"Then I heard Grady ask, 'you sure you don't know where we are already, being how you know everything else, including my cell number! Now, Ms. Kay, how in the hell did you get that?'

"Then a totally different voice came through his phone, and it was Melissa. And she had China with her. 'I gave her the number, Dad, so she could call you and let you know that China and I are all right!'

"I saw the calm over take Grady, and for the first time ever, he had a tear coming down his face. But it was just a relieved tear of joy y'all, and I had one in each eye as soon as I heard China's voice. We went back to Ms. Kay's apartment and went upstairs to get our daughters and hear their story. Melissa started the conversation off after we hugged them both and made sure they were okay. Grady had been the only dad that Melissa had ever known, so she called him Dad most of the time. 'Hey, Dad, I know you were worried when you heard that I was with Red, but I wasn't with him like you may be thinking.'

"'You have no idea, Melissa, what I was thinking, but I can tell you this! I didn't raise you to be with no pimp!'

"'Daddy, Red doesn't call himself a pimp on account of how society views them now! He refers to himself as a gentleman of leisure.'

"'What's the damn difference?' Grady asked. Now I thought I knew what a pimp was because of my association with them when they came in the pool hall to gamble, and based on the way they talked and the cash they carried around, they seemed to be living well from their craft! I had seen them many times with beautiful women who looked like they were proud to be where they were, but I really never put much thought into that game because I was taught to get my own money from the gambling table, so I did!

"Then China spoke, 'Well, the media portrays pimps as guys who kidnap women and make them do what it is he wants them to do against their will. Now I'm not saying there's no guys out there like that, but they are skimps, not 100 percent real pimps! That's why Red would never call himself a pimp because he doesn't operate like that, and he frowns down on the ones who do. Red is completely sucker-free, Dad, and he don't mess around with the wannabes because they give guys like him a bad name. Plus, he has nothing in common with them at all! Every lady Red has is definitely there because she wants to be, not because she has to be. And from what I have seen firsthand with my own eyes, a lot of them girls would self-destruct without him.

"'Most people think that girls who choose that lifestyle come from broken homes and low self-esteem! Daddy, that is far from the truth as a one-dollar bill to a hundred-dollar bill. Some of these ladies are from very good homes, some even born with a silver spoon in their mouth. Some people are just different than others, and that's just how it is. I've seen girls who can't kick the drugs on their own, but I've seen him get them off and keep them clean. He doesn't beat his ladies like the stereotypes suggest, but he might slap the shit out of a bitch though.' China and Melissa slapped a high five on that because they both thought it was kind of funny.

"'I'm not going to lie. I did too. Daddy, if a lady decides at some point that she wants to give that life up and do something else, Red has no problem with that at all. In fact, he tells them to invest their money wisely because one day, that game will become old, and they will be left out in the cold if they don't have an endgame to this particular lifestyle. One thing I learned from him is you have to do something with that cash that you make, like investing it to come back and take care of you one day. Red is very intelligent because he knows that if you treat those ladies right, they always come back when things get tight! Sometimes, he won't even accept them back if they have gotten scandalous or drugged out real bad!

"'Everything is not for everyone, and that will be the first thing that Red tells you. In fact, I have seen Red with my own eyes tell a young lady that he didn't think she was cut out for this life, and after that, he bought her a plane ticket home and gave her enough money to last her until she figured out what it was that she really wanted to do. Two weeks later, after she spent all the cash Red had given her, she was back by her own admission and has been doing the damn thing at a very high level ever since!

"'See, with Red, it's by choice, not by force. The pimp has whores that may sell a little something to get that cash because that's the only game he knows to give her! But Red, a true gentleman of leisure, has ladies of the night with a side of bitch added, and they sell nothing but game. And their prices are very high! Now I don't know about the rest of those guys because I have never been with them, but Red walks a different walk and talks a different talk and has the empire to prove what he says works. Dad, remember when you said that sometimes you have to do wrong in society's eyes to set yourself up to do right in your own?'

"Grady and Ms. Kay both looked at me as if they couldn't believe I would have those kinds of conversations with my daughter. Grady said, 'Great talk, Charlie, way to go.' But China and I have had no secrets because she knew I didn't have a nine-to-five, so when she was old enough to notice that, I had to explain to her why I didn't get up at the crack of dawn like the rest of the working class and go out the door with a cup of coffee in my hand too.

"'Yes, I remember having that conversation with you, China, but I think you might be off a little bit by what I meant.'

"'I don't think so, Daddy. You just look at it different because I am your daughter, and I fully get that.'

"'China, I'm your father, and I won't have you being a lady of the night for a guy like that or any other guy.'

"'I feel you 100 percent, Dad, and that's why I am here with plans to get that cash for myself. I'm sure Red knew Melissa and I were with him to only pick his brain for the real, uncut game, not the fame! Charlie, Red's ladies don't sell their bodies for sex, even though society would have the public believe that! Red's game is top flight and tight, and he taught them something completely different than selling their bodies for chump change. He said a woman don't have to even do that if she doesn't want to. Instead, he tells them that conversation rules the nation, and if they really pay attention, they will find out all they have to do is ask for help.

"'Beautiful women have an advantage over the plain-Jane type of women, and that is why Red only accepts the most beautiful, exotic-looking ladies that the world has to offer! To Red, appearance means everything in that business. Red says that if you're not a dime, then don't even waste his time. Every man wants attractive women, and sometimes, he feels obligated to help her out if she needs some assistance, especially if the one at home has let her appearance go down some. I think some people forget that the same thing that they did to get their significant other is the same thing they have to do to keep them from having roaming eyes for someone else!'

"Then Melissa took over again! 'Uncle Charlie, Red never ever tried to get us to be a prostitute on account of who are fathers are, so he just let us answer the phones and book calls for his other ladies. We didn't make as much money as the other girls, but we did learn the business of distributing calls. So now we are going to give Ms. Kay a run for her money!'

"Ms. Kay winked at them and raised her glass as though she welcomed the challenge. Grady and I looked at each other; as if both our daughters had just lost their damn minds because there was no way in hell we were going to give our blessing to what we had just heard!

"'What, Melisa, you think your dad and I are going to just agree to this?'

"Melissa looked at China, and they slapped each other a high five like they had thought this through way before they called us to Ms. Kay's penthouse apartment! 'Dad, I wish y'all would give us your blessing on our business plan, but you really don't have to because China and I are grown now.' Grady told Melissa and China to go get in the car and that we would discuss this on the way home. 'Dad, there is nothing to discuss because our minds are made up. Dad, we're good right here.

We're going to spend the night at Ms. Kay's house for late-night girl talk, and we will be home tomorrow or the next day.'"

"Ray Ray, your sister is asking for you!"

"Okay, Mom, tell her I'll be right there! Hey, Charlie, this conversation is far from over with, buddy. I'll get back at you on the flip, so keep your cell on your hip!"

"Bet that, Ray Ray, tell China to give me a call later too, man."

I went in to visit with my sister, but I hurried up and cut it short because I had a lot of unanswered questions left! Since Charlie had already bounced, guess who was going to be on the receiving end of the questions I had now? That's right—China! We told everyone good night early because I had big-time questions now!

As China and I walked to the car, her intuition kicked in. She snuggled up on me, locking her arm around mine while looking up at me with those hazel-green eyes. "So did you and Charlie talk?"

"Yeah, you can say that, but we were interrupted by my mom calling me in because I hadn't seen Gladys yet. China let me just go ahead and get this out there! You building this team, is that something you learned from Red?"

"Yes, Ray Ray, that is where the idea originated from, but I have put my own spin on it."

"Have you ever been with another woman, China?"

"Hell nah, Ray Ray where did that come from? The way I see it, if the plumbing don't fit, then I must acquit!"

"Oh, you're going to go all Johnny Cochran on me now, huh?"

"Ray Ray, I know women who like other women, but I'm strictly dickey, Ray Ray. And I never even fantasized about being gay. That's just not who I am. I know sometimes I can be a bitch, but there is something you need to always remember about me, Ray Ray. I'm your bitch, and I like being your bitch! [My amygdala released a shot of dopamine at that point.] Ray Ray, I have met girls who want to play on both teams, but I only can see myself playing on one, if you know what I'm saying." She leaned over, rubbed the inside of my thigh, and said, "If you didn't know, maybe we ought to call it an early night so I can remind you."

You know how everybody has that sweet spot when it comes to a fine woman? Well, that was definitely my sweet spot, and she was well aware of it. So yeah, I knew exactly what she was saying. To make sure I understood, she kissed me very softly while biting my lip as she pulled away ever so slowly. "Do you know what I'm saying now, Ray Ray?" (Shit, I was about to OD on dopamine now!)

"Yes, lil momma, I think I do. So tell me how Charlie and Ms. Kay linked up, China."

"Aw, it wasn't a long-term thing between those two because Charlie had his own ideas and only wanted to be a gambler. Ms. Kay wanted Charlie to be in control of all those ladies who she had working for her to make the competition back off her some. Plus, she liked him very much. The competition knew she didn't have a man, so they used to try and strong-arm her out of her business for that. Charlie stepped in for a minute as her man and all that went away, not because people feared him but because they just respected him for the way he carried himself. Daddy has to be active, not lounging around in penthouse apartments all day and answering phones. That just wasn't his thing."

"Hold on, China. Were you working for Ms. Kay when she was with your dad?"

"Hell no, Ray Ray. By the time they messed around, I was on my own, doing my own thing. Just so you know, Ray Ray, my thing was booking calls for the ladies who worked for my escort service, not actually doing the calls!"

"Charlie would have never gone for that shit! China, are you telling me what I think you're telling me?"

"Why do you think Ms. Kay comes to Charlie's place and gambles still? It's sure not because she needs the money."

"I don't know, China. Why?"

"It's because she still has an itch for Charlie, and everybody knows it, including Chanel! Charlie doesn't step out on Chanel though. I know that for a fact about Daddy."

"China, do you realize that you have called Charlie Daddy twice now?"

"Yes, and I'm glad that I can do that in front of you now. Aren't you?"

"I don't know what I am right now other than shocked, but confused is still there too. Okay, China, back to Stacey! You knew her before now too, didn't you?"

"No, Ray Ray, but I have seen her before in my traveling days when I was in that life. She worked at after-hours poker games when you thought she was in school probably, but I didn't know her then or you. But I did lock eyes with her on several occasions while coming and going on my business encounters. Since I was in that life, I looked at Stacey like she was a lean, mean, moneymaking machine just by how she kept herself up. I kept a little blue book with exclusive clients in it, and young women like Stacey were on the demand from these kinds of clients. I wanted to talk with her about the business, but I was always in a hurry and never got the chance. The way she locked eyes with me, I think she was curious some about my lifestyle. We just never got a chance to sit down and talk."

"China, how does that madam thing work?"

"Why, are you interested in being a gentleman of leisure, Ray Ray?"

"I don't know about that, China, but I know I need to know as much about it as you and Stacey seem to know! So catch me up to speed, please!"

"Okay, Ray Ray, the madam job is to do all the marketing, as far as paying for all the advertisements to make her phone lines ring with clients. She also has drivers to take the ladies to appointments if they don't have their own car, and there is a fee for that too!"

"China, where does she find ladies who want to be in the life?"

"Most of the time, they find her by her ads that she has posted up everywhere, and also, word of mouth goes a long way too. She also has her lawyer draft up rules and regulations for all her clients and ladies, in case a lady tries to do some extras with a guy that is not part of the madam's rules and regulations."

"Oh, I get it . . . The madam is not promoting prostitution because that would fall back on her if a lady got busted for prostitution!"

"That's right, Ray Ray, and it keeps her business on the legit side, and that is very important if you're going to be in that lifestyle for a while. These ladies are escorts only, and anything else is prohibited. The rules are explained from *A* to *Z*, not *A* to *C*, to all parties involved. The clients and the ladies must sign a consent form to be kept on file just in case somebody wants to go rogue!"

"China, how does the madam make her money though?"

"Fees, Ray Ray, lots of fees! She is in control of everything coming in and going out, and all calls from clients come through her. She books calls for her ladies with the upscale clients and charges both of them a booking fee. When you're doing this all day every day with multiple women and clients, at the end of the year, you just might need some jelly jars, Ray Ray!"

We both laughed at that remark because I had heard that so many times that it was starting to sound like a logo or something.

"I don't know, China, sounds like a lot of work and stress."

"Ray Ray, let me explain something to you right now! It is, and you have to be cut out for it because sometimes, you don't get to sleep as much as you would like, especially through the holidays because that's when clients are really active the most. I would never go back to that, and you know why? Because I don't have to! I did that to give myself a cash flow jump start, and now that I have that, it's on to bigger and better things. Ray Ray, let me explain something to you right now! When I did my thing, I was one of the best that ever done it. I say one of the best because Ms. Kay has always been the best and probably always will be. But I learned mostly about the business from her, so that made me one of the best. I like the idea that you and Charlie got about the after-hours casinos. Ray Ray, you don't strike me as the kind of guy who wants to live check to check, working on somebody's job!"

"You're right about that, China. I want to live free and enjoy life, not just exist! Time is a virtue, and it don't wait on anyone. Sometimes, you have to take a shortcut and go with what you know, and I know gambling!"

"Well, there you go, Ray Ray. I will have three houses closed sometime next week, and it will be time for you to go with what you know! Did you look at the house for Stacey yet?"

"No, I haven't had a chance yet with all the other stuff going on China, but I will put that as top priority on my to-do list tomorrow morning."

I dropped China off because it was starting to get late, and she had to get up at 5:00 a.m. to get dressed for work. Before she got out of the car, she looked at me with an erotic, sensual look that made me want to turn the engine off and go upstairs with her, but I had way too much to do for an early night. "Ray Ray, you know I love you, right?"

"Sure, I know that, China. Why would you ask me that?"

"Ray Ray, there were times that I thought you would leave me if I revealed everything to you all at once, so that's why I decided to not to tell you everything in the beginning of our relationship. But you always stayed around and put a smile on my face, and sometimes, I desperately needed that."

"China, where would I be if I didn't know you? I find myself asking that sometimes, and the truth is, I don't know, and I don't want to ever find out."

"Ray Ray, you know I can hear you, right?"

"I damn sure hope so, girl. Now give papi a kiss and get out of here because I got people to see and places to be, lil momma!"

"Speaking of being a mother, you know, I want a son. Or whatever God gives us, I will be happy!"

"Whoa! Where did that come from, China? I'm not ready for a kid yet. I'm only twenty-one years old."

"Calm down, Ray Ray. I'm not talking about right now because we're not that established financially yet, but someday, we will be."

"Okay, China, there you go confusing me again."

She smiled and said, "Papi, I am not going anywhere. You're stuck like Chuck with me, so just put it back on cruise control and enjoy the ride."

"China, I like being stuck like Chuck right now, whoever he is, and you know how you say how I put a smile on your face? Well, you also know how to put one on mine. Now get out of here so you can get some rest before you have to get up and go to work. You know five a.m. comes early, and I'll see you later on."

I watched her walk all the way to the front door, thinking about how cool that might be to have kids of my own someday before I chucked up the deuces and burned rubber out of there. I called Stacey and told her to get a good night's sleep because I was taking her house shopping tomorrow.

"Ray Ray, I don't know what to say, but what time will you be here?"

"I thought you didn't know what to say."

"Aw, you funny, Ray Ray."

"I can't really tell you that because it depends on what time I come in from the pool hall. Stacey, you know daylight be catching me on the way home most of the time, so let's just see what happens."

"Okay, Ray Ray, I'll link up with you tomorrow then. Looks like we are back tight, huh?"

"Yeah, I would say that, Stacey." Then I hung up the cell and headed straight for the pool hall to link up with Charlie!

Before I got there, China called to remind me that there was blunt of some kush in the glove compartment if I wanted to get my mellow on again.

"Thanks, lil momma, I just might do that." I lit it up and cranked those Bose speakers to the sound of Kid Ink's "Time of Your Life"! I was bobbing my big head so hard that I dropped ashes in my lap and almost burned the jewels! Now you can pull and squeeze almost anything on a man and he can recover from it, but you have to be gentle with the jewels, that's all I'm saying!

When I arrived at the pool hall, the game was in full effect, and Charlie was at the table, doing his thing of cutting the craps game while calling bets at the same time. He could multitask better than any gambler I had seen since I walked through that pool hall door about three years ago. He could place ten different bets with ten different people and never forget whom he was betting with or how much the bet was. I mean, he was better than good. He was a veteran gambler who knew everything about the craft of gambling that only a pro would know! But even he had a weakness just like everyone else, and it was about to get exposed again!

"Hey, Ray Ray, I'm glad to see you show up. I was starting to think you didn't like money anymore or something."

"Aha, I see you trying to tell jokes."

"What do you mean by that, Ray Ray? My jokes are always on point."

Ms. Kay busted out laughing and said, "That was the best joke of the night right there, Charlie, because you have never been as funny as you are handsome, man."

"Ray Ray, does she know I can hear her?"

"Yeah, Charlie, I think she does."

Everyone laughed and continued on with the craps game. There were some new players at the table that I didn't recognize. I looked at Charlie, and he gave me the signal that they were marks that gave up rolls on the points. They dropped a cool two grand in about forty-five minutes, giving up those rolls on the dice, and then they went out the door to get more cash. I thought that was kind of odd because they had to know by now that it was a hard bet to make, let alone win it.

When I came to the table, Charlie pretty much just left all the marks to me to concentrate on the more seasoned gamblers like Ms. Kay and all her cash! Me myself, I like to see those forty double Ds on Ms. Kay jump around when she became excited. I'm kind of a breast man too, and that was just a beautiful sight to see for any man. She was Charlie's girl long enough to not be a mark, so she was hard to handle when it came to gambling because Charlie had shown her the right way to gamble. When she bet the dice in, she knew how to push that money at whomever was calling her bets. Most of the time that would be Charlie because he was the only one on deck that had enough cash to call her bets!

Ms. Kay wanted to break Charlie because she thought if he didn't have any money that would drive him back to her, if only if it were for financial gain. She didn't care what made him come back to her, as long as he came back. But Charlie loved Chanel, and he wasn't going anywhere! Ms. Kay liked to sip on a glass of champagne every now and then, and when she did, she went after Charlie like a leopard after an elk! "Charlie, do you still think about me?"

Charlie looked straight in her eyes for a second before he said very softly, "Sure I do, Ms. Kay! But not as much as I think about Chanel."

"Ouch, struck me right in the heart, Charlie!"

"I know what you're getting at, Ms. Kay, but that life just wasn't for me. It's too much work."

"Ain't that a bitch? I did all the work. All you had to do was keep me happy, and you couldn't even do that! Counting money is too much work for you, Charlie?"

He responded once again in a very soft voice, "I'm counting money right now, but I'm doing it the way I want to do it. And I'm good with that, so place your next bet, please!"

Ms. Kay didn't like something like that said to her, especially in front of people, because where she was from, that was known as capping, and she didn't like being capped on from anyone! She looked at Charlie with a very serious look and reached in those forty double Ds and took out twenty grand and threw it in the box, and the whole pool hall got quiet. Ms. Kay's money was longer than I-35, so she could call whatever bet she liked. "That's my next bet, Mr. Charlie Soft. Can you fade that?"

Charlie counted it to make sure he could call it, although he knew it was way too much to place on one bet. But Charlie hated to be bullied at the craps table, especially by Ms. Kay, and that was his weakness about to be exposed again! He told me to run the dice game for a minute until he got back from his office. Even I had a bad feeling about betting that much cash in one bet because Ms. Kay had a reputation for getting ahead of you and walking out the door, leaving you with no way of getting even! The probabilities were in Ms. Kay's favor, and even Charlie knew that. But like I said, he hated to be bullied, and that was his weakness. He came out of the office with Chanel close behind and had her count out twenty grand. Chanel knew that Charlie and Ms. Kay had a thing once. But she trusted her man, so she never doubted Charlie's loyalty!

It took her a while because that cash was not all hundred-dollar bills, and Charlie didn't trust counting machines. But Chanel had counted cash like that many times before, so it only held the game up for a minute. When she was done counting the cash, she handed it to

Charlie, and he threw it in the box to me to fade Ms. Kay! Before I threw Ms. Kay the dice, I tried to get Charlie's attention because he was off his game, betting like this, but he wouldn't even make eye contact with me. Ms. Kay picked up a green die and a red one and slung them down the table. I hurried up and stopped the roll of the dice because you cannot shoot two differently colored dice out there like that because that is what is known as a horse and a mule, and a horse and a mule have never pulled the stagecoach together. She was feeling her drink some and she thought that was funny. But Charlie and I didn't! That could have created a big problem if I had let them dice roll across the table like that!

Then Ms. Kay said, "Charlie, are you a little nervous?"

Charlie wanted to prove to Ms. Kay that his money was just as long as hers, but Ms. Kay knew it wasn't! The talk around town was that Ms. Kay had as many as twenty-one girls working for her and received at least a grand a day from each of them. Charlie couldn't compete with that! But he came back at her with that soft voice. "I was wondering the same thing about you, Ms. Kay . . ."

Ms. Kay was good at exposing people's weakness, and that was exactly what she was trying to do by betting so much cash in one bet! "Ray Ray, this is about eight hours' worth of work for me. You better tell your boss he is way over his head on this one." I looked at Charlie with great concern because Ms. Kay was right, but he still would not even make eye contact with me.

"Ms. Kay, are you going to roll the dice or just cap all night?" Charlie asked.

"Oh, you think I'm just capping, Charlie? Ray Ray, throw me the green dice, and let me show Mr. Charlie Soft how big money eats up lil money."

I threw Ms. Kay the dice, and she blew on them very seductively while looking at Charlie straight in his eyes. Then she slung them down the table until they stopped on a bright 7! She looked at me and said, "Let it ride if Charlie is going to fade me!"

Charlie finally made eye contact with me, but it wasn't a confident stare like all the other times before. Instead, it was more of a concerned look! But he had an image to protect, and he had jumped out there in the water like that with no life jacket. So either he was going to learn to swim in deep water or drown trying! "Ray Ray, give her the dice and let her roll!"

"That's a forty-grand pot, Charlie. You got me?"

"Like a ball in a glove. Let her roll forty thousand!" Charlie said.

She picked them up again and blew on them like before. And she slung them down the table again, and they stopped on 11! Now, readers, you know 7 or 11 on the first roll is a winner all day every day, and she was sixty grand up just like that! She ordered another drink and turned around and gave Charlie the stare-down look, like a boxer does his opponent before the fight begins. "Let it ride," Ms. Kay said.

"Roll her, Ray Ray!"

"Wait a minute," Ms. Kay said. "Money on the wood always makes gambling good, don't you agree, Charlie?"

Charlie was always a gentleman, even under pressure, and losing that kind of cash that fast had to be pressure. You know, they always say pressure will bust a pipe. Well, even Ms. Kay knew Charlie's pipes couldn't stand too much more of that kind of pressure. Ms. Kay still had an itch for Charlie, and she was still feeling some type of way because he left her to do what Charlie was born to do—be a gambler! Charlie called Chanel over with the money bag and took out eighty grand, and the whole pool hall got quiet again.

You could only hear the jukebox playing "Baby I'm Scared of You" by Womack & Womack when Ms. Kay rattled the dice around in her hand and slung them down the table again! They seemed to take longer this time before they stopped on 4, tray 7. That was a 160-grand pot that she had in the box, and I doubted that Charlie had 160 grand still in that money bag!

"Let it roll again, Ray Ray, if your boss is going to fade me." I didn't even look at Charlie this time. I just threw Ms. Kay her 160 grand and told her to count it fair and that she would find that it was all there! "What, your boss is through fading me?"

Charlie didn't even say anything. He just turned and walked into his office and slammed the door!

"Yes, he is, Ms. Kay. Tonight is your night, so enjoy it while you can."

"I sure will, Ray Ray, and tell Charlie that if he needs money, all he has to do is to link up with me. We can work something out, I'm sure."

Ms. Kay always walked around with large amounts of cash, and nobody never even thought about robbing her because they knew better. The word was out! She was hooked up big-time with the underworld, so everyone knew what that meant! There were rumors floating around that long ago, two guys robbed her at gunpoint. The word around town is she Jimmy Hoffa'ed them, and that meant they were never seen again! She picked up her cell, and about five minutes later, two guys showed up who looked like they played professional sports to escort her to her limo!

I let one of the up-and-coming apprentices of the pool hall sit on the rack (run the game) while I went to check on Charlie, because I knew he was not cool right now, and Charlie was always cool. I knocked on his office door, and Chanel opened the door with a look on her face that I had never seen before from her. But I did recognize the look. It was a very serious look, and the outcome is never good with a look like that! To put it mildly, let's just call it a look of concern on her part. She grabbed her keys and stomped out of that door like she just might not be coming back!

Charlie spoke, "This is not going to be good, Ray Ray. I have just lost Chanel and the baby with that move I just made, man!"

"Wait, what do you mean by Chanel and the baby?"

"Ray Ray, Chanel just found out today that she is expecting."

"Charlie, that's great news, man. You're going to have a kid come into this world. Man, you have lost big before only to triple it on the comeback, so what's the big deal?"

"Ray Ray, it wasn't a big deal until I lost all that money to Ms. Kay of all people. Chanel is not stupid, Ray Ray. She knows what Ms. Kay is trying to do, and the cold thing is she thinks Ms. Kay just got a little closer to pulling it off! I just lost more money out there tonight than I have in my entire life, Ray Ray, and I done it in a very stupid way at that! One hundred forty grand chasing twenty grand; I know better than that, Ray Ray!"

"Charlie, why'd you let Ms. Kay bully you like that? You know better, Charlie, and that's why you lost like that! You weren't gambling. You let her get under your skin! You were trying to get lucky, man, and if I were playing like that, you would ask me if I were crazy or something! So I have to ask you, Charlie, are you crazy?"

He just looked down at the floor because he knew he could gamble better than that! I just wasn't going to just stand there and let him feel bad because Charlie was my man, so I broke the awkward feeling by changing the subject. "Hey, Charlie did you and Uncle Grady ever have to cash in on the favor that you both owed Ms. Kay?"

"Yes, we did, and we had no idea that she was going to do that!"

"Do what, Charlie?"

"She had big-time clients coming into town that loved to gamble. To repay the favor that we owed, we had to set up magnetic pool tables in her spot with the magnetic dice to match! We also had to host the crooked game, and her clients didn't have a snowball's chance in hell to win. We scammed everyone in the joint for her, and we only got a small fraction of the money that night. She counted out 500,000 right in front of us when the game was over but only gave Grady and myself 25,000 apiece. One Shot was furious, but he knew her reputation and damn sure didn't want to get Jimmy Hoffa'ed. So he did what every smart gambler does—live to place your next bet another day."

"Wow, Ms. Kay got it like that?"

"Yes, she does, Ray Ray, and she has had it like that for quite some time now. Some people say she is connected to the mob, but she has never admitted that to me! Why do you think I really left a beautiful woman like that? It's not her that you have to worry about. It's the high clientele list that she has in her pocket that makes her dangerous. Ray Ray, never underestimate the power of a soft, flexible vagina, man, because it's ranked up there right with the almighty dollar, I would say. She knows a lot of secrets about a lot of people, and some of those people would do anything for her to not let those secrets get out. She plays the leverage game very well, Ray Ray, and that is her strength. And those forty double Ds don't hurt either. She was always in her office on the phone with the door closed sometimes, and that just made me feel uncomfortable sometimes, ya know? Ray Ray, can you cover the closing on the property, because I have no cash on me right now, man!"

"Charlie, that was all your money? I know you didn't just gamble off the house money."

"Ray Ray, just cover it, will you? Give me a few days, and I'll get it back to you."

"Okay, Charlie, but you better never get out of line like that again."

"Bet, Ray Ray, never again."

Charlie had plenty of cash. He just had it put up somewhere that only he knew where it was, and he just had to have time to get it when he was all by himself. Charlie and I were cool as a fan, but I didn't even know where he kept the bulk of his cash, maybe in some jelly jars somewhere. After all, he learned everything he knew from One Shot (Grady).

I went back out front and took the game back over because I needed to try and scratch back some of the cash Charlie had donated because that was exactly what he did—donated it off—because he damn sure didn't play for the money. He tried his luck and ended up getting fucked, because being lucky is for your everyday schmuck. I stayed there until 7:00 a.m. and hadn't come close to what Charlie had lost. Charlie left around 3:00 a.m., so I had to lock up.

After I did, I went home to get some sleep because I was going to have a very busy day. China was already at work, so I made me some boiled eggs and oatmeal and went to bed. Sometimes, I would do the vegan thing and go without meat for a while when I thought my waistline was getting too big. If I wanted a woman with a slim waist and who was extremely cute in the face, I had to lead by example. I take great pride in the way I come out of the house each morning. I guess you can say that I lead a high-maintenance lifestyle as well. I have to have a manicure and pedicure on the regular, just like any well-groomed person. How am I going to be with a well-groomed woman when I'm not well-groomed myself? You know, a man gets what he goes after, and I'm going after that well-groomed lady because that's what I like. And if we have anything in common, she'd like a well-groomed man.

I heard the key unlocking the door, so I rolled over and glanced at the clock, and it read 7:00 p.m.! I jumped up like I was late for an interview or something, noticing I had overslept! It's kind of funny because China knew just what I was jumping up for, and that was one of the things that I loved about her. She was always on point! "Ray Ray, don't worry about it. There is always tomorrow."

"Damn, China, I didn't mean to sleep that long. Call Stacey for me and tell her what happened."

"Nah, Ray Ray. That's something you're going to have to do. Besides, isn't she at work already?"

"Yeah, she probably is. I'll call her in a few minutes."

"Ray Ray, you kind of stood her up, and I think you should know this right now about women. If a woman really cares for you, she will hang on to your every word, so I think you need to watch what words you put out there. I might not show it, Ray Ray, but I would be furious if you told me you were gonna take me house shopping and you weren't responsible enough to set your alarm clock."

"What are you saying, China?"

"I think you need to get dressed and go to her job. She will be glad you did. Trust me on that, Ray Ray! There is nothing more important to a woman than attention!"

"Is that right, China?"

"All day, every day, Ray Ray. You better ask somebody."

We laughed.

"Come here then, pretty lady, and let me give you some of that attention right now!" I grabbed her hand and pulled her to me and returned that soft bite on the lip that she was ever so famous for, and then without warning, she let out a moan that always made me weak in the knees.

"Not now, Ray Ray. You have work to do. Go make her feel like she is part of the team, player!"

I hadn't thought about it up until now, but I guess my lifestyle did kind of portray that. It is what it is, so I gave China a rain check on that moan she displayed and got dressed and drove down to the club where Stacey worked. As soon as I entered the club, I saw her behind the bar, mixing drinks. Her smile lit up the dimly lit bar like the sunshine, and I could tell just by that smile that she was glad to see me. I sat down on one of the bar stools and ordered a cup of joe because if I was dreaming all this, I might just need that coffee to wake me up. She had on a navy-blue dress, and I noticed the color right away because she knew that was my favorite color as well. I couldn't help but smile because to me, that meant she was trying to see if I would even notice.

"Hey, lil momma, I like what you're wearing!"

"I thought you might, Ray Ray, because blue is your favorite color, isn't it?"

"Aha, a woman that pays attention. I like that. Stacey, I'm sorry I overslept on you like that, but I had a long night."

"It's fine, Ray Ray. There is always tomorrow."

I looked at my watch, and it read 1:15 a.m.!

"You know, Stacey, tomorrow is not a promise to anyone, so can you take off right now?"

She knew where I was going with this, so she said, "Give me a minute, and I'll be right back." She went to the back, and when she returned, she had her coat in hand, biting down on that pinky fingernail.

I thought to myself, *there will be questions.* I still had the address of the house that China had given me, so I punched it in the GPS, and away we went. Before I even had a chance to make a comment, she was quicker on the trigger with the questions and the comments. "Ray Ray, let's talk business first."

"Okay, Stacey. What you got?"

"I got clients for us already because a lot of guys who used to come to the underground poker games I worked in have come through here already, and I have told them that I will keep them in the loop when our thing pops off."

"I like that, Stacey, and I'm sure Charlie and China will too. But right now, let's go get you into your own spot because we're pulling up to it right now."

She turned and looked at it, smiling, and asked, "Can we please go inside, Ray Ray?"

I called the realtor's number that was posted in the yard, and when the lady answered, I told her I was outside the home and that my lady would definitely like to see the inside. She asked if we could wait because she was only five minutes away, and I agreed to that because I knew this house would just make Stacey's day! I always liked putting a smile on someone's face because to me, that says "Hakuna matata!" (No worries, and yes, I watched the Lion King too.) The place was a no-brainer, so I signed on the dotted line and dropped the deposit in cash and went furniture shopping.

Stacey was so excited that she sung this little song all the way there. "Lucky for you that's what I like" was what she kept singing while kissing me on the cheek, and right at that moment, I knew I still had feelings for her. But make no mistake about it. I cared very much for China as well!

You know how most women are. They want to look at every piece of future in the store before they actually pick out something. Now most men, on the other hand, would be happy with just the floor arrangements that were on display. I wanted to leave the furniture shopping all in her hands and just go to the car, but China's voice popped up. "Ray Ray, there is nothing more important to a woman than attention from her man!" So I grabbed her around her slim waist and tried to enjoy it as much as she did.

All that was working just fine until we got by those TV sets. Wouldn't you know it, I walked by a sixty-two-inch TV airing a championship Mayweather fight, and Stacey immediately lost her shopping partner because I was going to watch this fight! I told her to pick out what she wanted and bring me the tab! She responded with "Not on your life, Ray Ray. I also am a big Mayweather fan, and the shopping can wait!" Now that was the Stacey that I remembered! Watching sports was a big part of our relationship back in the day, but the only difference now was, I bet cash on sports.

There was a guy there that I had to relieve of his cash because he didn't want it. Anyway, that was the way I looked at it if he was going to bet against Mayweather! I will never forget that shopping trip in the furniture store because the guy was talking so much smack about

Mayweather that I had to check and see if he was a gambling man! He was talking a lot of smack, saying that Mayweather was afraid to stand toe-to-toe and fight.

Before I could even comment on what he said, Stacey took over. She looked at me and said, "Ray Ray, move around. I got this one, okay?" Apparently, Stacey had been keeping up with the sport because she let the smack-talking gentleman know a thing or two about boxing. "Hi, I'm Stacey, and if you know anything about the sport of boxing, you would know that's what a skilled boxer does, hit without getting hit! He is a boxer, not a fighter, and there is a difference."

The man replied, "Young lady, my name is Cody Visor, as in Visor furniture, and I own this store among other things. And I also am a betting man."

"Well, Mr. Visor, my man and I are here to buy some furniture for our new place, and he also is a betting man! So I'll tell you what. If your guy wins, we will pay double for the furniture that we pick out. And I'll tell you right now, we need a house full. But if Mayweather wins, we will walk out of here with free furniture. That's how confident I feel right now!" She turned and looked at me, and I shrugged my shoulders, wondering how much furniture she planned to buy.

Then Mr. Visor asked me, "Are you condoning this bet, young man?"

"Why yes, sir, I am. I got my woman's back, so I guess that you have yourself a bet. By the way, my name is Ray, but everybody calls me Ray Ray."

"Well, Ray, let's shake on that bet like real men do, and I hope you brought your checkbook."

"Mr. Visor, I brought something better than a checkbook. I brought cold, hard cash, so I hope that is all right with you."

"Oh yeah, Ray, cash is just fine. In fact, I prefer that over a checkbook any day! Well, the bet is on, so let's check it out, Ray and Stacey!"

I took about five grand out of my pocket, and Mr. Visor's eyes lit up like Fourth of July, and the bet was on! Mayweather entered into the ring like he always did, confident and flamboyant, and the Mayweather fan base went wild! Since we were in a furniture store, Stacey and I took a seat on this navy-blue love seat that we fell in love with right away. The bell rang for the action to begin, and Mayweather's opponent wasted no time trying to knock Mayweather's head off! Mayweather bobbed and weaved for the first four rounds with his opponent throwing everything at him but the kitchen sink. Mr. Visor was still talking smack as if he didn't know what was coming, but I'm sure he had seen this technician at work before. And he knew that Mayweather was not a front-runner. He just didn't like the guy for whatever reason that he himself had. At the beginning of the fifth round, Mayweather stopped bobbing and weaving and started planting his feet with every hard shot to that kid's body, taking the wind out of him more and more with each shot!

Stacey leaned on my shoulder and said, "It won't be long now, Ray Ray, because this kid doesn't have much wind left now." At that point, Mr. Visor started talking to the TV set as if the guy he was betting on could actually hear him. Halfway through the fifth round, the kid didn't have any gas left in his tank, but he wouldn't go down. He should have though, because by him still standing Mayweather unleashed so many punches that the kid's own corner threw the towel in right before he kissed that canvas. When the kid finally came around, he seemed to be furious at his corner for taking so damn long to throw that towel in.

I looked at the store owner and said, "We will be taking this blue couch along with that same TV set that your boy got his ass kicked on, if you don't mind, sir."

The furniture store owner responded with "A bet is a bet, Ray, so enjoy your shopping spree free of charge on me."

Before Stacey and I got started on our shopping spree, I made sure Mr. Visor had my number in case he wanted to come down to the pool hall and try to win his money back, because that's the kind of gentleman I am. He said he liked to play pool, so he would for sure be calling one day soon! After Stacey and I finished furniture shopping, we returned to the owner to ask him when we could expect delivery. He said we could expect it anytime we wanted to, but we would be just expecting unless we paid for the delivery! Stacey and I looked at each other with this confused look because we thought the bet covered all that, but Mr. Visor quickly let us know that the bet just covered the furniture, not the delivery cost! I gave him two hundred for the delivery, and ever since then, I made sure I had a full understanding about proposition betting and everything else too.

I left the store and called China once I got in the car to tell her that Stacey was all set.

"Great, Ray Ray. Where is Stacey now?"

"She is right here in the car. Would you like to speak with her?"

"Yes, I would, if you don't mind, Ray Ray."

"Hold on. Here she is."

"Hey, China, what's going on? Oh, girl, I'm so happy right now. I love the place that you picked out."

"Whoa, Stacey, how do you know that China picked it out?"

"Ray Ray, who is the real estate agent, China or you?"

"Stacey, you know I can hear you, right?"

She burst out laughing so hard that she dropped the phone. I picked it up and put it on speaker to hear China's response to all this and she was laughing just as hard.

"Ray Ray, your family is right. You should have been a comedian or something, man. Hey Ray, the houses that you and Charlie wanted is ready. All I need is the cashier's check and it's a done deal."

"China, I know you got that part, right?"

"Yes, I got it after you bring me the money, Ray Ray."

"Just take it out of the deposit box and go take care of it. I need to keep the cash I have in my pocket for gambling."

"Okay, I'm getting dressed now to go and take care of that."

Then Stacey asked, "Hey, China, do you mind if I tag along, because I really don't have anything else to do at the present time?"

"Sure, girl, have Ray Ray drop you off at my place, and we will go take care of it together like a team trying to get to the Super Bowl."

I dropped Stacey off and headed down to the pool hall to inform Charlie about the news. When I entered the pool hall, all the pool tables were full, and that was a good sign of what was about to come. Charlie wanted to have a sit-down with the team so we could discuss what everyone's role would be, so I called the girls and told them to come to the pool hall for a meeting after they were done.

# Putting It All Together

"Ray Ray, what time did you set the meeting for?"

"Charlie, you really didn't give me a specific time, so I told the girls after they took care of their business would be good."

"That's fine, Ray Ray. That will give you and me time to go over some things."

"Like what, Charlie?"

"Like putting it all together, man, from the bottom to the top! Ray Ray, if we do this right, we will be set for life, and all we have to do is keep them gambling! Ray Ray, you're a long way from across those tracks that you left back in Texas. And I only say that because I know you got a thing about railroad tracks, but you're going to have to get over that, man. And let's go get this money, man. You down?"

"Charlie, I can't believe you just asked me that. Of course I'm down like Charlie Brown."

"Who the hell is Charlie Brown, Ray Ray?"

I laughed. "Charlie, don't even worry about it, but I will say this. You need to get out more if you don't know who Charlie Brown is, man. Just a little advice, brother."

"Okay, funny man, point taken. Now can we get back to business?"

I was laughing hard. "My bad, Charlie. What were you talking about?"

"Ray Ray, we're going to build a company with the team that we have here, and I have just the strategy to achieve that goal. [I was all ears.] There will be three spots, and the girls will be sort of like overseers over them; China at one location, Chanel and Stacey at the other two."

"Wait, Charlie, those girls don't know anything about running a craps game or any other game."

Charlie laughed and said, "Maybe the other girls don't, but you know China does."

"Yes, you're right about that, Charlie. She could do it if she had to, and I'm sure she would be good at it too. In fact, I think she is just as good as you are, Charlie, and I'm sure you taught her all that she knows and some."

"What can I say, Ray Ray, the girl is a fast learner in just about anything that she wants to know. But no, Ray Ray, they will just keep the books and manage the clubs as far as how much money will be coming from them every night."

"Okay, Charlie, but where will our staff that we will need come from?"

"Good question, Ray Ray. That is exactly what I want to talk to you about. Since a lot of these guys will be people who we think we know pretty well, make no mistakes about it. There will be sharks in the water, and sharks stay hungry! Listen closely, Ray Ray, because you're about to enter a whole other world, but I think you're cut out for it because it's in your bloodline. The cash will be coming in so fast we won't have time to count it, but make no mistake about it. We will make time." He started laughing. "There are some major sharks in the water, and when you have money, those sharks smell blood! Everybody wants to be a winner and will step on anyone in their way to achieve that. If you're going to be dealing with people, then you have to become a people person. You have to watch their body language as well as what comes out of their mouth because most of the time, it will display itself in just normal conversation. Different people have different needs, and the ones who have the less needs will be the most unlikely to betray you that fast, friend or not. So it is very important to know what all your employees' needs are, especially the needs that they don't tell you about!

"I met a guy once, and the way that he got his rocks off was to point out everyone else's discrepancies rather than his own that he never took time to look at. He thought he was above and beyond anyone else in his little feeble mind, and the sad thing about it was, he really did believe he was perfect. The guy was such a hater that it oozed out of him no matter how hard he tried to hide it. He thrived on everyone else's faults but his own, and for some reason, that made him feel like he was above everyone else. There were some problems in this guy's life somewhere, and he would literally pick at people just to belittle them in some kind of way. And for some strange ass reason, that made his day.

"Everyone has some kind of an addiction, whether it is drugs or a spouse, but more times than others, it's just plain, simple greed! They'll want what you have, and what you have may not even be money that they want. It can be something just as simple as your style and how you carry yourself. All these addictions are very hard to overcome, but greed is the most dangerous by far because there are no boundaries with these people! Don't get it twisted Ray Ray, money is the root of all evil, and the people who are filled with greed are the real sharks in the water, and they will chew you up and spit you out if ever given the chance to.

"Never let your staff know your strategy or your plan because they need to concentrate on what they are hired to do instead of what you are doing! Never debate with these people because they are only trying to find a weak spot in you and figure you out. Speak very few words because the less you say, the stronger you will seem, and that will always keep the cowards at bay! Always stand on what you believe in and let others who want to be in your circle know what your beliefs are as well because that will let them know how not to come at you. Never be an ass-kisser because those whose asses you kiss will never like you. But one thing about it, Ray Ray, they will respect you, and that is the most important thing. You can't please everybody, and you're a fool if you even try. So stay in your lane and keep away from lames, and you will be fine. The first law of nature is self-preservation, so make sure that you're good first before you do anyone else.

"Now I have some people in mind for our staff, and most of them have not been tested yet, but that will be your job, Ray Ray, after I send them to you. So use good judgment, young man. What about your boy Anthony, Ray Ray? Have you been in touch with him lately?"

Needless to say, I was kind of shocked by Charlie bringing Anthony's name up for this staff because what he really thought about him wasn't good in the past. "No, I haven't seen him in a while, but I will put the word out that I'm looking for him because now that I think about it, he is kind of responsible for my success by bringing me inside this billiard room that day I met you, Charlie."

"Check him out first, Ray Ray, before you hire him because if he hasn't cleaned his act up, we can't use him. Remember, no weak links if we are going to make this thing work. Ray Ray, I know that you hate going down across those tracks, but those are the people who need our help the most."

"Yeah, Charlie, since you put it like that, I will go down across the tracks by the liquor store. Let's see if we can clean up some of those guys' lives for them by giving them jobs."

"I like that idea, Ray Ray, because that's letting them know you haven't forgotten where you come from, and I think that will go a long way with them. Ray Ray, we all have to have a reason to get up in the morning, and I think that those guys get up for the wrong reasons. So let's see if we can change that, and after that, the ball will be in their court!"

"Bet, Charlie. I'm on it, brother!"

I jumped in that Audi and burned rubber out the parking lot to get this thing in motion once and for all, and I was kind of excited to give those guys a second chance that society was not willing to do. When I got to the railroad tracks, there was a train coming, so I had to come to a stop for a minute. While sitting there, I thought about my mom for some reason and how special she was to the family. Doing something good for someone else has always been a thing that was instilled in me by my parents, I guess, and over the years, I have been taken advantage of by some, but I get up and brush myself off and do it all over again because I truly do believe that God is watching. Just like my mom said, "Our blessings come from God, not man!"

Most of these guys made mistakes in their lives for mostly just trying to eat the only way they knew how and nothing more. Now I'm not at all saying that a guy shouldn't be punished for his crime, but you have to be fair and make the time fit the crime. It's the same crime with different outcomes for the brown-skinned people than those of the Caucasian persuasion! I didn't say it. Statistics did! Not everyone has that fairy-tale ending, especially if they are not given a beginning in life to even start with. Statistics have been saying that for years—that blacks and Latinos have been shedding the most tears because of their kids getting gunned down in the streets by cops. I don't think the parents were asking for too much when they just want what any parent would want—for the unjust killings to stop! It's no secret. Brown-skinned people have been getting the short end of the stick in the courtrooms since courtrooms were built, but nothing ever gets done about it.

"Why you think that is, Ray Ray? I think the poem you like, 'America, the Two Sided Story,' says it all, Ray Ray."

"Charlie, I grew up with most of these guys, and they got caught up doing whatever it was that they were doing. They will pay for it for the rest of their lives if something doesn't change, and I am willing to give them that change. Anthony and I always had that connection like good friends did, so I really set out with him in mind to pull him out of the gutter if that was where I had to go find him because that's what you do for a friend! You bring him up, not tear him down."

# Running into Robert

I pulled up into the little strip mall where most of the people who were down on their luck at the time hung at, expecting to run into Anthony. I dressed for success when I wasn't going to the gym, so I knew I had to speak their language to get their attention because it's hard-core across the tracks, and you'll get slapped for looking at somebody the wrong way if you're not careful. I opened the door on that fine automobile and said, "Hey, any of you motherfuckers seen Anthony lately?"

A thin light-skinned brother walked up to the front and said, "If it ain't Ray Ray's ass down here, slumming with the slumlords!"

I recognized the voice, so I took a long stare before I noticed that I hadn't seen this guy since junior high school. It was my childhood friend Robert, and he didn't look like life had been treating him very well. So if I could not find Anthony right now, I would start with him. (Like I said before, that's what friends do.)

"Hey, Ray Ray, how in the fuck are you, mayne?"

"Well, well, if it isn't my main man Robert. What's buzzin', cousin?"

"Mayne, ain't a damn thing good around here. Take a look around."

"Yeah, I see that, but I'm here to try and change that, brother. You want a job to earn some real money?"

Robert was originally from Memphis, Tennessee, so instead of pronouncing the word *man* like most of us do, Robert said *mayne* when he talked. I always thought that was kind of unique and funny at the same time. "Hey, Ray Ray, you remember that little light-skinned girl back in school with the blue eyes that had your nose open big enough to drive a Mack Truck through it?" He started laughing.

"Yeah, man, I remember. Her name was Marsha Brown, and those blue eyes did have me fucked up a little, Robert, real talk. Anyway, man, back to why I came down here."

"Talk to me, Ray Ray, and I'll talk back, mayne!"

"Well, Robert, I have a business proposition for you if you're interested."

"Talk to me, Ray Ray, and I promise you that I'll talk back."

I started laughing. "Still the class clown, huh, Robert?"

He smiled and said, "Come on, Ray Ray. What you got for me, mayne?"

"I'm opening some after-hours spots, and I'm going to need some guys who I can trust."

"Ray Ray, this may come as a surprise to you, but does this look like where the reliable guys hang out?"

"Robert, sometimes cash has a way of making unreliable people be reliable, you know what I mean? At least for a while, until they have everything they need from you. Robert, I really have not seen you since high school, and even then, we ran in different circles. So how you been?"

"Ray Ray, you don't have to be a rocket scientist to figure out I have been going through some things, mayne! I had a job once working for this maintenance company, and do you know that they paid me minimum wage with no benefits whatsoever? And that shit is legal. I got up and busted my ass for these people for three years with only a fifty-cent raise the whole time, mayne! You can't live on that shit, only survive! I ended up more broke than the day I started, so the way I look at it, it's just modern-day slavery. I heard they are getting ready to start charging money for air to just breathe, Ray Ray! You know what that means, mayne?"

"What does that mean, Robert?"

"That means I'm about to be a dead motherfucker, Ray Ray. That is what it means, mayne."

I started laughing. "Robert, you're still crazy as hell, man."

"Ray Ray, the way I see it, the powers that be want you to have one idea and one idea only- How to make it to work every day to a job that only allows you to just pay your bill. Long as that's the only idea you have, you damn sure don't have the time or the cash to think about how to come from under that weight that you have on your shoulders. You're working for handouts, not advancement of any kind. That shit just barely keeps you breathing, so if that rumor about them charging for air is true, I'm going to flat line, mayne! I'm so broke that I can't even pay attention, so how in the hell am I going to pay for air? That's all I'm saying."

"Yeah, Robert. I don't know how that can be legal or who is responsible for designing such a law, but they sure didn't have poor people's interest at heart when they did so! Robert, the way I see it, that kind of law just keeps the wealthy rich and the poor like crabs in a barrel, pulling each other down, making it almost impossible to reach the top. But I did say almost impossible, my brother, because I have a plan for success and nothing less, man. You down, Robert?"

"Mayne, I'm down like a first-day clearance sale. Sure, I'm down, Ray Ray. What do I got to lose?"

"I don't know, man, you might have your own blueprint to success that you're not telling me about."

"You're a funny man, Ray Ray. Don't patronize me. I know I'm one of those crabs in that barrel that you're talking about! I have been down so long that I have forgotten which way is up!"

"That's all in your mind, brother. Up is still in the same place it has always been, looking toward the sky. What if I gave you a chance to start that journey back across that bridge to the good life that people from across the tracks only dream about?"

"Okay, Ray Ray, you got my attention. What you need?"

"I need some security guys for starters. You know, some big guys who are good at working the doors and who can take care of business if they have to!"

"Sure I do, Ray Ray. How much does a job like that pay?"

"One hundred dollars a night, seven nights a week."

"Shit, I can't fight, but for one hundred dollars a night, I sure will give it a try! Ray Ray, I know guys who will beat you to death for looking at them wrong. Have you forgotten what goes on around here? For a hundred dollars a night, there is no telling what they might do."

"Hold on, Robert. I'm looking for guys who are cool, calm, and who do not want trouble but who won't run from it either if there ever comes a time to make a stand."

"I understand what you're saying, Ray Ray, and I think I know of such guys. Now take Billy, for instance! Billy just came home from Iraq, and he is going through some kind of sleeping disorder and don't sleep that much at all, if he sleeps any. He went over there and fought for a country that seems like they don't give a damn about him or what he did over there, and that shit weighs heavy on his mind every day! The guy's physical appearance is horrifying to anyone that looks at him. He damn near looks like the Thing off the movie *Fantastic 4*, mayne, and I'm not just making this shit up, Ray Ray! He came home from that war all messed up in the head with that post-traumatic stress or something like that. I do know if you put him on that door as security, people will think twice about starting trouble, and you can take that to the bank and cash it out, mayne!"

"Okay then, Robert. Billy sounds like a guy I can use, so get him and all the rest of the guys who you think might be a good fit for security and make sure they're all together and all cleaned up. Meet me at the Charlie's billiard room tomorrow at noon."

"Fa sho, Ray Ray. I'll see you then."

"What about Anthony. You seen him lately?"

"I don't see him that often, but I hear he lives across town with his baby mother. And judging from our last conversation, I don't think he likes the way things have turned out in their relationship. I think her name is Terrie or Teresa or something like that. Anyway, she has about four kids, and only one of those kids belong to him. And I think it has been taking its toll on him. Mayne, he used to hang out with us all the time, Ray Ray. Now she won't let him go anywhere without her ass tagging along, mayne! And the cold thing about it is, she steps out on him every chance she gets! She got my mayne all messed up in the head, and a lot of times, she leaves him home with the kids so she can go out with her friends to the nightclub and shake her ass all night! What the fuck, Ray Ray. What mayne is going to go for that shit?" He started laughing hard. "Anthony used to be strong like a stiff drink of Hennessy, mayne. Now he's just watered down Kool-Aid, mayne. It's just so sad. Anthony used to be hard in the paint, mayne!"

"Hey, Rob, unfortunately, there are guys out there like that. I'm just not one of those guys, man."

"Hey, Ray Ray, I think the proper way to describe that is, we are not one of those guys because you know I wear the pants with my women."

"Shit, mayne, you got to get a woman first, and that blow-up doll you got don't even count."

"Damn, Ray Ray, you got to be kidding. She don't? Shit, mayne, I was going to bring her to the pool hall tomorrow to see if you guys can hook her up with a job too. I mean, we can set her in the back room for customers. You know, have a little red-light special or something."

"Rob, you are still a class clown, huh? What you going to do? Pimp your blow-up doll?"

"Hey, Ray Ray, don't hate. I got to get paid too. The bitch eats a lot." We both laughed. "Hey, Ray Ray, you know word on the street is, Anthony's girl flirts with every guy who she thinks is cute, and the way I hear it is, she thinks they all are after a few beers! But the cold thing about that is, he knows it and goes right back to it. He must know something I don't know. That pussy must be gold-plated or something, and he must be waiting for her to die to snatch it out and cash it in. I'm just saying, Ray Ray, I ain't ran into no gold-plated pussy before, and if it's going to clip my nuts like that, I don't want to, shit!"

I laughed. "Robert, you should be doing stand-up or something because you're funny as hell, man. You got my sides hurting from laughing at your silly ass."

"Where is that mayne's pride, Ray Ray?"

"Hey, brother, we like who we like, and that's all I can tell you about that."

"But, Ray Ray, most of the time when I come over, she is passed out drunk on the couch with those kids just running back and forth, having a free for all or some shit! A man can't go out like that, Ray Ray. You need to go find your boy and save him before it's too damn late, mayne!"

"Yeah, I hear you, Robert, but it's not like hanging out in front of this liquor store has benefits either. You know what I'm saying, man? Besides, having somebody is better than having nobody, or so I've been told."

"Ray Ray, are you implying that I don't have a woman?"

I laughed. "Robert, I already told you that the blow-up doll don't count, so stop trying to include her."

"Damn, Ray Ray, I'm glad she is not here to hear that. It just might hurt her feelings." We both cracked up laughing and slapped high fives again and again before we got back on the subject of Anthony. "I tell you what, Ray Ray. I'll track Anthony down for you if you need me to."

"Do that, Robert, and here is my number. So call me when you find him, no matter what time it is."

"Got it, Ray Ray, but I have a little favor to ask."

I already knew what the favor was that he was going to ask, so I reached in my pocket and pulled out some cash. "Robert, call everyone over who you plan to bring to me tomorrow because I have something to say to them." Now don't get it twisted. I once saw Robert take a knife from a guy that was much bigger than he was and beat him with the butt of the knife until he was unconscious, then he sat there until the guy came to and knocked his ass out again with one punch! That kind of thing goes on every day across the tracks with him because Robert hates bullies with a passion! One thing about Robert is, you can question his intelligence all you want. But if you really want trouble, just test his manhood, and you will be sorry that you did!

He turned to the rest of the guys and said, "Listen up, motherfuckers. My main man Ray Ray got something to say to you ungrateful bitches!"

They all stopped in their tracks and asked, "Who the fuck is Ray Ray?"

I looked them all right in their eyes one guy at a time before I spoke. "I'm Ray Ray, and I have work for some of you. But there is a catch! Now with this money that I'm about to give you, there are two things you can do with it: buy a drink and continue killing yourself or buy some food. It's your choice. But if you show up tomorrow with alcohol on your breath, this job will be over for you before it even starts! I'm looking for some guys who want to make some improvements in their lives starting tomorrow. Now I know some of you won't make the cut, but that's okay because everything is not for everybody. But for you guys who want to stand on your own two feet for a change, I would buy some food and give up the drinking and come to the pool hall tomorrow with this ugly motherfucker right here, and we will take care of you. Oh yeah, all you guys will receive gym memberships because you will have to stay in shape, and that is mandatory if you come."

They looked at me like I was speaking another language or something, and that was kind of funny to me. But I meant every word of it. China, Stacey, and I worked out at least four days a week, and we took being healthy very seriously.

"Ray Ray, it's good to see you, mayne, and I'll be there."

I handed everyone a twenty-dollar bill before I jumped back in that sedan and burned rubber out of there. When I returned to the pool hall, the girls were already there, waiting in Charlie's office, discussing the layout for the after-hours casinos. I stepped in to hear Charlie's breakdown of my uncle Grady's plan, better known as One Shot!

"Chanel, I need you to be in charge of all the waitress and bartenders in the casino that you will be assigned to, and China and Stacey, I need you to do the same. It will be mostly bookkeeping that you will need to pay attention to for the liquor and the rest of the bills. Ray Ray, I need you to oversee the security and pick up all the money from each spot after every shift. You got some guys lined up for that?"

"Yes, I think I do, Charlie, but I will know for sure tomorrow."

"Okay, Ray Ray, I will make sure I collect all the house money every four hours from every spot. Now at some point, we will need to get some sleep. That's why we will all need a lieutenant, and even that lieutenant will need a deputy. Okay, China, let's talk location. What you got?"

"I have two of the best high-class spots in the suburbs that you can have, and they both used to be country clubs."

"Nice, China, and where is the other one located?"

"The other one is a perfect location because it's right across the street from the bar where Stacey works across the tracks. There are always people coming and going, so there is always traffic. And that's a very good cover for our business, don't you think?"

"Yes, China, I think those two country clubs are perfect, but you know how your man is about railroad tracks!"

China looked at me with a concerned look and grabbed my hand and pulled me to her real seductive like, and right when I bent to get a sympathy kiss from her, she put her right hand up and put her brakes on that kiss with a friendly smooch on the face and told me to grow a pair! Everyone in the room laughed, and so did I. But I still wasn't feeling those damn railroad tracks.

Charlie knew I wasn't either, so he looked at me and asked me, "Ray Ray, you good with this? If you're not, man, we can always find another location. It just might take some time, that's all."

"Nah, Charlie, I don't want to hold up the money train, man. I'm good with it. Let's do it!"

"Okay then. We have three days to put a staff together, so let's get busy!"

On Monday morning, we had things in order. By Monday night, all doors were open for business, just like we planned! All three places were packed with people from all walks of life, and the one thing they all had in common was they all just wanted to have a good time. And a great time was what we gave them! We had drinks and food, and for the grand opening night, we had buy one get one free for the first three hours, and we made a killing on that alone!

I met Billy for the first time, and I had to agree with Robert. This guy was built like a tank, and nobody in their right mind would want a problem with this guy. He had a very deep voice, although he didn't talk that much. He carried a look on his face that spelled all business, and if you really didn't have business with him, it'd probably be best just to keep it moving!

After the first month, we split half a million dollars five ways after paying off the staff, so the way I looked at it, there was no way that a nine-to-five could compete with that, so I was in like Flynn staying down for the crown! Robert had cleaned up his act, right along with ten other guys from down on the block, and every day they thanked me for pulling them out of that legal trap hole that society calls a liquor store. These people had given up hope and turned to dope, and it made me feel good knowing I had something to do with turning their lives around for the time being anyway. I still hadn't heard from Anthony yet, and the number that Robert had was disconnected.

# Bumping into Anthony

One day, I was at the grocery store and bumped right into Anthony and his girlfriend. Right away, I noticed the thing about her that probably caught his attention too before she had those kids. It seemed that she was very attractive back in the day, but you could just tell that the years of alcohol abuse and drugs had taken its toll on her. And that probably led to her insecurities and why she needed to tag along behind him everywhere. I went right up to him and said, "Damn, brother, you're a hard man to find these days. Where you been?"

When he turned around, he seemed glad to see me! "Aha, man, just working, you know, trying to keep my head above water, man. Hey, Ray Ray, I hear you're Charlie's right-hand man now, and I can't say I'm surprised because he liked you from day 1."

"Well there's more to that story than I can explain right now, so can we link up later, man?"

He turned and looked at his girl, as if he had to get her permission first, and she gave him a look like she was not feeling that at all! He turned and looked at me, as if to be saying, "You see what I have gotten myself into?"

"Leave me your number, Ray Ray, and keep your cell on your hip, and I will get back at you on the flip."

We both kind of laughed at that remark because we used to say that back in school. I jumped back in my car and called China to see if she wanted to grab some lunch, but she and Chanel were already doing just that. Stacey was taking a nap, so I decided now would be a good time to check on my family since I hadn't been over in a while. I pulled up, noticing how my mom's house was not up to par with my own and decided it was time for her to enjoy some of the fruits of my labor. I had so much cash that I was running out of places to hide it, so I figured it was time to spend some on my mom. I had a catalog of some nice homes in my glove compartment, so I took it inside for her to look at.

Gladys and the rest of the family were sitting around and watching TV when I walked in, so me walking through that door gave them plenty to talk about. My sister Carol was the first one to make a sarcastic comment, like she always did. "Well, well, if it ain't the prince of the city." She started laughing. "Hey, Ray Ray, you're just like Uncle Grady now, huh?"

"What is that supposed to mean?" I asked.

"I mean, look at you, man. You're him reborn again. The way that you dress and the ladies that you have, even the cars that you drive. I mean, you're Grady all over again, man."

I knew that was coming, so I tried to change the subject by showing my mom the brochure that I brought in.

"Those are nice, son. Are you going to move there?"

"No, Mother, I'm moving you and the family there as soon as you pick out one that you like."

"Ray Ray, that's very nice, but I can't afford a place like that."

Then my bigheaded sisters snatched the magazine and started to pick one out for Mom, but I didn't care if it got them off my ass.

"Ray Ray, you already do enough for me. Spend that money on your family, why don't you?"

"Mother, don't you know? That's exactly what I'm doing. You guys are my family, and nothing will ever change that."

"Aha, those are awfully sweet words coming from such a devilish person."

"Shut up, Carol, because you're the one with the devil horns growing out of the side of your head. Mom, can I temporarily suspend Carol from the family until further notice?"

"That's funny, Ray Ray. You know you can't live without me."

"Well, I would like to try it out for a million years and see how that feels."

Then Mom said, "Speaking of the devil, Ray Ray, when are you going to go to church with me? You know it's been a while."

"Yes, I know, Mom, but I just haven't had the time."

"Boy, I can't believe you just said that because there should always be time for God in your life, and if there's none, something is definitely wrong that needs addressing. Ray, you know you don't have to be Ray, you know you don't have to be in a church for God to hear you, right? God hears and sees everything that we do, so that means his lines are always open, no matter what time it is. So have a talk with him to let him know how you're doing spiritually in life from time to time. Ray Ray, always take God with you wherever you go, and you will be all right, son, as long as you let him guide you through life because without him, you're just a lost soul!"

"You're right, Mother, and I'm going to make time for him as soon as I get you moved into that house."

"I tell you what, Ray. You come to church with the family this Sunday, and then I will consider your proposal."

"Mom, you drive a hard bargain, but I accept it."

Just then, my cell rang, and it was Anthony calling. "Where are you, brother? Are you ready to link up with me?"

"Yeah, Ray Ray, I'll meet you at the pool hall in thirty minutes. And I got some news that you can use, but you're not going to like it!"

"Bet, see you in thirty! Well, Mother, I have to go take care of some business, but I will be back on Sunday morning to take you to church."

"I'll be looking forward to it, Ray Ray, so don't let me down."

"I won't, Mom. Now give me a hug and take this money and buy that little praying dog some dog food because she looks like she is getting skinny."

"Yes, she is, but it's more old age than anything because you know she is about twelve years old now."

"Mother, isn't that like 120 in dog years?"

"Don't say that out loud like that, Ray. That will hurt her feelings, and you know she is sensitive about her age."

I started laughing. "Nah, Mother, I didn't know that, but how can you tell that she is sensitive about that?"

"Watch, Ray Ray! Dominic, you're getting old!"

I couldn't believe it . . . She jumped down and out of my mother's lap and ran to the corner and stood up on her hind legs and put her two paws together as if she were praying to be young again. My mother thought that was cute, and frankly, I did too. "Mother, that dog needs to be in the circus somewhere because that is definitely a circus act that people would gladly pay to see."

I jumped in my car and headed across the tracks, looking out of my car window at the city, noticing how across these tracks, some of these people never had a chance from day 1, mainly because of just simple lack of information. The information that I had, I had gotten from gambling. And I had the blueprint on the pool table and the craps table, and I wasn't taking any prisoners. I was kicking ass and making sure they remembered my name.

When I got to the pool hall, Anthony was already there, talking with Charlie, and I could just tell when I pulled up that the news that I could use had reached Charlie's ears before mine! With the way they both were looking at me, I could tell it was something serious! "Ray Ray, let's go to my office right now!" I didn't know what all the secrecy was about, but I knew I wasn't going to like whatever this was about just by watching their body language.

As soon as that door closed, Charlie looked at Anthony and said, "Tell Ray Ray what you just told me!"

"Ray Ray, I know who broke into your sister's house!"

My eyes immediately turned red with fury. "Well, don't keep me in the dark, man. Give me all the news."

"My little cousin just got out of jail, and he said there was this guy in there bragging about whose house he had broken into, and judging by what my cousin told me, I think that may be the guy."

"So what makes you think he is the guy, man?"

"Because he also mentioned your sister's street and some jewelry that he supposed to have taken from her house afterward."

I never told anyone about the jewelry but Charlie, so maybe this was the guy! "Okay then, how can I find this motherfucker?"

"Calm down, Ray Ray, and listen for a minute, will you? The guy is still in jail on a thousand-dollar bond that he doesn't have, so I'm not aware of when he gets out."

I didn't want to sit down. I wanted to ride on this guy and let him know that he had messed with the wrong guy's sister.

"Wait, Ray Ray, let's be smart about this because we don't need you fucking yourself off over this guy, especially since things are going right for us."

"Charlie, I can't let him have a pass, if that is what you're suggesting."

"Oh, hell no, that's not what I'm suggesting at all, but we don't need something like what you're thinking coming back on us, even if it's years later."

Then Anthony said, "I know how to take care of it Charlie, so listen up. Here is what we will do. Bond him out and hire him to work for you. That way, we can take our time to make sure he is the guy that we want. If he is in jail running his mouth, it's just a matter of time before he talks about it here, so we just got to wait him out and stay patient."

"Nobody can know about this but the ones who are standing here right now, you feel me?"

"Loud and clear, Charlie. Just let me know when he is free! Anthony, you did well, so welcome to the family. Now you're one of us, so go handle that."

"I'm on it, Ray Ray. I'll go and post his bond right now and let you know when he hits the ground. He is always bragging about how many people he knows, so he will brag about getting bonded out, whether he knows who done it or not. I'll just find a guy or a girl who knows him and pay them to post the bond. After the guy pays the bond, there is no need for him or her to stick around, so I will send them on their way because the less they know, the better! I will stick around and offer him a cigarette and a ride home, and the rest will be history."

"You got a guy for that, Anthony?"

"Sure do, Charlie. I just got to make a few calls, and it's done."

Well, I can tell you this much, the guy never saw it coming until it was too late, and for whatever it's worth, nobody has to worry about that guy anymore because he also got Jimmy Hoffa'ed!

# Things Couldn't Be Better

Almost four years had gone by, and now I was almost twenty-five years old going on thirty because I had experienced many things in my short life. And things couldn't be better. The after-hours casino spots were running like well-oiled machines with the poker tables and craps tables full every night. I have a very good security team, and on a particular night, they proved their worth! There was a guy at the poker table who had lost what we call don't-go money because it was money that was meant to be paid for something else before he gambled it off, and it wasn't supposed to go. He had a little too much to drink and started to be rude to the rest of the packed crowd. I thought that could be bad for business, so I had to get him out! I called Robert over the security radio and let him know that the club had a problem and I needed it to get taken care of immediately!

Now this guy thought he was Billy Badass until the real Billy Badass showed up. You know, that false courage called alcohol would do that to us sometimes, and like I said before, Robert hated bullies! But I will say this about Robert. He tried to be reasonable by trying to talk some sense into the guy, knowing that the guy had a little too much to drink. When that didn't work, he called Billy the Fantastic 4 guy over for some assistance. When Billy walked up, the guy who had way too much to drink almost shit in his pants when he saw Billy! (Hell, the guy may have shit because the odor in the air did change some.) The guy was so startled just by Billy's appearance that he forgot about Robert. While the guy was watching Billy's every move, Robert took that as a cue to do what he did best. You would have thought Robert worked at KFC with the way he served that three-piece knuckle sandwich to the guy's face! The guy fell to the ground, asleep and bloody, and had to be taken out on a stretcher. After that, we didn't have any more problems in that club.

Everything was good as of now, and the "fork in the road" image came in my mind. And I knew I had to have an endgame to all this one day, just not today! Sometimes, you take that fork in the road toward success, and sometimes we take the wrong road of a life filled with stress. But if you don't ever take a chance, how will you ever find that road to happiness? What happened here in my life happened so fast I never even thought about how lucky I was to meet Charlie Soft! Charlie did not only give me a shot at learning something different; he also did that for many other people as well. I had broken my leg back in high school, so there was no way in hell I was ever going to play professional sports. I was twenty-five years old now and had everything that a man could want. Not until I go back across those tracks where it seemed like nothing back in high school.

There was no way in hell I was ever going to play professional sports, so if Charlie had not taken me under his wing and taught me how to play pool, among other things, I would be somewhere in a factory on somebody's assembly line where it's either too cold in the winter or to damn hot in the summer, not good! I'd probably have some lead supervisor that rides around all day, watching me, because he hated me as he didn't have my personality or swagger!

I realized just how lucky I was! On the other side of the tracks where I was from, bad things happen every day like it was normal shit! In fact, it happened so often that it did become normal for some after a while. It was not that the people were bad; it was mostly the situation that they were put in that made them do desperate things more often than others. And sometimes, it would lead to some jail time or an early death. So if you ever got the chance to get away from that and go make a better life for yourself, you take it, no matter which fork in the road leads away from there!

When I went shopping, I didn't even look at the price tag anymore. I just bought it if I wanted it. Now I was not rich, but I sure was living like it. I could live in the best homes that money could buy and in any neighborhood and travel to any state I damn well please! I was not driving China's sedan anymore. In fact, I had cars of my own—a new black Escalade, a drop-top Corvette, and the love of my life, the new 550 Mercedes-Benz—with the five-bedroom house to match! Stacey also was enjoying the fruits from our labor, and with her and China now real estate partners, things were way beyond my expectations! We all were making money and pooled our money together to keep all the bills up and keep things running smoothly.

Charlie and Chanel had a two-year-old son now, and everyone called him CC. And he was the most handsome and intelligent little kid that you would ever want to see. Stacey and China had really bonded together, and I had an all-star team. And we were all living the good life. Ms. Kay was still doing her thing on a high level and still had that itch for Charlie, but Charlie was still keeping his distance from her if it was not gambling related. My family had moved out of the old neighborhood across those tracks that I hated even driving across, and life was pretty good for them as well.

We had a crew of thirty members, so Charlie and I were just collectors now of the cash from the three spots, plus the pool hall. And we had so much cash that we were running out of places to put it, so now I was thinking of jelly jars for real now! China and Stacey bought up so much real estate that we had to hire a whole different crew and lawyers just for that.

One night, Ms. Cardi B was coming to town, so I decided it was time to just kick back and have some fun and take a break from the paperwork that I had to look over every night. All work and no play makes Ray Ray stressed out a little sometimes, so I was going to have some fun with my girls. Everyone wants the good life, and no matter what your field is, you're going to have some stressful days accomplishing that! As far as I was concerned, I wasn't just going to make money, I was sure going to enjoy it as well. Working a dead-end job and living from check to check just wasn't going to do it for me either. Just like it wasn't good enough for my uncle Grady, it damn sure wasn't good enough for me also, and that was my motivation to keep things in order. I was almost twenty-five years old and had already seen and spent more cash than some people would ever see in their lifetime entirely.

Now I'm not going to go all Facebook on you because that has never been my style. You know how some people put their whole life story on Facebook? They put what light they're sitting at in their car and which way they are about to turn, along with everything else that they can think of. All I know is, if you have that much free time on your hands, maybe you should get a puppy or something is all I'm saying. I don't know. I never had that much time, I guess, because I always had too much on my plate just from my day-to-day activities.

I was young with a lot of cash, and being entertained had always been at the top of my bucket list. And I was in the mood for some hip-hop. I called Charlie to see if he and Chanel wanted to go with the girls and me to let their hair down for a minute and check out Ms. Cardi B, Jhené Aiko, and Ray Sremmurd. Charlie had never had the pleasure of seeing her in a concert. Hell, Charlie never saw anybody in a concert because he never took a day off to just enjoy himself a little. I told him that he didn't know what he would be missing if he didn't go because it was going to be a show that would be off the charts!

"Ray Ray, I would love to go, but I have some club business I need to take care of first. But it shouldn't take all night, so go ahead and pick up Chanel and me those tickets and drop them off at my house. We will pick them up and join you guys later."

"Bet, Charlie, I can do that for you, man, but what club business you got to take care of that you haven't shared with me?"

"Nothing major, Ray Ray. Just got a report that someone has been skimming off the top, so I'm going to take Robert and go handle it."

"What do you need Robert for, Charlie? Just fire whoever it is, and come on, man!"

"That is exactly what I plan to do. But you know how some people take the bad news of getting fired, so I'm taking Robert with me. After that, I will go home and change, and Chanel and I will meet you guys there."

"Not a problem, Charlie. Just make sure that you show up because you know those front-row seats for this kind of show won't be cheap, brother."

"Ray Ray, as much money as you are raking in, I know you are not complaining about spending a little. You can't take that money with you, so enjoy it while the getting is good, my brother."

"Charlie, I'm sure you're the one saying that to me right now, when you never go anywhere and enjoy yourself even just a little bit."

"Ray Ray, I enjoy life more than I might let on. Just waking up every morning with Chanel next to me is enjoying enough, and you can quote me on that, my brother from another mother."

"Charlie is Chanel in the car with you right now, because you're putting too much on that!" I laughed. "You sound like you're trying to convince her instead of me. Is she right there with you, because it sure does sound like it?"

He laughed and said, "Just get the damn tickets, smart-ass, and I'll, I mean, we will meet you there."

After that statement, I knew for sure she was in the car with him, and that was kind of funny. I called Anthony and told him that Charlie and I were going out for the evening, so he had to make sure everything was running just as if Charlie and I were right there. He would be in charge of everything until further notice. "Whatever you do, keep an eye on Robert because you know he can be a hothead sometimes."

"I got you, Ray Ray. Go on and have some fun, man. I got this!"

After that, I called Stacey and China and told them the news, and they were just as excited as I was because Ms. Cardi B and friends were hard to get tickets for, especially front-row seats.

Most guys would love to be in my position. I mean, life was better than good because I had two beautiful, smart women that wanted to see me win when most guys had trouble just holding on to one. Even after working hard all week and bringing her home his paycheck, she still is not even close to being satisfied, and in most cases, she is just a paycheck away from leaving his hardworking ass all by himself! Hey, like my Dad always said, "You get what you go after, and I wanted it all." I know it sounds strange to the conventional kind of people, but there is nothing conventional about how things go down across the tracks! Having two women that know about each other and respect each other at the same time is way beyond the conventional kind of guy's mind. But coming from across the tracks where I was from, we just had that swagger that was hard for any woman to resist! What man wouldn't want more than one woman at his disposal that sees to his every wish and, from time to time, will even make him a hot dish? You know how some people say that blessings come in many disguises? Well, at that time, I really felt my blessing was my lifestyle, and what a lifestyle it was!

"Hey, China, can you and Stacey be at the same location dressed already, or is that too much to ask?"

She laughed. "Nah, papi, we not going to work you that hard; you can pick us up at Stacey's house. Ray Ray, Daddy and Chanel are coming too, right?"

"Yes, but they will meet us there later because he has some kind of club business he needs to clear up first. Anyway, that's what he told me."

"Okay, Ray Ray, give us about an hour, and then pick us up."

"Okay, I'll see you both then. Please be ready because I don't want to miss the opening act."

I put the pedal to the metal and hit the freeway headed to the big house to get cleaned. I felt good about my life at this point. I mean, I had everything that a man could dream of. I had not one but two beautiful women, and we were all go-getters when it came to that cash. And we all pooled our cash together to make things happen, just like a team would do. It took me about forty-five minutes, and I was out the door, ready to relax and enjoy the entertainment for the evening. When we arrived, the whole parking lot was full, so I guess I wasn't the only one that thought they were worth seeing. We walked in like superstars, dressed in all blue. Stacey was in navy blue, China was in light blue, and I myself coordinated with both women with a dark-blue jacket on the outside and a light-blue on the inside. I also had long dreads now past my shoulders, and when we walked in, we turned heads all the way to our front-row seats. We made it to those seats just in time to see her coming to the stage.

Ms. Cardi B was just in the middle of talking about that quarter lick when I noticed I had not heard from Charlie yet! I called his cell, and it went straight to his voice mail. I thought that was kind of odd because of all the years we had known each other, that had never happened, not even once! When I couldn't get an answer, I told Stacey to call Chanel's cell and see what the business was. She did, and the same thing happened with her. Then she looked at me with this concerned look on her face after Chanel's phone went to the voice mail and said, "Hmm, that's strange, Ray Ray. I have never gotten Chanel's voice mail before. Maybe they turned their phones off because they wanted to catch up from being backed up, if you know what I mean!" I smiled at Stacey because I knew exactly what she meant by that statement. I had said it to her way to offend.

"Charlie wouldn't tell me to pick up tickets for him if he wasn't sure he was coming. He just doesn't do things like that. I'll give him a minute, and if he hasn't called me back by then, then I'll get worried because Charlie is one of the most responsible people I know!"

China was so into the concert that she didn't even realize that I was feeling a certain kind of way right about now. I tried to put Charlie in the back of my mind and enjoy Ms. Cardi B, but something was not right!

# When Things Go Bad

Charlie kept a safe in the floor that nobody even knew about except me. I mean, his own daughter didn't even know about it. It was not that he didn't trust her; he just thought it was something she did not need to know about for her own safety! I don't know what made me think about that now at this particular time, but I did! When the concert was almost over, I noticed that Charlie or Chanel never called back. Now I was concerned! I tried to call Anthony and Robert, and neither of them answered. But their phones didn't go straight to voice mail, so now I was kind of tripping!

"What's wrong, Ray Ray? You have a look on your face that I don't like."

"It's probably nothing, but your dad or anyone else on our staff isn't picking up. And that does concern me a little!"

"Well, if it concerns you, it's scaring the hell out of me, so can we leave right now?"

I didn't even hesitate because Charlie was my man with the master plan, so you know I was on the way! We all scurried to my SUV, and away we went to the location where Charlie was supposed to be! The speed limit was seventy miles an hour, but I was cruising at one hundred because I had a bad feeling brewing inside my gut. And so far, that gut feeling had never been wrong! The girls kept dialing everybody's numbers, but they still didn't get any kind of response from anyone who they tried calling. The closer I got to that exit, the more of a bad feeling I got because Charlie had never not answered his cell for me. We began to hear sirens as we approached the exit, and in the back of my mind, I just knew that sound had something to do with Charlie and Chanel! I looked toward the stars, and a cloud of smoke was coming from the club's direction. That bad feeling grew more and more until I turned on that street, and what we saw made our jaws drop into our laps.

Someone had set the club on fire. Anyway, that was what I was thinking, and there was hardly any part of it standing when we got close enough to see it. There must have been at least ten fire trucks there, along with the whole police department, and the girls screamed so loud that I thought the windows shattered with those high-pitched screams. The flames were so high that you could feel the heat from blocks away, and I was standing there, searching for some kind of explanation for what I was experiencing. But no words would come out, just tears! I couldn't talk or breathe. Man, I just dropped to the ground, only to find China already there. Stacey never even made it out of the car. Instead, she just balled up in the back seat, not wanting to witness what was going on right here, right now!

Police and ambulances were everywhere, and I knew that at some point, I would have to talk to them. But I welcomed the opportunity because someone had to be held accountable for this treachery! The word spread very fast because my phone was ringing off the hook, from Ms. Kay to Red and mostly all the other gamblers that frequently catered our spots. And there was way too many to mention, so we were gonna keep it moving. I know Charlie was loved by many, and all the high rollers were hitting my cell to offer any kind of support if any were needed. And that just reminded me of the grace and charm that he carried every day. The place was not even open for business yet, so only some of the staff was inside. The only question now was who was in there?

# Brannon

A detective who went by the name of Brannon walked over to my car to ask me some questions as I watched one of our after-hours spots burn to the ground! I stood there in disbelief and silence, watching it, because I didn't know what else to do!

"Ray Johnson, is that correct, sir?"

"Why yes, it is. Do you know who done this?"

"No, sir, not yet that is, but what makes you think that someone did this?"

"Because buildings just don't burn themselves down like that, Detective Brannon!"

"Mr. Johnson, there are a lot of reasons that buildings catch fire, and I'm sure you have watched enough TV to know that. We have many things to look at before we can come to that conclusion, but I'm curious as to why you may think that someone did this on purpose."

"I don't know why or what I'm thinking right now, Detective Brannon. I just need to know who was inside there!"

"We have to let these people do their jobs, Mr. Johnson, before we can determine anything at this point. It's just too early in the investigation. The forensic team has a lot of tests to perform before we can give you any answers on anything. In the meantime, can you come down to the station and shed light on what goes on here at this address and just who you think is responsible for this?"

"Detective Brannon, I have a feeling that you already know what went on at that address, so let's cut through the chase, please, and find out how many of my people were in that damn building, if you don't mind, sir!"

I could tell this was going to be a very long night, but I assured Detective Brannon that I would be there as soon as he needed me to be because I would not be able to function until I found out what the hell happened here tonight! China had already retreated back to the SUV to check on Stacey because she was still balled up on the floor in the back seat of the car, making a whimpering noise that I will never forget. In fact, I can hear it now, and it was making me get goose bumps! I walked back to the SUV very slowly, with my head racing a million miles an hour. My body was so numb that I could not even feel my own footsteps! I got behind the wheel and just sat there, listening to Stacey's and China's whimpering for at least thirty minutes before I even started the SUV! The radio came on blasting, but I quickly hit the mute button because I just wanted silence at the moment so I could think!

"Stacey, China, I have to go down to the police station and talk to this detective, but I can drop you both off if you're not feeling up to this."

They both answered simultaneously. "Hell no. That's my father in there, and we are a team. And we all will deal with this together like a team does, Ray Ray!"

In another situation, I would have felt good about this unity that I just witnessed, but this was a whole different kind of situation that I felt the need to handle alone! Readers, I'm a very big Marvin Gaye fan, and when I turned the radio back on, Marvin Gaye was asking me, "What's Going On?" (I know. Ironic, huh?) I tried to think about what Detective Brannon said about buildings sometimes catch on fire from faulty wiring or something, but in the back of my mind, there was a person who was responsible for this fire. And I would not rest until I found out who that person was!

# The Police Station

When we got to the police station, Detective Brannon was waiting for us, so we entered his office to see what he had found out. There were missing-person pictures all over his wall, but the one that stuck out to me the most was Marvin Anderson! He was the guy who had broken into my sister's house years back and apparently was still missing! I had watched enough cop shows to know that an experienced detective never let you know that he was on to you. I didn't stare at the picture long enough to make him think I knew something about this missing poster that was stapled on his wall. I only glanced at it.

"Mr. Johnson, I know this is a very bad time for all three of you right now, but I have a job to do. So let's go over some things, and I will try to get you out of here as quickly as possible!" He wrote down all our names and excused himself to go into the next room, where there were other detectives awaiting him. At least, that was the way it seemed to me at the time. When he came back into the room, he looked me straight in my eyes and asked me how many people were in that building! I informed him that the girls and I were at a concert that Charlie and Chanel were supposed to link up with us at later, so we really didn't have no way of knowing that. He asked a variety of other questions, as was to be expected, before his desk phone rang. When he hung up, he asked if we would come down to the morgue to identify some bodies.

# Losing Dear Friends

Stacey and China screamed with those high-pitched, ear-piercing screams, and the fire burning down that club was displayed in my brain like a 3-D movie all over again, sound effects and all! We all took that seemingly long walk down the corridor to where the dead were kept, and if you have never made that walk before, there is no way I could come up with words to describe that feeling. But I could tell you this, it was an experience you don't ever want to have! When we entered the room, there were five body bags on five separate steel tables, so we started with John Doe number 1! Detective Brannon looked each of us in the eye before he told us to brace ourselves because he knew this was something that people don't do every day.

He started to unzip the first bag, and I could tell before that zipper was barely open that it was one of the guys who Robert had hired who went by the nickname Cash! The girls did the high-pitched scream thing again, but this time, I was expecting it because Cash was a likable guy. He was one of the few guys who had an endgame to the hustling life, and he attended college every morning to insure that he would not do this forever. China and Stacey admired that about him and would always offer to help with any homework that he might need some assistance on, so yeah, they felt some kind of way about that kid. And it hit them hard and me too! All she and Stacey kept saying was "Not Jason, Ray Ray, not Jason!" Jason Daily was the kid's real name, and I knew I was going to get feedback from this kid's family because like I said, he was a likable guy who had his head on straight!

The next bag that he began to unzip belonged to a very pretty young lady who went by the name of Sunshine, and she rightfully deserved that name because she was always smiling and that would make you want to smile too, even if you were having a bad day. You know how sometimes we just need to talk? Well, she was definitely that kind of person that would lend you an ear and make you feel like she really cared about whatever it was that you were going through. My dad was like that too, and I saw my dad in her. So I had a very special place in my heart for her and often told her that. She lit up anyone's dark day just as if she had pulled the curtains back and let sunshine into that dark, gloomy day that you were having. Her real name was Sonia Valdez, and she was a spicy little thing and brought joy like the holidays whenever she came to work. Everyone loved Sunshine for more reasons than one but mainly because she seemed to be so happy all the time, like she didn't have a care in the world. She was one of Stacey's closest friends and also her right-hand girl down at club when she took time off to just get some sleep. She also worked out with Stacey sometimes, and that was something that they both enjoyed. Stacey really considered her as a real friend, and Sonia would often spend the night at Stacey's when she was just too tired to drive her home. So yeah, Stacey took that real hard! Now I don't have to tell you that the high-pitched screams came again because they never really stopped from Jason's body bag!

By the time Detective Brannon got to the third bag, there were no more tears to shed. We were all out of tears and cries, so by the time he pulled that zipper down, all we could do was stare at Robert's dead body. We squeezed one another's hands until they started turning blue. My knees buckled from seeing my friend lifeless on that steel table, and I had to hold on to the wall just to keep my balance! Yeah, that fucked me up for a minute because the last time I saw my friend, he was walking and talking, so yeah, that fucked me up big-time! Stacey and China backed up and sat on the little wooden bench that was over by the wall, but I walked up to my friend and saw how bad his body was burned. Through the burned flesh, I could see he had a hole in his head with dried, burned blood on his face. I quickly went from a state of depression to being mad as hell because somebody had shot my friend before they set that building on fire, and I didn't need a detective to tell me that. At that point, Detective Brannon walked up to me and asked me if I knew who could have done this. "No, sir, but I damn sure am going to try my best to find out."

"Well, Ray Ray, let us do our job because we have the resources that you don't have, or maybe you do. I really don't know you that well."

I stared at him for a second because I knew that he was implying something, and I wasn't going to feed into it right here, right now! "Detective Brannon, with all due respect, can we get to the reason that we are all here, identifying my friends!"

He gave me the curious look, like he was trying to figure me out, before he unzipped bag number 4! It was another female waitress who we all called Shortstop, and probably not for the reason that you think. Shortstop earned her name by always making just one more short stop before she came to work, and that always made her late. We all loved her though, and she would be greatly missed! On the last body bag, China and Stacey returned to the steel tables because there was only one more bag to be opened, and Charlie or Chanel was not there yet. But this was the moment of truth because one of them was going to be in that bag for sure!

Detective Brannon told us to brace ourselves again before he proceeded. He unzipped the bag very slowly because he didn't know any more than we did, but when he unzipped that bag, it was a guy lying there who none of us recognized, and he also had a gunshot wound. In fact, he had three! Now I can't even begin to tell you all the thoughts that raced through my mind or what order that they even came in, but the first question that came to mind was, *where the hell are Charlie and Chanel and Anthony?*

Then Detective Brannon said, "Ray Ray, we know that you and your buddy Charlie run after-hours spots, and we pretty much leave you guys alone as long as there is no funny business going on. But this is what I would call funny business, wouldn't you say, Mr. Johnson? Look at Charlie and his friends lying there all shot up and grilled up like a bratwurst hot dog. Are you going to stand there and tell me that you don't have a clue who did this? Who would do this to Charlie and your friends, Ray Ray? And what reasons would they have?"

Then I said, "Detective, I really don't know because Charlie pretty much stayed to himself, but you're right about one thing and one thing only! Those are all our friends except one, and I don't know who that guy is. I have never ever seen this guy before in my life! Detective Brannon, I have some news that I think you can use because that is not Charlie lying there at all!"

"Are you sure about that, Mr. Johnson?"

"If you don't believe me, ask his daughter, who is standing right here, right now beside you."

Detective Brannon looked at China, as if asking her if that were true, and she obliged him by saying, "Yes, Charlie is my dad, but that is not him lying right there!"

He stepped in the washroom to use his phone, and when he returned, he thanked us for coming down to the precinct to answer some questions and said he would be in touch. We all walked out of the precinct with more questions than answers, but as you might imagine, that would line up with all that has happened! We kept our question to ourselves until we sat down in that SUV because we all lived by the same law! (Never let anyone outside the team know what you are thinking!) My mind began to backtrack the nightmare, and up until now, I really never thought about it. But I didn't see Charlie's car at that burning-down club's site, so where was he and Chanel and Anthony?

Stacey said, "Let's drive back down to that club to make sure because we won't be able to sleep until we know for sure."

"Shit, Stacey, with all that has happened, we won't be able to sleep anyway for many nights to come. I'm sure of that."

By the time we got there, they had put up caution tape all around the club, but that didn't stop us from parking and walking to find out what we all needed to know! Sure enough, when we walked to where Charlie parked his car each and every night, it was not there, and that made all our minds take off, racing around that fast track of mystery! Just then, my cell rang, and the caller ID read Ms. Kay! I put the call on conference call so everyone could hear the conversation we were about to have.

"Ray Ray, are you guys okay?"

"Ms. Kay, didn't you ask me that when you called earlier? Hell nah, we're far from okay!"

"Yes, Ray Ray, my apologies to you all. I know you all have lost some dear friends tonight, but at least Charlie and Chanel weren't in one of those body bags down at the morgue!"

Now I don't have to tell you the look that came over all our faces because it was most apparent that Ms. Kay knew more than the police did at this juncture of the investigation. "Ray Ray, this is a conversation I'd rather not have on the phone, so can you come to my place right now, please?"

"I'm on my way, Ms. Kay!"

# The Shakedown

Now as you could imagine, the conversation in the car was full of questions between us, but the one that was at the top of everybody's list was, How in the hell could Ms. Kay know everything we had done up until now at this very minute? The car was pretty quiet after I hung up the phone until China said, "That bitch!" Now let me just show you how we all thought alike. Stacey and I didn't even have to question what bitch China was talking about because we all thought it. China was just the first to say it out loud! The only way Ms. Kay could possibly know what she knew was through Detective Brannon, so we all had the same question! What kind of a relationship did those two have for her to get information from him that quickly? Then I started to wonder if Ms. Kay was whom he called when he stepped in the restroom back at the police precinct.

When we pulled up to Ms. Kay's penthouse, she was already sitting outside on her penthouse balcony. I couldn't wait to take the elevator to her floor, and neither could China and Stacey! The valet guy parked my SUV, and we took the elevator to the penthouse floor.

"Come in, and let me say once again, my condolences for your friends."

"Thanks, Ms. Kay, but where are Charlie and Chanel and Anthony? I'm assuming that you know Detective Brannon also because how else could you know what you know?"

"Yes, I do, Ray Ray. He is an old client of mine and owes me a favor or two, so he feeds me information from time to time. But the one thing that he doesn't have a clue about is where the rest of your friends are, and neither do I!"

As soon as she said that, my cell rang with a blocked number, and my gut told me this whole scenario was about to get worse than it already was, if that was even possible! Blocked calls are never any good, and after that night, I never would answer a blocked call again! The blocked caller said, "Ray Ray, if your people are as important to you as I think they are, it's going to cost you to get them back!"

I quickly put the phone on speaker so that everyone there could hear the conversation because as God is my witness, I didn't want to hear what I was about to hear by myself! I motioned for everybody to be quiet so I could try to make out this voice that I was listening to and also every detail that he asked. Ms. Kay reached for her own cell, as if she just might be getting ready to call Detective Brannon, but I motioned for her to put her phone down and let me see what was going on first!

"Ray Ray, I need you to get one million dollars together in one hour, and I will call you back with further instructions about where to bring it. And, Ray Ray, if you want to see your friends again, don't call the cops because that will just complicate things, and I'm sure you don't need any more complications at this point."

"Wait a minute, I need more time than that to get that kind of cash together, and I also need to know which of my people you have."

"Well, let's see, Ray Ray. How many of your people are missing?"

Then I said, "Wait. I'm going to need more time than an hour, and I need you to tell me I have that!"

Then he hung up. Now, readers, I couldn't possibly tell you everything that we discussed in that hour, so I'm going to ask you, what would your conversation be like at a time like that? As I was thinking back, China had the most riveting statement! "Ray Ray, don't fuck around with these guys. I don't want anything to happen to Daddy or no one else. We have lost enough already."

"Ray Ray, I think you should let me call Brannon because China is right. You don't want to fuck around with these guys!"

"Hold on now, Ms. Kay, not just yet. Let me think for a minute, please!"

Stacey was wide-eyed and whimpering still, and after hearing that for a while, my mind was made up. I wasn't going to take the chance of involving the cops and get my remaining friends dead. No way. I had lost too many dear friends already, and I wasn't about to lose any more. I asked Ms. Kay if I could speak with her in private because with what I was about to suggest, Stacey and China were not going to agree because I was going to go get my people myself!

"Hell no, Ray Ray. Whatever you got to discuss with Ms. Kay, you're going to do it right here, right now because we are all a team, remember?"

I looked at the clock, and we had fifteen minutes before that hour would be up. I never really got a conformation on whether or not I had more than the hour that he demanded at first, so whatever I was going to do, I had to make it fast! "Ms. Kay, I need some of your hard hitters to watch my back because I am going to get my people."

"Ray Ray, you're not about that life. But I do have some people who are, and you won't even have to be involved. Just give me the location after you get it, and I will take it from there."

Now I didn't want to owe Ms. Kay another favor because there would be no telling what I would have to do to repay it when that time came around. But time was running out, so I had to make a decision quickly. On that note, the phone rang on cue, and it was the call I had been expecting.

"Ray Ray, do you have what I want yet?"

"Yes, but I'm assuming this is not your first rodeo, so let me talk to my people before we go any further."

Charlie was the first to speak. "Hey, Ray Ray, where are China and Stacey?"

"They are right here, Charlie, right along with Ms. Kay. Where are Chanel and Anthony? Are they all right?"

"Yeah, everyone is alive and well, so get these gentlemen what they ask for so we can get up and out of here." Now that was just like Charlie. The bad guys may take his life, yet he still referred to them as gentlemen. "Ray Ray, the cash from the club is now at the big house, so go do what you have to do!"

Then the bad guys spoke, "Okay, enough of the pillow talk. Do you have what I asked for or not?"

"Yes, I do, so where am I bringing it to?"

"I'll call you back soon, so be ready to ride."

"China, you and Stacey go to the big house and get what needs to be got and meet back here!"

"Hell no, Ray Ray, you're coming with us. Counting out that much cash is going to need all three of us, so come on, man!"

I didn't really think about it, but she was definitely right. That was going to be a lot of cash, but it was only a small drop in a big bucket to get my friends back unharmed! I could always get more cash, but friends like these only come around once in a lifetime. So I would pay whatever they demanded. Even if I didn't have it, I would get it somehow!

Then Ms. Kay said, "I have a van downstairs with baby seats and all. Take that because you will be inconspicuous. You don't need to be riding in something so flashy with that kind of cash!"

"Bet, Ms. Kay, I appreciate that."

I never took anyone to the big house except my family, and Charlie and Chanel were part of my family. But just to make sure Ms. Kay was on the up and up, I asked her to come along too. I didn't trust her like that, so I figured that I would keep an eye on her to make sure she didn't call Brannon behind my back. I asked her to ride along to help me count. She was cool about it and jumped in the van and drove me all the way to my house, baby seats and all, but Ms. Kay was no crash dummy and knew exactly why I asked her to ride along! She still had that itch for Charlie, and I knew she would do everything in her power to make sure he had a safe return. So I did trust that!

As we were pulling up to the big house, my cell rang with the blocked number again, and the voice instructed me to meet them in Club 2000 and make the drop! Right away, I got a bad feeling because Club 2000 was across those railroad tracks that led to the rough side of town, and you already know how I feel about those railroad tracks!

"Hold on a minute, Ray Ray," Ms. Kay said. "We're not going to walk into an ambush, so let me make a call and get the right people in that club before we get there."

Then the girls said, "Yeah, Ray Ray. We are club owners, not gangsters, so let Ms. Kay do her thing!"

I knew Ms. Kay had a long reach in the underworld, and now might be the time that we needed that reach. So I let her make the call. Up until now, all I ever heard Ms. Kay speak was English, but when she made that call, she let me know just how intelligent she really was because she spoke in a language I didn't recognize. And that blew me away! Stacey caught on to the language right away because she had taken the Italian language in college, and she knew exactly what Ms. Kay had said. When Ms. Kay got off the phone, Stacey said, "Ben fatto," which means well done.

Ms. Kay winked at her and said, "Grazie" in Italian, and China and I looked at Stacey and shrugged our shoulders, as if saying, "Where the hell you learn that at?"

"I took Italian in college, but I didn't think I would ever get a chance to use it. But I'm glad I took the course now."

When we got to the big house, I sent China and Stacey downstairs to collect the cash and wait for the call again from the bad guys, and Ms. Kay stayed on her cell, speaking Italian to whomever was on the other end of that call! My cell finally rang with the blocked call again, and I received the instructions to come inside by myself to make the drop. I wasn't about to put anyone else in danger, so I looked at everybody else in the car and said, "This is where you guys get off this train. I'm going in alone."

I never had a reason to carry a gun, but in a case like this, I was strapped like Marshal Dillon with the Glock that I brought from the big house! Whatever the cost, I was bringing my people home, or I wasn't coming home myself. I made that up in my mind just like that! Many things were running through my mind, but what was at the top of my thoughts was not losing any more of my friends, even if I had to give my own life up to accomplish the task at hand. Robert, Shortstop, lil Cash, and Sonia Valdez were still horrible images in my head, and that had my blood at boiling temperature!

Ms. Kay's cell rang, and it was her people, letting her know that they were at the club, locked and loaded, and would be on standby for whatever she wanted done. I looked at her and thanked her for her assistance, but now I needed to do this alone. "Ms. Kay, I need you to take care of my beautiful ladies while I go do what I have to do, so take them to your house and wait for my call."

Ms. Kay said, "Hell no, Ray Ray. We all have a stake in this, even me! If anything happens to Charlie and I know I could have stopped it, I wouldn't know how to live with myself afterward! I am still very much in love with him, and I'm sure you all are very aware of this because it isn't a secret. My people inside that club won't let anything happen to us, so let us do what we have to do. And there is nothing else to even talk about."

Just at that moment, I heard my mother's voice saying, "Ray Ray, whatever you do, always take God with you, and you will be all right." So I pulled the van over and turned the engine off for a minute. I looked everyone in the eye and asked that they join me in holding hands for the Serenity Prayer that I had heard my mother say so many times. "God, grant me the serenity to accept the things I cannot change, the courage to change the things that I can, and the wisdom to know the difference."

The van was in silence while I started the van back up and drove to the club across the tracks where the bad guys had instructed me to be. But on our arrival, Ms. Kay noticed some of her people sitting in the parking lot, and I felt a little bit safe. Ms. Kay reached down in her bag and took out three more Glocks and gave them to China and Stacey, and there was nothing I could say about it because I'd rather they be tried by twelve than carried by six, if you get what I'm telling you right now! If this turned out bad, I wanted them to be able to protect themselves at all costs.

I was not about to walk into a crowd with a million dollars in a duffel bag, so I instructed them to keep it in the car until I had proof that my people were all right. I cocked my Glock and got out of the van first, not knowing how many of Ms. Kay's people were waiting inside, but Ms. Kay assured me they would reveal themselves only if they needed to and not until! I paid the door price and walked inside and surveyed the club to see if I could recognize the bad guys who had called my cell earlier. My cell rang again, and I was instructed to wait at the crowded bar until someone approached me with what to do next. I ordered a Perrier water and tried to act calm in this nightmare that I could not seem to wake up from, but my trigger finger was itching to get my people back home at all costs.

Then it happened. A guy who I had seen at the pool hall way back approached me and asked how I was doing tonight! I looked him straight in his eyes and asked him where my people were. "In time, Ray Ray, in time! You know, we both lost friends tonight, so let's take this nice and easy so there won't be any more casualties tonight."

He asked me to follow him to the back room, where I was relieved of my firearm, and that made me feel kind of naked. The more I looked into this guy's eyes, the more I remembered where I had seen him before. He was one of the marks who I had relieved of his cash in less than an hour, and the way he lost it now made me think he was just in there to case the place of who was who. Because nobody bets those sucker bets expecting to win, unless they know absolutely nothing about gambling.

"Did you bring what I asked you to bring, Ray Ray?"

"Yeah, I did, but you're going to have to show me that my friends arc good before we take that step."

"Ray Ray, I could kill you right here, right now if you don't do what I say."

I was on the other side of the tracks now, but I was more mad than scared. But I knew I had to keep my composure together for Charlie and my friends to make it out of there alive! "Yes, I know that, but that's not going to get you what you ask for, now is it?"

He looked at me as if he was trying to size me up so or something, so if that was the case, I was sure going to let him know to get the right size! At this point, I had made my mind up that I was not going to leave there without my friends!

The club music was so loud that I knew that if there were gunfire, nobody would hear it, and I didn't know if that was good or bad at that point! He picked up his cell and told whoever was on the other end of that call to bring in my friends, so they did! Charlie, Chanel, and Anthony were brought in the little, tiny back room with blindfolds on, and that made me furious, with a heartbeat that I could hear over the music.

"Ray Ray, I'm assuming that you have the cash close by, maybe even in the car, so this is how this is going to go. One of my guys will walk out to the car with you and get the cash, and after we count it, I will let your people go!"

I didn't want to take the bad guys to that van because of who I left sitting inside of it, but Ms. Kay was no crash dummy, so I assumed she knew what was about to go down, especially if her people were in the club, watching the whole thing go down!

# Ms. Kay's Power

We made our way through the crowded club, and even though my heart was beating a thousand miles an hour, I remained focus on the task at hand. My intuition was right though because when I got to the van, China and Stacey were gone! Ms. Kay was sitting there with a whole differently colored duffel bag sitting in her lap, and I knew right away that this was no ordinary woman by far! She had the heart of a gunfighter, and she was letting it be known to everybody who was paying attention, even me! I knew Ms. Kay still had deep feelings for Charlie, but up until now, I guess I really did not know just how deep those feelings were. China and Stacey were sitting close by in another car, out of harm's way, that Ms. Kay's guys had brought across those tracks to the parking lot of a club where you would not catch me at any day of the week.

The bad guy bent down to see who were in the van before he noticed it was just one person, and that one person was a woman. "Ray Ray, is this what you call backup for tonight?"

Ms. Kay only smiled at his comment because obviously, he didn't know who this woman was, but he was sure about to find out!

"Hey, bag lady, the bag, please" is what the bad guy said.

"Whoa," Ms. Kay said, "If you want this bag, you're going to have to come and get it because it's much too heavy for a lady to pick up."

She hit the automatic locks so he could climb in, but he was not trusting that move at all. So he took his cell out to call the guy that was seemingly in charge. But before that guy on the other end could even answer, Ms. Kay's guys ran up out of nowhere and pushed the guy in the back of the van, and I was just as surprised as he was. The only thing was, they were not there to hurt me. Ms. Kay was in the leverage business, and just like back in the day when she found out who One Shot and Charlie were so quickly, she also knew who this bad guy was just as fast! Before I knew it, Ms. Kay's guys had a gun to his head, and right away, he started pleading for his life! After he was secured in the back seat of the van, Ms. Kay started speaking that Italian language again to her guys. They took out a folder, and in it were pictures of the bad guy's family. And that quickly made him rethink just how this was all going to play out and how precious life is.

Ms. Kay said, "Tell me, Raymond. Do you love your family?"

Raymond looked at Ms. Kay with his mouth wide open, but no words would come out. And I thought to myself, *how familiar this scene looks to me right about now!*

When Raymond finally did get some words to come out, all you could hear him saying over and over was that it was not his idea at all. I told him that it really didn't matter whose bright idea it was because he went along with it. "Should have thought it through before you signed on this rodeo. Now you're just as guilty as the guys inside who thought this whole thing up!"

I didn't know how Ms. Kay knew what she knew as fast as she did, but one thing I do know was, she did it very well and very fast! Ms. Kay looked at me and asked, "How you want to do this, Mr. Black?" And I caught on right away that she wasn't going to use names that she didn't need. So I climbed in the back seat, thinking about my friends lying down at the morgue, and I cocked my 9 because Raymond just might be making that trip tonight if I didn't get my friends back in one piece!

Then I looked at Raymond and said, "This is how this is going to go if you don't want to take a trip to that morgue where my friends are getting prepped for a dirt nap that they will never wake up from! You're going to call your guy and tell him to bring my friends out, or I will turn your lights out right here, right now, got it?"

You know how they say that the eyes don't lie? Well, Raymond could look in my eyes and tell I was not fucking around on this one, because no matter what, I was not going to lose any more friends tonight. Also, I made sure I told him exactly that! He made the call, and so did Ms. Kay to let her guys know the play. The bad guy (Raymond) made the call and told his boss that there had been a slight change in plans because he was staring down the barrel of a Glock! The bad guy on the other end of that cell agreed to exchange one body for one body, but he would not release Charlie until he had the cash! I thought about it and realized a bird in the hand was worth two in the bush and took the deal because like I said before, I was not about to lose any more friends tonight! The mastermind bad guy inside the club waiting for a payoff told me to bring the money inside the club, along with his friend Raymond, but Ms. Kay and I had an idea of our own!

"Hey, Ray Ray, you know that you can't walk in there with that cask, don't you?"

"Yeah, I thought about that the minute that I got the call, but it's my friends in there. And I would gladly give up the cash if I think that it would get them all home safe."

"Ray Ray, how do you know this guy even remembers what you look like?"

"I'm assuming he was the other guy who was with this guy when they came into the pool hall that day, but I don't know that for sure."

She picked up her cell and spoke Italian again, and five seconds later, there was one of her guys, picking up the bag. The only thing though was this guy struck a very strong resemblance to me, only a little taller. Ms. Kay handed him the bag that was in the back of the car that contained no cash at all, only wet paper napkins. Ms. Kay saw the surprised look on my face and told me this guy was definitely about that life, so my people were in very good hands. She said this guy would be the new Ray Ray who would walk in with the money and would do whatever it would take to walk out with my people, even if he had to give his own life in the process. The guy looked so much like me that I had to wonder if there was something that my mom forgot to tell me! He walked up to Raymond (the bad guy) and took the butt of his pistol and cracked him in the top of his skull to let him know he was not messing around.

I looked at Ms. Kay. She was smiling while she made this remark to me, "Ray Ray, Mr. Brown is ex-military. What you want me to say?"

Even though Mr. Brown looked a lot like me, he also spoke the Italian language, and that kind of fucked me up for a minute, as you might imagine. After Mr. Brown scooped Raymond up off the ground, he made him call his boss and tell him everything was a go and that he and Ray Ray would be coming through the club door very soon.

Then Ms. Kay took charge like she had done this before, and that gave me some confidence that all would turn out well. "Ray Ray, jump in the back seat and change shirts with Mr. Brown because it would be better if he shows up wearing the same shirt the bad guy had last seen you in. The pants really won't matter because it's dark inside, and he won't even be focusing on that anyway. So the shirt will be fine."

"Hold on, Ms. Kay. What am I supposed to do if I am not taking the money in?"

"Why don't you go with your girls to the house, Ray Ray? I got this. Besides, this is really not your thing. You're a hustler. Stick to what you know because you don't want to cross that line!"

I knew what she was trying to tell me, but my friends were in there. And if I went that far to call you a friend, then there is nothing I won't do for you.

Mr. Brown marched the bad guy in the club at gunpoint, and I don't know what happened after that because Ms. Kay and I went and joined China and Stacey still sitting in the van. Ms. Kay and I were in the process of explaining what was about to go down, and the next thing I knew, people were running out of the club from the sound of gunshots. Ms. Kay's cell began to ring, and when she answered, she spoke Italian again. Stacey knew every word that was being said, and after about two minutes of listening to Ms. Kay, she yelled out, "Drive, Ray Ray. Drive to the front of the club right now!"

Ms. Kay paused her call just long enough to repeat what Stacey had already said, so this must have been serious if they both were shouting the very same thing! China took her Glock out and racked it back, and so did I before I started the van and drove off to the screaming crowd that was running from the club! Stacey was very smart, but she wasn't as hard as China and I. So she got down on the floor of the van, just in case all hell broke loose! When we got to the front, Ms. Kay's guys had Charlie, Chanel, and Anthony standing there, waiting for us to pull up and pick them up. As they got in the van, I could see blood spatter on everyone's clothes, so I knew someone had gotten shot. But it wasn't any of my people, so I drove off as fast as that baby momma van would go with the cash that we had brought still in the duffel bag! I drove out of the club parking lot. I could see the guy who I switched shirts with and who played me in my rearview mirror, ripping off my bloody shirt and tossing it to the ground to pour lighter fluid on it and blazed it up by the flick of a cigarette butt!

I thought to myself as I was driving away, *Man, I am glad this guy is on our side because he brings a whole new meaning to the word* brave heart.

Ms. Kay had saved Charlie's life, and I was sure that would be something that he had to consider down the road when she made a pitch for him again because I was pretty sure she wouldn't forget to bring it up. Everyone was talking and hugging so much that my ears were going off like high-frequency radars, trying to pick up on every conversation that was going on in the van!

Then Stacey asked Ms. Kay in the Italian language, "What happened inside that club?"

Ms. Kay responded back in Italian, "Stacey, the less you know is probably better for everyone." Then she gave me the look as if Stacey was asking too many damn questions! Now at the time, I didn't know what exactly was said, but I could tell by Stacey's reaction that it was something she thought about and what it really meant coming from such a woman as Ms. Kay!

There was a lot of emotion in that van that night, as you could expect. There were too many to even remember them all. We were just blessed to get our friends back in one piece, and we owed it all to a woman who loved playing the leverage game and making people owe her favors! She was very good at it, and that kind of concerned me some because I knew now she had some leverage on us!

I had to drive across the railroad tracks in order to get to the freeway. I remember thinking how seemingly nothing good happens across the tracks, and I approached them with caution! I drove the van back to Ms. Kay's penthouse to get my SUV so I could be on my way back to the big house to put the cash back where I got it from. Chanel thanked Ms. Kay for doing what she did because if she hadn't done what she did, she might not even be alive tonight!

Then Ms. Kay said, "I appreciate that, Chanel, and I'm not going to lie to you. You know I still have a thing for Charlie, and I was not going to let anything happen to him or to the people he cares about, including you."

Chanel was a little impressed, but in the back of her mind, she knew that her saving Charlie's life might just be the fork in the road that would lead to her leaving later because Ms. Kay was only looking for a way for everyone to owe her a favor for something. What she wanted most of all was my friend Charlie! But Charlie still had two after-hours spots going, so he didn't feel the need to get in bed with Ms. Kay, even though she had saved his life. And he let that be known to everyone in that van, including her! Ms. Kay hated rejection, so that did not sit well with her. But she respected his decision for now, even though deep down inside, if you really paid attention to her, you could just tell her wheels were turning. Now seeing the power that this beautiful woman had, I knew her still having that itch for Charlie might not turn out to be a good thing, unless she got her way. And that did concern me more than I let on because this woman was just as dangerous as she was beautiful. That was scary!

What happened here tonight will stick in all our minds until the day we all die, and if anyone brought it up besides the people who were there, we would just say that it was just a made-up lie! When Ms. Kay was no longer around us, we all agreed not to talk about it among anyone but ourselves because Ms. Kay had eyes and ears everywhere, and this woman was dangerous with contacts nationwide, including Detective Brannon!

# Trying to Get Back to Normal

When we finally got home, nobody could sleep, as you might imagine, because too damn much happened in only a short period of time. There were a lot of conversations going on, and the most talked-about topic was Ms. Kay and Detective Brannon! One thing we all agreed on was, this was not over because the cops had to be at that club by now because there had been gunfire. I was expecting a visit from Detective Brannon at any moment because, apparently, more people had been shot down at Club 2000 across the tracks!

As I said before, there were many emotions going on, but I could look in Stacey's eyes and tell that she didn't sign up for this. China didn't say anything at the time, but I could tell. She was a soldier and was fighting this battle to the end! I tried to comfort Stacey by telling her that we would be okay because we still had a cash flow that was coming from the other two after-hours spots and the real estate was great too, but she grabbed my hand very firmly and asked me, "Do you think that I am thinking about money right now, Ray Ray?" Before I could even answer her, she said, "Y'all don't get it, do you? Or do you all just not want to talk about it? This is about how Ms. Kay got us all by our hair, and she could pull it as hard as she wants to. And there is nothing that we can do about it! This is far from over because now we are all going to owe her a big favor, and we all know it."

Stacey was no crash dummy either, because everyone thought it, but Stacey just spoke on it first. Just then, my cell rang, and you can just guess who was on the other end—Detective Brannon! "Ray Ray, we have a problem, but it's nothing that a duffel bag of cash can't fix. So if you want to go on living your life as you have been, I'm going to need that bag of cash!"

# Things Go from Bad to Worst

Charlie looked at everybody with a long glare before he spoke very softly, "Ray Ray, give me the bag, and I'll go meet this Detective Brannon and see if we can work this all out."

China spoke, "Daddy, you do realize that if we let him extort us like this, we will only be opening the floodgates that we can never close!"

I took a look around the room and at everyone's expression in the room, and you could just tell by the reactions on everyone's faces that China had spoken the truth. But what else could we do?

Chanel spoke, "Charlie, as bad as I hate to suggest this, there is only one thing left to do. Call Ms. Kay and give her what she wants because she is the only one that can get Detective Brannon off our asses so that we don't have to give away all that cash and go on with our lives as we know it! Until we can relocate out of town somewhere else, we need to buy time right now."

For the first time ever, I heard Charlie get loud! "Relocate? Did you all just see the kind of power she has? I hate to put it like this, but the power of many vaginas is a very powerful tool. And she has clients everywhere that owe her favors behind that pussy who can't wait to pay one of those favors off. I can't play with power like that because that will put us all in jeopardy, and you guys know that. For all we know, she could be behind Detective Brannon calling me anyway. I mean, how else can he know about the cash that's in a duffel bag that fast?"

Chanel walked over to take her cell out of her handbag and handed it to Charlie. "Make the call, Charlie, or open the floodgates. Your call!"

Now, readers, I don't have to tell you that there were all kinds of mixed emotions going on in the room right here, right now!

"Wait just a minute, Charlie," I said. "This has to be voted on by everybody because this is a team thing, remember?"

Chanel spoke, "Not tonight it isn't! Charlie, if you don't make this call, I will take lil CC, and you will never see us again. Now make the call, please, and give her what she wants!"

Charlie softly took the phone from his lady's hand and made the call on speaker because a man's son was a reflection of him. He sure wasn't going to risk lil CC growing up without him in his life, and he could tell that Chanel meant what she said!

When Ms. Kay answered, you could tell that she was anticipating the call just by the way she answered. "Hello, guys. Is everything all right, Charlie?"

"Ms. Kay, I think we need to have a conversation, but not over the phone."

"Why sure, Charlie. How long will it take you to get here? I was just about to order some food. Can I get you anything?"

Chanel was watching Charlie's body movement because she wanted to see his every emotion. "That's very thoughtful of you, Ms. Kay, but I don't have much of an appetite right now. I'm sure that you can understand why."

"Of course, Charlie. I understand. See you when you get here!"

Charlie turned to kiss Chanel on the cheek before he left, but she wanted no part of his affection right now. I knew right then and there that there was a very big storm brewing in her head right now! Stacey had been quiet though all this, and I was starting to wonder about her as well!

I said, "Hey, Charlie, you need this bag, don't you?"

"I don't think so, Ray Ray. Ms. Kay doesn't want the money. She wants me, and that should concern everyone standing here in this room!"

After Charlie left, I felt like I had to be the one to keep the team from falling like dominoes, so I started with Charlie's lady, Chanel!

"Hey, Chanel, this is just a test, and we are going to get through this together."

"Don't worry, Ray Ray. I would never take lil CC from Charlie, but I had to make him think that so he could feel like he had more to lose than just money."

Stacey got up and went into the bedroom, and I knew I had to go say something to try to get her back on track. Before I could even get started, China pushed me to the side and went straight to where Stacey was and said, "Girl, you know, Mama said there would be days like this, so suck it up and stay focused because it's still about the money. Don't kid yourself."

Then Chanel said, "Listen to her, girl, because she is right. It's always about the money. We all have become accustomed to a certain lifestyle, so we can't let this change the plan!"

Stacey let go of China's hand and stood up and looked at everybody before she said, "Don't y'all kid yourselves because what has happened tonight makes it about staying safe. I think you're all rushing to a decision that you may regret later. Let's just wait until we hear from Charlie before we know for sure where this path that we seem to be on leads."

Then in unison, Chanel and China held hands and said, "Wherever this path takes us, we will stand by our men 100 percent."

And let's not forget that Charlie was also China's father, so we knew she would stand strong like a soldier. With Stacey a little on the shaky side, I knew I had to have a private conversation with her to see where her head was really at. Before I could even do that, Charlie called and said everything was all good and that he would be here soon, and I relayed that message to everyone there. Stacey looked at me as if she didn't think everything was good and asked me if I could take her home because she was very tired. That was completely understandable because we all were. But I knew Chanel and China would not rest until Charlie walked through that door, and frankly, neither would I!

When Charlie did walk through that door, China and Chanel ran up to him and hugged him as if he had just come home from a very long trip. But Stacey just stood there like she had something else on her mind, and she looked scared to death. I quickly asked Charlie to fill us in on the conversation between him and Ms. Kay!

"Okay, team, this is the deal. The only way to make Detective Brannon back off is to let Ms. Kay think she is part of our team and that I myself have a relationship with her just like you have with China and Stacey, Ray Ray, and that's the only deal there is for us, like it or not! I know you guys don't like dealing with her, but we have to be smart about this because she knows way too much about all of us, and she will use that leverage to her advantage if she has to."

"Wait, Charlie, are you saying what I think you're saying?"

"Yes, Ray Ray, I am. Her business is now part of our business, but that will stay between us, not the staff. There is no need for them to know about us being in bed with her, after all that's happened. Now I'm sure you all are very tired, so let's all try to get some sleep and pick this up tomorrow. I know you all have your own places, but you're welcome to spend the night right here. We have enough rooms for you all to do that."

Stacey spoke, "No, I want to sleep in my own bed, if you don't mind, Charlie."

"Sure, Stacey, I understand. Go home and get some sleep, and we will talk tomorrow."

I really had a bad feeling about leaving Stacey all alone by herself because clearly, she was still standing on shaky grounds! I asked China to spend the night with her so I could think about where this was all going without having to worry about Stacey's state of mind! "Sure, Ray Ray, anything for the team." But you could just tell that China did what she did because Stacey seemed to be falling apart, and the last thing we needed right now was a weak link!

# Sunday Morning

I woke up not even knowing what day it was, but I was quickly reminded by the call that woke me up.

"Ray Ray, son, have you forgotten your promise to me? It's Sunday morning, and I don't want to be late for church."

Oh, snap. With all that had happened, I had completely forgotten about my promise to go to church with my mother. I had never lied to my mother before, and I sure wasn't about to start now. I jumped up and took a shower and got dressed and went out the door, thinking about how I had always been taught since my adolescent years that God performs miracles, and I was thinking I just might need one today. When I picked up my family, I said nothing about what had happened at the club, but I didn't have to because the club that had burned down had been all over the news. And my mom definitely watched the news every day!

"Ray Ray, I didn't think you would make it to church, but I'm glad that you did, son, because God tells me that you have a heavy heart about something. You want to talk about it?"

"Mother, I know that you watch the news, and you know that the club that burned down was my club. So is there anything that you want to ask me?"

"Yes, Ray Ray, there is something that I want to ask. Is your heart right with God? If it isn't, I think it's time that you have a talk with him. You know what I am saying to you, son? Now I'm not going to preach to you, son, because I don't want to take the minister's job, but

I do want you to use me as an ear if you need to get something off your chest. I'm your mother, son. Maybe I can offer you some kind of guideline if you need me to."

"Mother, there is something that I always wanted to ask you. When you picked up and just left your friends back in Texas, was that hard for you to just leave friends that you had known most of your life?"

"Yes, it was, Ray Ray, but you have to understand something. There is a big difference between friends and acquaintances, son. Friends will be with you forever. Whether it be in the form of a weekend phone call or a monthly letter, friends will always be there, like a solid marriage, son. Why you asking?"

"Well, Mom, I have always been straight with you, and you have always been straight with me. And I know you know what path that I have taken in life, but unlike Uncle Grady, I have always had an endgame. I'm thinking maybe that time was yesterday."

"Son, remember what your father used to say to you?"

"Yes, Mom. If it feels right to you, then it probably is right, but if it feels wrong, then it probably is. But he never told me how to get out of feeling like I'm trapped!"

"Son, that's easy. Just eliminate what makes you feel trapped, and if your friends feel the same way—trapped like you do—then discuss this trapped feeling with them also."

I smiled at my mom because she knew exactly what I needed to hear. She knew the whole team was going through some things because of that club being burned to the ground without me giving her details of the whole night's events. That's my mom. She knows!

Have you ever showed up in church when you haven't been in a while and the nice people who are your mother's friends want to ask you all sorts of questions? Now you know the life you have been accustomed to doesn't coincide with church regulations, so you just do the best you can with your answer. After church was over, I went and had Sunday dinner with the family, and I had been missing that so much that I fell asleep in my dad's old La-Z-Boy chair and slept until my mother tapped me on the arm to say, "Son, your old room is waiting for you."

I looked at her and smiled, and she led me to my old bedroom. I lay on that bed and slept like a baby until my cell started blowing up. It was Anthony! "Hey, Ray Ray. Are we opening tonight? Because we have a few shaken people on staff now on account of what happened to some of our staff at the other club, ya know?"

"Yeah, I know. Where are you? I'm on my way to you now."

I got off the phone and kissed my mother and told her I loved her, and out the door I went for what was already shaping up to be an interesting day! I called Charlie to see what was going on, and he said that when everyone got up, Stacey was gone and that she was not answering her cell!

# Stacey Gone Again

"Okay, Charlie, I'll try her in a minute. But right now, I'm going to pick up Anthony because we might have a problem with some of our staff, and I'm sure you know why."

"Sure I do, Ray Ray. Do what you have to and tell Anthony not to mention anything about Ms. Kay, please!"

"Fa show, Charlie. Keep your cell on your hip, and I'll hit you on the flip." I scooped up Anthony to get a rundown on what was going on with our staff.

"Hey, Ray Ray, if you don't know how to fix this problem, let me enlighten you. It's simple. Just double everybody's pay and watch how fast that shaken problem goes away."

I didn't have a lot of time on my hand for negotiation, so I told Anthony to make it happen.

"Ray Ray, you know, I miss the hell out of Robert, Cash, and Shortstop, man. And every time I go to work, I will still be looking for them."

"Yes, me too, Anthony. They will be missed by everyone, but don't let the staff know anything about Ms. Kay. We don't need them tripping on that! Make sure we pick up the tab for whatever their families need, including their funerals, and make sure I get the ticket personally. Not Charlie, me!"

"Ray Ray, can I ask you a question?"

"Sure, Anthony. What you want to know, man?"

"What's this thing you have about railroad tracks, man? I mean, are you superstitious or something?"

"I don't know, Anthony. I guess I am. I got my first and only whipping in my life playing down on the railroad tracks when I was a kid, and whenever I cross railroad tracks, let's just say I don't like crossing them. The shit that happened at that club that night was across the tracks, you know that?"

Anthony was laughing. "Man, you are superstitious, huh? Ray Ray, if you really believe that bad things happen while being around railroad tracks, then you need to stay away from them because we are what we believe."

"Yeah, I hear you, brother. Hey, Anthony, I'm going to drop you off at my house, so take one of my cars and go let the staff know they will have a pay increase because I have pressing business to attend to."

"Got it, Ray Ray. I'll hit you on the hip later to let you know what's up."

After I dropped Anthony off, I picked up my cell and called Stacey's cell, expecting her not to answer because she had not answered for the team yet as far as I knew. The phone was answered on the second ring, as if she were anticipating the call from me. "Hello, Ray Ray. I'm at my mom's house if you're looking for me, and I don't want to be bothered right now. I just want to hang out with my family right now."

"Stacey, I know a lot has happened, but we need to stand strong in times like this. Remember, no weak links. Stacey, I'm coming over because I don't want to have this conversation on the phone."

"Ray Ray, you don't know where my parents live anymore because I moved them just like you did with your own family! What, you think I don't learn from your moves? You know, you have taught me a lot, Ray Ray, but the one thing you never bring up is your endgame to all of this. Or is that a conversation that you only have with China?"

"Stacey, where is all of this coming from all of a sudden?"

"Ray Ray, you really got to ask me that when so many of our friends are lying down at the morgue on cold stainless steel tables? This is coming from a tragedy, Ray Ray, a fucking tragedy, man! Have you forgotten those people were friends of ours? Ray Ray, what about

Jason Daily, whom you yourself named Cash? I know you have to feel something for that kid and his family! What about Sunshine, Ray Ray, a.k.a Sonia Valdez? You remember her?"

"Of course I do, Stacey. They were all also my friends too."

"She was my friend more than you will ever know, Ray Ray, and I don't know if I will ever get over her."

"I know you and she were tight, Stacey, but we will all miss her very much."

"Ray Ray, you know how the team always says that what we do in the dark will always come to the light?"

"Yes, Stacey, but where are you going with this?"

"If everything we do in the dark always comes to the light, then how come you never knew that Sonia and I were more than just friends, Ray Ray? Because China sure knew."

"Knew what, Stacey? What are you trying to tell me?"

"Ray Ray, Sunshine and I were way more than just friends. We were also lovers for at least six months, and China knew all about it the whole time!"

Now, readers, I don't have to tell you that there was a long awkward silence after that was said, just like the time before when we were about to break up and go our separate ways when she went off to college! (That same feeling was back!) Now, readers, I had never known any lesbian women personally, but this was right in my own backyard. And I was freaking the fuck out right now!

"Ray Ray, are you still there?"

"Yes, Stacey, I'm still here. I'm just in shock right now because I never thought you wanted to play on the other team."

"Yes, Ray Ray, I'm sure you are! You see, you spend so much time making sure money is coming through your door that you never realize what's going out of your door—me! All I needed was some kind of push to tell you, and this is it."

"Stacey, are you bisexual or something? Shit, I got to ask because you're confusing the hell out of me right now. Stacey, you and I have been intimate like rabbits since ninth grade. What the fuck, Stacey? Where did this come from all of a sudden?"

(I thought about what my mom had said about how I could talk to God at any time, at any hour, so I looked up to the sky and said, "God, I'm going to need some assistance on understanding this one!") The last time I checked, God created Adam and Eve, a man and a woman, so there's that!

"Ray Ray, I was never going to be first with you, and that was okay at first until I found Sunshine and let her into my life that definitely had a missing piece!"

"Stacey, are you saying you're walking away from the money and the team?"

"Fuck the team, Ray Ray. China knew about Sunshine and me from the very start. Did she ever tell you that she knew? Ray Ray, if I had known something like that about China, you think I would not have told you that?"

"Stacey, you're a little delusional right now. Let me come and pick you up so we can sort this all out."

"Ray Ray, there is nothing to sort out because I'm at the point of no return, and you know it. You will never look at me the same after what I have told you tonight, and don't lie and say we can put this all behind us because I know game when I hear it! Remember, I learned from the best. I learned from the team!"

"Stacey, you can't keep running in and out of my life like this. You're playing with my emotions right now."

"Ray Ray, when I came back to you, I came back for you! But the more time I spent around China, I began to like her as well. She was not having it though, and she quickly let me know that. I will be fine because I still have my property, and China made sure that I know everything about flipping homes. I can do this anywhere I decide I want to live on this planet thanks to her. I'm going to let you in on a lil secret, Ray Ray. China had this planned from day 1. She just went along with me being with you because I had something to bring to the table to benefit the team. China loves you very much, Ray Ray, and she will do anything for you. To tell you the truth, I kind of admire that about her. That's your ride-or-die chick, and she will do what it takes to get that cash for you! You got a down-ass bitch, Ray Ray, and she is more intelligent than you realize. Don't sleep on China, man, because after all, at the end of the day, she is still Charlie Soft's daughter first and foremost."

"Stacey, what is that supposed to mean?"

"Ray Ray, you and Charlie are best friends, and China is his daughter. It could mean many things, good for you or not."

At this point, I was asking myself, *is this bitch playing divide and conquer right now?*

"I've heard many stories about your uncle Grady, about how smooth he was with the ladies and all, so let's see how smooth you are when you go have that talk with China that I know you are just dying to have right now. Ray Ray, I love you and probably always will, but I need some time right now to sort things out in my head because so much has happened in only a short period of time. Right after this conversation, I'm going to turn my cell off and get some real sleep. God knows I haven't had any since this all started with the club burning down."

Now there was something that I never understood about people who say they still love you but do not want be with you, because if I have that strong of a feeling for someone and if I can call it love, then I will be with that person or at least try! I don't know how that can be.

"Okay, Stacey, I understand. Call me later on."

She was right about one thing. I couldn't wait to hear China's take on all that was said by Stacey.

# China's Side of the Story

I picked up my cell and dialed China's number but got no answer, so I tried it over and over until she picked up the phone. "Hey, baby, I'm sorry. I was asleep. What's going on?"

"I found Stacey, and I need to have a talk with you. Are you at home?"

"Sure, baby. Are you on the way? I'll make you something to eat if you're hungry."

"I'm hungry for information, and I don't think that you can put that on a plate, China!"

"Oh, Stacey told you about her affair with Sonia, huh?"

"Yes, she did, and I'm wondering why you didn't tell me because according to her, you knew all about it and she even made a pass at you."

"Ray Ray, come home, and I will tell you all about why I didn't tell you."

Now, readers, if there wasn't enough going on already with this other stuff, this would have taken over top priority because in a way, I felt like I had been betrayed by China and Stacey! On my way of driving to the big house, I couldn't help thinking about what Stacey had said about China! Stacey had been around a while, and she was just as sharp as the rest of us. I was kind of admiring how she had built China up and, at the same time, planted the seed of betrayal!

When I walked in the house, China had the smooth jazz playing, and I knew she was just trying to soften the blow about what she was about to reveal about Stacey and Sonia's lesbian affair that had taken place right under my nose. Since the opening of our after-hours spots, I had been very busy burning the candle at both ends, so I had not been spending much time cuddling with either lady. "China, did you know about Stacey and Sonia's affair?"

"Yes, I knew, Ray Ray, but I didn't know how to tell you something like that. After all, she was still holding up her end as far as making that cash for the team, so I said, if it's not broken, why try and fix it?"

That was one thing that I admired about China! You could never back her into a corner. She would always come out knowing what to say, so yeah, she was a down-ass bitch, if I say so myself!

"Ray Ray, we have an agenda to make enough money to end up with a lifestyle that most only dream about, and that's why as long as Stacey was pulling her own weight, she was serving her purpose. You have feelings for her, so this is something that I knew would change how you feel about her. I didn't do it. Stacey did!"

"Let me get this straight, China. You set her up to fail in my eyes?"

"Yes, I did, Ray Ray, so how do you feel about her now?"

"I feel betrayed by her for a second time, and I'll tell you right now, there won't be a third!"

"Well, think of it like this, baby. You gave her everything she ever wanted and more, and so did I! Even though she threw a pass at me, I never tried to catch it. Stacey tried to come on to me, but you know I don't swing that way, Ray Ray. So as soon as I knew Sonia played for the other team, I hooked them up so she would stay around. Yes, I kept her secret because if I had told you, what would you have done? I told them what they did in the dark needed to stay in the dark. The longer, the better! She said she loved Sonia, and every time you spent the night with me, she would always have Sonia come over and spend the night with her. I couldn't tell you that because you would have spent way too much time trying to understand how your first love changed uniforms!"

"Did Charlie know this too, China?"

"No, I never told him because he probably would have made me tell you. You remember that Charlie did tell you that there were things you didn't know about both of us, and that was before you knew I was his daughter."

"China, why would you not tell me what was going on with her a long time ago?"

"Because we needed her, Ray Ray, but we don't anymore because we can fill her spot overseeing the club with almost anyone!"

"Like who, China? Who can bring those customers in from that exclusive bar that she worked at downtown?"

"Ray Ray, that club has burned down, so we really don't have to get anyone right now until we decide to open a new location. And with all that has happened, I don't think we need another club right now until we see where this is all going with Charlie and Ms. Kay!"

China was right, but my feelings were hurt a little bit, though not to the point that I wanted to call Stacey. I was done with her, and this time, I meant it. Stacey had done well for herself because she had made enough money to invest in anything that she wanted to invest in and be all right down the road of life. She had her own home paid for and about five rent houses that she collected on every month, so yes, she was good financially. But emotionally, she had a long way to go because she still had a bad image in her head that would follow her for the rest of her life.

"Ray Ray, a lot has happened in a short time, and you need to relax. I know just how to do that for you. So go jump in the shower, and I will come and wash your back for you."

I wanted to be upset at China, but once she stuck that tongue ring out, I forgot what I even wanted to be upset about. *Fuck it. China is right. I need to relax some because I haven't done that in quite some time.* I was definitely backed up, so it would be kind of nice to just shut everything off, smoke a blunt, and get caught up. Up until now, I had been spending endless nights without any sleep, trying to make sense of all that happened.

The jazz was smooth and sounded nice, and it took me back down memory lane, when I first spent the night with China. And I was eager to drive back down that street with her in the car once again. I was in the shower for about ten minutes before the glass door opened on the shower, and I could smell the aroma of pot before she stepped in the shower with my favorite suit on—her birthday suit in 3-D. It went down until the break of dawn, before we both fell into a deep, coma-like sleep.

# Amanda Simmons

The next morning, China and I got up to get a quick workout at the gym before we resumed the nightmare that haunted everyone who was involved. The one thing about working out was that you forget about all your problems for the time being. You just put your earbuds in and are wherever you want to be in the world mentally.

We were on our second set of squats when I noticed a familiar face that I had not seen in a while, and even though she was far away, I could tell it was Amanda Simmons from the jewelry store at least three years ago! I didn't know why, but I felt the need to reintroduce myself. I guess I just wanted to see if she remembered me. Nothing got past China though, and the first thing she said to me was "Go for it, papi. She just might be Stacey's replacement if we decide to open another after-hours club."

I smiled at China and walked toward Amanda to see if she recognized me from three years ago. Before I even got all the way up on her, she looked at me and said, "Hey, Ray Ray, long time no see. What have you been up to? I even gave you my number, so why didn't you call me and invite me to the wedding?"

"Well, Amanda, there was never a wedding, so I couldn't invite you to something that never happened."

"Oh, I'm so sorry that things didn't work out for you. What have you been up to since we last met?"

"Well, Amanda, I never said that things didn't work out. I just said I never got married."

"Ray Ray, you don't have to say my government name like that. Just call me Mandy, please."

"Okay, Mandy it is. What have you been up to since the last time we saw each other? Are you married or do you have a boyfriend or something?"

"Ray Ray, if I didn't know better, I would think you were trying to flirt with me, asking all these questions, and I must let you know this off the top. I like it."

Just then, I thought about my uncle Grady and how all his lady acquaintances knew about each other, so this was a test to see if I was really anything like my uncle Grady. I looked down the gym floor at China, who was paying me no attention. She was on her cell, talking to her dad, the smooth-talking Charlie Soft, which I didn't find out until later. She made eye contact with me long enough to notice I was calling her to come to where I was having this conversation with Mandy.

"Mandy, I have someone I would like for you to meet. Her name is China, and we have a different kind of relationship than most. Are you cool with that?"

"Ray Ray, you're not on that swinger's shit, are you?"

"Hell nah, Mandy. China and I don't roll like that!"

"Ray Ray, I flirted with you the first day I met you, and if she doesn't have a problem with you talking to me, then I certainly don't. You know what they say about a woman, don't you?"

"Wait, Mandy, let me guess! Women don't want a man that another woman don't want, well, at least interested in. I'll say that!"

"You're absolutely right, Ray Ray. Are you going to let me meet her?"

China was already standing right there with a big smile on her face because she had heard Mandy's comment about how a woman doesn't want a man that another woman don't want, the same thing China had said to me a long time ago. The first thing Mandy said was about how beautiful China was. The Stacey thing came to mind, so I thought it was only fair that I ask Mandy this question. "Mandy, are you bisexual? I just need to know upfront."

"Ray Ray, China is very beautiful, but I only like men. Sorry if that offends you, China, but I don't roll like that."

"Mandy, no need to be sorry because I am strictly dickly myself, and that's how I roll. Now that we have that out of the way, Mandy, I hope to see you again. But for now, I have pressing business to take care of. Ray Ray, I'll catch up with you later. I have to go down to the office to close a deal, so I will leave you two alone to get better acquainted." She reached her hand out to shake Mandy's hand, and Mandy gladly accepted the handshake with a smile. China turned to me and kissed me on the cheek before she went out the door to jump in that cream-colored Mercedes and bounced!

"Ray Ray, I can tell she is a one-of-a-kind woman, and you must be very proud of her for letting you do whatever it is you want."

"Yes, Mandy. She is the rock of my foundation, and I couldn't have accomplished the things I have done in my life without her. But I want to talk about you, so tell me something about you that you think I ought to know."

"Well, Ray Ray, do you want the long version or the short one? How much time do you have to spare?"

"The short version will work for me right now, but if you give me your number, we can do the long version later on over dinner or something. Do you still work at that same jewelry store that I met you at three years ago?"

"Ray Ray, I don't work at that jewelry store anymore, but I'd still be there sometimes."

"Mandy, why would you still be at a jewelry store that you are not employed at anymore? I'm a little confused why you would do that!"

"Because I now own that jewelry store, along with two others inside the east mall and one in the west mall. Are you surprised because I'm only twenty-five years old?"

"Yes, and I think shocked would be a better assessment. How did you pull that off at such a young age?"

"Ray Ray, I thought you wanted the short version? If I tell you all of that, it will definitely turn into the long version, don't you think?"

"Mandy, you got me there. But I will say this, you're a very interesting person, and I think I want to get to know you better, if that's possible."

"Anything is possible, Ray Ray. Give me a call when you have time, and we can do the long version if you have that much time."

"Sounds good, Mandy. What's your number?"

"Ray Ray, I gave you my number once, and you never called. So you just have to come down to the store and get another business card if you don't have the one I gave you."

"Mandy, that was almost three years ago. I doubt if I still have that card, so why don't you just give me your cell and I will call you tomorrow?"

"Now, Ray Ray, where is the fun in that? If you're really interested in me, you will find me."

Then she turned and went to the ladies' locker room to take a shower, leaving me hanging about what her cell number was. I didn't like that, but I did respect it before I went out the door with a smile on my face, saying to myself, "Mandy, Mandy, Mandy!"

# Chopping It Up with Charlie

After the gym, I hit Charlie up to see where we were going to link up to discuss this "Detective Brannon and Ms. Kay" thing!

"Come by the house, Ray Ray, and I'll fill you in, man."

I got straight to the point when I walked in. "Charlie, what's going on with Detective Brannon and Ms. Kay?"

"Ray Ray, we don't have to worry about him as long as Ms. Kay is happy."

"Shit, Charlie. I don't know how to even take that."

"Relax, Ray Ray. You think all I learned from your uncle was how to gamble? Ray Ray, I'm a mack from way back. You better ask somebody." He started laughing.

"Charlie, now is not the time for jokes. How is Chanel taking all this?"

"Ray Ray, didn't I just tell you that I'm a mack from way back? Boy, you need to pay attention to what I'm saying sometimes." He laughed again. "What, you think you're the only one who can have more than one lady? By the way, Ray Ray, what's up with Stacey? She good?"

"Hell nah, man. That girl done went crazy, Charlie. She plays on the other team now."

"What's that supposed to mean, Ray Ray?"

"Well, apparently, Sunshine had a lick-her license, and Stacey saw the sign."

"Ray Ray, you're fucking me up right now! What the hell does a liquor license got to do with Stacey and Sunshine?"

"Charlie, now who is not paying attention? I said 'lick-her license,' not liquor license, man!"

"Ray Ray, get the fuck out. Are you saying what I think you're saying?"

"Charlie, that's exactly what I'm saying!"

"Well, how in the hell did you let that happen, Ray Ray? That's not good, Ray Ray. Does China know?"

"Yes, she knew before I did, and I'm feeling a certain kind of way about that too."

"Ray Ray, listen to me, partner, and listen very good! I don't care if you got to get Stacey a mail-order lesbian doll. You get her back at all cost! Ms. Kay just may take Stacey being independent and all as a weak link to her and her people. Ray Ray, you know that shit, man! Stacey has learned way too much about Ms. Kay, and they may not be good for any of us."

"Charlie, why am I feeling like I'm about to do a sequel of *The Godfather*, or maybe I should rephrase, *The Godmother*? Ms. Kay's starting to sound like Griselda Blanco or something, Charlie, so I hope like hell you really are a mack from way back and keep her happy!"

"Ray Ray, you got to get Stacey back, man. Where is she? Have you gone by her house?"

"I really don't know where she is. She wouldn't tell me. No, I have not gone by her house because she said she was at her mom's house. She said she was going to get some sleep, and she may call me after she gets some sleep."

"Well, shit, Ray Ray, go by her mom's house and talk to her."

"Charlie, it's not that simple. I don't even know where her mom's staying because she moved her whole family, and I don't even know when she did that!"

"Ray Ray, what did you just say?"

"You heard me, Charlie. I don't know where she is, but I will try to call her and try and talk with her."

"Ray Ray, you need to find her before Ms. Kay finds out. Have you forgotten how fast she finds out shit, man?"

"Charlie, what just happened to the mack from way back? Did he go on vacation?"

"Ray Ray, now is not the time. Find her before Ms. Kay finds out!"

I picked up my cell and dialed Stacey's number and got that sound that we all hate to hear when we think we're dialing the right cell number. "Due to customer's request, you have reached a number that has been changed or disconnected"! Now Charlie and I were really tripping because it was starting to look like Stacey had this all planned from the beginning! Charlie picked his cell up and immediately called China and told her the bad news and the reason that he thought the news was bad for all of us. China said she would go check with whom she thought Stacey might have told about her plan to be independent and get back with us when she could.

Just then, Ms. Kay called Charlie on his cell and told him to meet her for lunch if he could. "Ray Ray, I got this, man. Don't worry about my end. You just take care of your end, brother!"

# Secrets Come Out!

The staff we had left had heard many rumors about the club burning down, and Charlie and I had to come up with some kind of explanation to quiet down the rumors that were circulating! The best way to do something like that was to have a staff meeting and find out just how much they knew already. The only problem about that was, Ms. Kay was considered part of the team now, and she was bound to find out Stacey had adopted a Chinese name called One Gone! The only question now was, for how long? China could get no lead on where Stacey might have disappeared to, and Ms. Kay was going to find out she was missing in action sooner or later. There was no way around it!

The next day before the club opened, we called all the staff members to let them know there would be a staff meeting shortly after lunch at the club and that we would provide lunch, so they should show up hungry because we would have more than enough to satisfy everyone involved. Charlie, China, Anthony, Billy, and I got there before anyone else because we had to agree on what to tell them and how to tell them because this nightmare was never-ending, it seemed.

"Charlie, did you tell Ms. Kay about the staff meeting at noon?"

"Sure did, Ray Ray. She is a part of the team now, so I really had no choice. But she does not know Stacey has up and disappeared like Casper the ghost. Has anybody heard anything about her whereabouts or anything yet?"

Everyone shook their head no in agreement, and that was not good. Everybody in the room knew it. Then the quiet one, Billy, stood up and said, "In Iraq, there was a way that we had to deal with a threat, and I have no problem doing that if it ever comes to that!"

The room got kind of silent because we all knew what he was implying, and we were just not trying to go there, not yet anyway! Charlie thanked Billy for his input and loyalty, but he was not going that route because all he had to do was just smoothen it out with Ms. Kay when the time came, which was getting ready to be about noon!

When the doors opened for the rest of the staff to join the meeting, Ms. Kay was the first one through the door, looking like the high-maintenance woman that she was. Everyone was well into the catered food before Ms. Kay finally asked me, "Where is Stacey, Ray Ray? Is she not feeling well?"

Charlie looked at me for my response, so I just went with that for now. "Yes, Stacey is a little under the weather today, but I'm sure she will be feeling better soon."

Everybody in the room wished her well and continued eating their lunch for now. That was certainly possible, considering how cold the weather had been lately. After the meal was finished, the meeting started off with the rumors about the club burning down and the dear friends that we had all lost across the tracks! I looked at Charlie to see if he wanted to be the lead on this topic, but he gave me that famous wink as if he were saying, "Ray Ray, you got this one, so do what it is you do!"

I smiled at him with a wink of my own and stood up and cleared my throat to speak to the staff we had left in a language that they understood. "I know you all have heard all the rumors about Charlie and our friends and the club burning down. Now we can't bring back Cash, Sonia, or Robert, but we can make sure that the share they were receiving goes to their families as long as we keep that cash flow coming in that we all need to make it in this world today. We have lost the club down across the tracks, but we still have the other two that will almost keep everything just as it was. Nobody is going to look out for us, so we have to look out for one another, just like families do. We are living in a world where our opinions do not count because we are not the white-collar kind of people, if you get my meaning. It seems like in this country, only the wealthy get ahead, and they want you to think that if you're poor, you are better off dead. The history that they teach our kids in school is not accurate at all. In fact, the only time you see us in history books is when they need someone to blame for their fuckups and need someone to take a fall!

"Take my words and beware because the American dream for some has become a nightmare! What has happened to our club and dear friends, we cannot change, but we have to keep our heads up and still stay focused on what is most important: that cash in hand! Let's keep it 1,000 percent, people, not 100 percent! We can't do anything without it. Our good friend Robert said one day when we were just kicking back and joking around, 'Ray Ray, I hear they're getting ready to start charging for air to breathe. You know what that means?'

"I said, 'Robert, don't believe everything you hear because sometimes, people just make shit up for no reason at all.'

"'Well, Ray Ray, I sure hope not because if they do, your boy about to flat line in this bitch is all I'm saying.'" The staff was laughing. "Robert used to just say crazy shit like that all the time, and he will be well missed by all of us. I'm sure of that if I'm not sure of anything else! But let's not take our eyes off the prize and forget about why we do what it is we do. It's for the cash that we would not make anywhere else by working a nine-to-five! Now the cash won't alleviate the memories of our lost friends! Cash, Sonia, and Robert will always have a place in our hearts and leave a stain on our brains until we all leave this earth, but we have to stay in our lanes and stay focused on what's important, especially now! Us sitting here today is nothing short of a blessing because we all could have been in that club that night, but instead, we are here, learning tough lessons. Now if you don't mind, I would like to read you a poem written by a good friend of mine, and it's called 'Take a Look in the Mirror.'

"Sticks and stones can break bones, but words also can hurt . . . So the next time you talk bad about somebody, you should take a look in the mirror first! There's nobody in this world that is perfect, so to speak mean words about someone, ask yourself if it is really worth it. Just like your parents raised you . . . not to belittle people because whether you know it or not, your shit stinks too!

"Now for all of you here that don't know this beautiful woman, she goes by the name of Ms. Kay, and she is a very sophisticated lady, to say the least. If it were not for her, more of our dear friends would not be sitting here at this feast." I looked over at her and told her to stand and introduce herself since now she was part of the team! Charlie and China smiled with amusement, as if I had done a good thing.

Ms. Kay stood and said that she was glad to be part of the family and that she had always felt that she was somewhat part of the team anyway on account of how she had known Charlie for so long. Then she said, "I have been broke before, and I have had money before. And I think I'm going to prefer the choice of having it because every time the damn mailman shows up, he has in his hand some kind of bill that I need to pay."

I thought to myself, *Man, she is not lying about that.*

"Now when you have that cash, that bill is one less problem that you don't have to worry about, and you can go and address other problems that you have on your plate at the time. We should all be taking advantage of this quick cash that we are getting right now and take the time out to build your credit up and do as China, Ray Ray, Stacey, and Chanel have done in the real estate game. We can't be dumb about this cash right now. For you who have kids who want to give them a good education, this money will make sure that they don't end up on somebody's plantation. I don't have kids, but someday, I just might. After all, who do you think will have your back when you become old? And trust me, you will become old one day if you're lucky! Anyway, not only am I part of the team now, I have also chosen Charlie, and he is my papi now!"

The staff stood up and clinked their champagne glasses together before we turned on some smooth jazz and continued to wine and dine the rest of the afternoon away, with Chanel watching Charlie's every move!

# When Things Calm Down

It was two weeks later, and everything was back on track as far as the club business went, which was mostly gambling most of the time. Ms. Kay had not had time to ask me personally about Stacey's whereabouts because the business that made her famous kept her busy most of the time. At the same time, she had Charlie finally, and that kept her attention away from Stacey.

Since the club that China managed had burned down, she had started spending more time in her downtown office rather than the club life, and believe me, I had no problem with it. I think losing that many dear friends like that made her feel a certain kind of way—almost depressed! She didn't have that same glow in her eyes that she usually had. Even though I didn't show it like she did, I was going to keep it real! I was starting to have thoughts of getting out of that business because of those same friends I had lost also. It was just a thought though, and I kept that thought to myself until one day, I decided to go down to the jewelry store where I had met Amanda Simmons.

# Amanda Simmons Again

I parked my car and walked in, smiling at the thought of me surprising her. I just hoped she was at this location. When I stepped through the glass door, I didn't see her, so I decided to go get some assistance from the counter. "Excuse me, sir, but can you tell me where I can find Ms. Simmons?"

"Who may I say is asking, sir, if you don't mind?"

"Ray Ray, brother, just tell her it's Ray Ray."

He gave me the concerned look before he went to the back of the store, and when he returned, he gave me a number and told me Ms. Simmons would be waiting for my call. I took the card from the gentleman and walked outside and jumped back in that Escalade and Bluetoothed her ass. When she noticed it was me on the line, the first thing she said was "Hey, Ray Ray. Long time no hear, man."

"Yes, Mandy, I know. How have you been?"

"I'll tell you what, Ray Ray. Why don't you meet me at this cozy little bar right down the street where you're at right now."

"Bet, Mandy, give me the exact address, and I will meet you there right now." And she did. She was definitely right about one thing. It was a very nice, cozy little bar with a cozy little name to match—Mandy's Place! I went straight to the bar because I didn't see her when I first walked in, and I had no idea what kind of automobile she drove that might have been sitting in the parking lot because we never got that far yet in our previous conversation. She really didn't need a car to get noticed by me. She could have been walking with a bus pass, and she would still get my attention!

The gentleman at the bar wearing the name tag that read "Brandon" seemed to be expecting me because the first thing he asked was "Are you Ray Ray?"

I said, "I'm not even going to ask you how you know that name because there's only one way you could know something like that. It's Ms. Simmons, right?"

"Ray Ray, I see I have to get up early in the morning to get anything past you, man. You are sharp!"

I smiled and said, "No, you didn't!"

We both slapped high fives because the shit was funny. And then he pointed behind me, where a very beautiful woman was standing, looking like a Reese's Peanut Butter Cup. Yeah, that was my favorite. "Don't tell me. You own this too?"

"Brandon, you're right. You do have to get up early in the morning to get something past this guy." They both laughed in fun.

My response was "So y'all got jokes up in here, don't you?"

"Come sit down, Ray Ray. What have you been doing with yourself? I have not seen you or China at the gym lately."

"Yeah, I know. Many things have been going on in my life lately, but it's all kind of depressing at the time. And my problems are not your problems, Mandy, so let's talk about you, woman."

"Well, Ray Ray, there is really not much to tell. I work all the time and am pretty much a hermit without the religious discipline, if you know what I mean."

"Now, Mandy, this is one of those times where you and old Brandon over there may have just actually got earlier than I did this morning because I'm still asleep on that one."

"Ray Ray, I just told you that I practically work eight days a week, so I never have time to do anything else that's really fun, ya know?"

"Wait, Mandy, there are only seven days in a week."

"Yes, I know, Ray Ray. Now do you see the problem?"

Now you would think old Brandon working behind the bar would have plenty to do since he was a bartender, but no! He was over there, laughing his ass off, all in my Kool-Aid and don't even know the flavor.

"Ray Ray, don't mind him. He's just having fun with you because he knows I like you."

"Hold on, Mandy. Did you just say what I thought you said?"

"Ray Ray do you really want to set yourself for another punch line so old Brandon can Shit himself laughing over there? Well Amanda... since you put it like that, he'll yea!! I would love to see old Brandon shit himself, and I hope the rest room is all out of toilet tissue too! She busted out laughing but I was serious as he'll! I actually wanted to see him run to the restroom to only find out the tissue was all gone! I wondered how amusing he would find that punch line! You know what Mandy, if you really like me how about us getting a little privacy from old Brandon over there. Sure Ray Ray, we can go in my office or upstairs, you're call!"

"Sure, Ray Ray. We can go in my office, or we can go upstairs, your call."

Marvin Gaye was playing in the background, and as you all know by now, I am a big Marvin Gaye fan and will be until the day I die. "Can you hear the music this clear in your office, Mandy?"

"Sure you can, Ray Ray. This place has state-of-the-art everything from front to back. Do you want to go in my office and check it out, Ray Ray?"

"Sure, Mandy, why not?"

"Well, I can think of a few reasons, but I won't go there with you right now, Ray Ray."

I always listened like a counselor, and I know everything said is said for a reason. And I knew what she just implied meant something sexually. We went into her office, and what an office it was! She had the professional-type conference tables with a state-of-the-art intercom system with the full works, big-screen TV and all.

"Mandy, where are you from? Because I know you're not from around here."

"Why would you ask that, Ray Ray? What gave it away?"

"I would say the exotic look was my first clue, and then there is your accent to drive it home."

"Well, my dad is from Cuba, and my mom is from Puerto Rico. But I went to college in Cali."

"So that's where the 'Reese's Peanut Butter Cup' look come from, huh?"

"I don't know what you're talking about, Ray Ray."

"Yes, I know. That's why you're smiling right now, and don't try to hide it."

"Not in a million years, Ray Ray, not in a million years!"

I thought to myself, *that's a hell of a commitment, a million years.* "Mandy, how did you get all of this at such a young age?"

"My parents have always been in the diamond business way before I was born, so I kind of grew up with it in my blood, sort of, I guess."

"Mandy, as fine as you are, why don't you have a man?"

"Who said I didn't have a man? I need to talk with them right away for starting such a malicious rumor about me."

"Hold on, Mandy. You're confusing me right now. I just assumed you didn't have one because you seemed like you liked me a little."

"Ray Ray, you should see the look on your face right now. You're just too easy, man." She was laughing hard.

"Okay, Mandy, you got me again, but can you be serious for a minute?"

"Ray Ray, I have to be serious all the time because all I do is work, so let me have a little fun, baby, tonight, please."

*Did she just call me baby?*

"Ray Ray, I got this feeling that you're not your everyday, typical man the first day I met you, and I was kind of disappointed when you came in the jewelry store looking for an engagement ring."

"Why, Mandy? I never got that feeling from you that day."

"Of course you wouldn't have. I had to respect that and remain professional in my store. One thing I will never do is fool around with a married man again."

"Wait, Mandy, you were letting a married man hit that?"

"For two years, Ray Ray. He kept his wife a secret from me. I worked so much that I'm not that demanding of a man's time, and he took advantage of that for almost two years."

"Mandy, where is this guy now? I mean, do you guys still talk?"

"No, once I found out, I just changed my number and went back to working myself to death every day and just staying to myself. Ray Ray, I don't know what you're into, and I really don't care as long as your thing doesn't interfere with mine. I think I would like to get to know you a little better, Ray Ray, if you think you also would like to get to know more about me. And believe me when I tell you what you know about me now is very little. But I am curious about the kind of relationship that you and China have that she don't mind you talking to me because let's keep it 100 percent, you don't see that with the housewife type."

"Oh, that? Well, Mandy, China is definitely cut from a different cloth, but we kind of just clicked from day 1. I grew up in a pool hall across the tracks, and I guess I have always been different than your average guy. I'm just different."

We sat there and talked in her office until closing time. We talked about everything from my little puppy Fluffy all the way up to Stacey before Mandy had started getting a clear picture of the life of a hustler!

"Ray Ray, it's getting late, and I do have to get up early in the morning. So when will I see you again?"

"Mandy, I was just wondering the same thing, girl, because you're the one who works eight days a week."

"Yes, you're right, Ray Ray, but some way, somehow, I would like to make it happen."

"Mandy, I think I would like that very much. So you hit me on the hip, and I will hit you back on the flip."

"I definitely will hit you on the hip, so make sure it don't take that long to hit me back on the flip." She started laughing.

"Hey, Mandy, you need me to walk you to your car?"

"No, baby, I have security for that."

"Well, shit, can they escort me to my car while they are waiting on your pretty ass?"

"Sure, if you would like, Ray Ray. I'll have Brandon walk out with you."

"That's quite all right, Mandy. I got this. Call me to let me know you made it home safe, okay?"

"That's so nice of you, Ray Ray. I sure will."

I jumped in my SUV and called China to make sure she was all right because after all, she was still depressed over losing dear friends like that. She didn't answer, so I went down to one of the after-hours spots to see how everything was coming along. The first people I saw when I walked in were Charlie and Ms. Kay! I had been avoiding her mostly for the time being, but I got this gut feeling she was about to ask me about Stacey.

"Ray Ray, good to see you. Where is Stacey? I have asked everyone about where she is, including Charlie, but everyone is acting like its classified information."

I knew if I told her the truth, it was going to fall back on Charlie because he should have said something first. At least, that was how she was going to look at it! I looked at Charlie as if I didn't have a choice. I had to tell her even if it threw him under the bus or not! I was finally cornered, and I didn't know what to do because if I told her a lie, she was going to know it was a lie. So what do I say? "Ms. Kay, can I talk to you in the office, please?"

"Ray Ray, what's wrong? Is Stacey okay? Is she hurt or something? Charlie, why does Ray Ray want to go in the office just to tell me where Stacey is?"

Charlie looked at me and said, "Do what you have to do, Ray Ray. We've got to tell her!"

"Oh my god, someone please tell me she is all right before I have a nervous breakdown or something."

"Ms. Kay, you might want to have a drink on account of what we are about to tell you."

"Shit, guys, you're scaring the hell out of me right now. Can you please just tell me! Wait, if you're getting ready to give me some bad news about Stacey, then you're right, let me brace myself and have me a strong drink! Bartender, give me a double on the scotch!"

"Bartender, can you make it two?" We all looked up because we recognized the voice without even seeing the face! Ms. Kay was the first to jump out of her chair and run and hug this woman with the voice that we all heard many times over and over. When Charlie made eye contact with me, I had a more puzzled look on my face than he did! All I could do was shrug my shoulders in a suppressing kind of way because I was just as stunned as everyone else!

"Hey, Ray Ray, thanks for sending my family and me on vacation for that week in Vegas. I really needed to just get away for a while after all that has happened. Thank you. Ray Ray, I know that you have a birthday coming up next week, so I thought I would pick you up a little something while I was in Vegas. And I hope you like it. I have to go to the car and get it, so Ms. Kay, what's up with that drink?"

"Oh, it's coming, baby. It will be here when you get back!"

Now, readers, at this point, I didn't know what to say because the last thing I wanted was to let Ms. Kay know what really happened, and thank God I don't have to because Stacey just walked through the door, in the nick of time, like nothing had ever happened! She excused herself and went out to her car to get my early birthday present. To tell you the truth, my birthday was so far in the back of my mind that I had really not paid much attention to me even having a birthday coming soon.

When Stacey returned, you would not believe the birthday present she had under her arm! He was all black, with four white paws and a white-tipped tail and wore a name tag around his neck that spelled "Fluffy" and I don't even have to tell you that my jaw dropped to the floor! At that point, I didn't have to put on an act like I was surprised or something because I really was. This woman just walked in like nothing had happened with this little cute puppy that looked exactly like my childhood puppy Fluffy and I was sitting there feeling ecstatic. Now I'm asking myself, how many more surprises does Stacey have up her sleeve?

Everyone is admiring this little bundle of joy so much that nobody even paid attention to Detective Brannon when he approached the bar and ordered a drink. But Charlie and I did, and we gave each other that look that spelled trouble.

Volume two coming soon...

Does Ms. Kay really believe anything that Stacey just said?

Why did detective Brannon all of a sudden just show up?

Amanda Simmons—what connection does she have with Ms. Kay?

99 Questions Volume Two is coming soon!

.    .    .